HEIRS OF MONTCLAIR

THE GWENNIES

ISBN: 978-1-7645095-0-3

First Edition | 2026

Self-published by the authors.

Cover design by **Maria Necula** – coverbound.co.

<u>Authors' note</u>

Heirs of Montclair is the first installment in the H.O.M Series.

It is set in America, Florida in the year 2037.

This book contains scenes that may be triggering / upsetting to

readers.

It is suitable for 18+ due to these factors.

Thanks for reading, enjoy!

Trigger warnings

Eating Disorder/Body Dysmorphia

Drugs

Guns

Graphic Violence

Needles

Explicit language

Abuse

Experiments

Torture

To the readers who find beauty in crumbling worlds,

may your heart stay unbroken and your bookmarks

never lost.

xoxo, The Gwennies

Chapter 1

Is this a cult?

Wes.

I wake up choking on air that tastes like metal and disinfectant, like someone scrubbed the room so hard they erased whatever used to be here before me. The first thing I notice is the light. Not bright, worse. Flat. White. Like it's pressing directly behind my eyes. My head throbs, and when I squint, pain lances through my skull so sharply it makes me swear out loud.

"Shit."

My voice echoes. That's when I realize I'm not alone.

There are five body-shaped capsules lining the walls of the room, all open, all identical, all very much not something I recognize. I'm sprawled half-out of one of them, limbs tangled like I was dumped here instead of laid down.

I push myself upright, heart hammering. I look down to see I'm wearing a grey shirt and matching grey pants, soft and stretchy, kind of like hospital scrubs. No logos. No pockets. No shoes. Just fabric and the creeping sensation like I've been *standardized*.

I run a hand through my hair. Black and still mine. Short, messy, like I forgot to comb it for a week. Hell, I don't know how long I've been strung up in this *thing.* My skin looks pale under the light, almost sickly, and my eyes, Jesus, my eyes sting like hell. Blue. That's the only upside of this migraine: confirmation. At least I know what color my own damn eyes are.

Four other teenagers are sitting up in capsules, looking just as wrecked. They look around my age, seventeen.

Across from me, a girl with long, curly blonde hair clutches her shirt away from her body like it personally offended her. Her face is scrunched up in pure disgust, brown eyes flicking around the room like she expects to catch something. She's average height, skinny, posture stiff, like she's already decided she hates this place and everything in it.

Next to her is another girl, shorter, softer somehow. Long, dark hair falls straight down her back, and her eyes, a greenish blue, move carefully, dissecting every piece of information in the room. Olive skin with a calm expression. She looks like she's trying to be gentle with the situation, which feels wildly inappropriate considering, *where the hell are we?*

Two guys stand near the far wall.

One of them is huge. Like, six-foot-two minimum, shoulders broad enough to block a door. Dark brown hair cropped short, arms packed with muscle, tan skin and jaw clenched so tight I can practically hear his teeth grinding. He scans the room like he's preparing to break something or someone, if given the slightest excuse.

The other guy's tall too, pretty jacked but not like hot head over there. Blonde hair, wavy and short, green eyes wide with confusion but not fear. He looks... weirdly chill, all things considered. Like he woke up in a nightmare and decided to wait until it was all over.

None of us say anything for a few seconds. What do you say in this kind of situation?

Finally, the blonde girl breaks the silence. "Okay," she says, her voice sharp. "What the actual hell is this?"

Good question. I open my mouth to answer, then realize I don't have one.

"I don't remember getting here," the calm girl says quietly. "I don't remember... anything after, she stops, brow furrowing. "After running." That word punches something loose in my head.

Running, shouting.

Fear so thick, I could feel it stuck in the back of my head, making my stomach flip.

"I remember my name," I say. "Wesley. That's... that's something, right?"

The chill guy nods. "Yeah. Same. Name's still there. Parents too. Sort of. Like... snapshots."

The big guy exhales through his nose, clearly pissed. "No phones. No bags. No exits."

He's right. The room is sealed. There are no windows and only one door. That's when the blonde girl suddenly yelps.

"What?" I ask.

She spins around, shoving her hair aside. "There's something on my neck."

My pulse spikes. We all reach back at the same time, *she's right*, there's a mark. Right at the base of my skull. It was raised and rectangular. I drag my finger over what feels to be jagged lines, tracing what I think are numbers. Almost like a barcode off an item. *Is that what we are now? Items?*

"What? When, how the fuck did I get this?" I say, my fingers shaking.

Before anyone can answer, the door slides open. Three adults walk in, all smiles and soft voices and hands already reaching out like they were expecting us to be crying.

"Good evening," one of them says brightly. "You must be disoriented."

No shit.

They touch our shoulders, guiding us out of the room. Speaking like therapists and kindergarten teachers, however, they're dressed like nurses.

"Get me out of here. Now. I don't know who you think you are? But I'm not staying here one more minute." The intense guy barks. He almost goes to barge past the freaky ladies. However, the only guard in the room caught his attempt, pushing him back into us.

The man was wearing a dark navy combat uniform with a helmet that included eyewear covering his entire face, just a foul voice booming through. "Don't even think about it."

"Everything will be explained soon," One of the other women assured us. "For now, you should shower, eat, and rest."

I don't trust people who smile this much.

We're led through a sterile, brightly lit hall. One of the nurses points to a door to her right, claiming that as the showers. We then go through a door on the left. Inside is a temporary sleeping room with neatly arranged beds. They tell us it's night and that assembly will be at nine in the morning sharp. That 'we'll receive instructions then.'

Assembly? So what? This is some kind of school.

I lie awake staring at the ceiling, fingers pressed against the mark on my neck, wondering why it feels like something is watching me from the inside.

The morning starts with an alarm; it sounds like it was designed by someone who hates joy.

Through an intercom in the room, a calm disembodied voice tells us to dress in the uniforms that have been placed at the bottom of our "beds". Pearl white shirts with navy blue blazers, pants and skirts for girls, along with some sweatshirts. *You've got to be kidding me.*

I arrive to "assembly". A large room that reads, *assembly hall*", packed with teens all dressed in the uniform, the walls bear with only three colors. White, gold and navy-blue. It looks like a real normal school, that is until I remember what I woke up in a couple hours ago.

I'm late. *One minute. One stupid minute.*

A staff member blocks my path, smiling tightly. "Detention."

"What?" I snap. "It's my first day."

"That doesn't matter. Rules apply immediately. Isolated Detention."

Isolated Detention. What the fuck? Is that supposed to scare me? I mutter a string of swears under my breath as I take my seat beside the other four teens I woke up with.

Suddenly, a robotic voice booms.

"Why are you here?"

The students respond in perfect unison.

"To be improved."

The words crawl under my skin.

"Does improvement require consent?"

"No."

"Who leaves unchanged?"

"No one."

"And if improvement takes time?"

"We will remain."

Is this a cult? It was a pledge, a warning. I don't know what could have happened for me to end up here.

Suddenly, a tall, dark woman, wearing a deep-toned blue dress steps on stage. Her hair tightly tied in a low bun, her eyes piercing through the crowd of students.

"Welcome students to another year at Montclair Academy. To our new students, welcome. I am the headmistress of Montclair Academy."

So, she runs this child kidnapping center.

"I'm sure you have many questions. Our private school is well taken care of and very generously funded by the most elite, wealthy families, such as your own. Montclair is responsible for students becoming the best versions of themselves, fixing behavioral issues so that the younger, next generation can thrive and succeed."

She remains cold and composed. "Of course, young people are vital in protecting and securing the integrity of the free world. We must not allow... outside minds to take over our society."

Outside minds? What, does she mean people with other opinions other than these fucked up adults? I scan the rest of the room, my eyes falling above the stage, the school's crest, a slogan under it, 'Montclair Academy. Reform. Correction. Excellence.'

"With our school's focus being perfection, please understand that following school rules will grant you rewards, breaking them will result in isolated detention. I'm sure you don't want that just as much as we don't want to give it. All students will be preparing for the reform trials, a final test to see if you have been able to successfully pass the year. So please children, as your reform trials begin, try to remember that your parents made the right decision in sending you here. We all just want what's best."

My chest tightens.

No way my parents did this. This place wants what's best? Best for whom? Because she sure as hell didn't say for us. The two boys beside me whisper something under their breath. A security guard appears instantly, smacking both on the back of the head. They glare. The guard glares back.

"Now, for all the new students, you must stick together in your assigned sector groups. Make some friends, evaluations of students are done both individually and as units. If you cannot adapt to your group, you will be deemed unfit for what comes next." Her voice booms around the room.

I shiver. *What comes next?*

The headmistress then wishes us luck for the year and leaves. A staff member dismisses us to class. As we stand, I glance at the others. We all have the same thought. Whatever this place is, it's not a school.

And it's already decided what we're going to become.

Chapter 2
Another year. Another group.

Wendy.

I've learned you can tell a lot about children by how they leave assembly.

The obedient ones walk fast, heads down, already folding themselves into the shape the school prefers. The troublemakers look around like they're memorizing exits that don't exist.

These five do neither.

They drift out together slowly and uncertainly like the floor might disappear if they trust it too much. I smooth my apron, paste on my warmest smile, and step into their path before any staff with less patience decides to intervene.

"Right this way, dears," I say, voice light. Practiced. "Since you're new, I'll give you a little tour."

They stop and stare. No one says thank you.

Or anything at all.

That's fine. Silence is common on the first day. I prefer silence to the burning questions of, *"Where am I? When can I get the hell out of here?"*

As we walk, their footsteps echo loudly in the halls. The boy with dark hair, the one that was late, *'Whitmore'*, keeps his hands shoved into his pockets, jaw tight, eyes flicking everywhere. The tallest boy walks like he's restraining himself from punching a hole in a wall. The blonde boy looks calm, but it's the kind of calm that comes from disbelief, not peace.

The girls stick close together. One of them watches everything. The other watches nothing but the floor.

I clear my throat cheerfully. "Why don't you all introduce yourselves? It's good to know who you'll be sharing a sector with."

Nothing. Not even a glance at one another.

I laugh awkwardly, just a touch too high. "Alright then, in your own time."

We reach their sector door. Boys' rooms on the left, girls' on the right. Symmetrical. Orderly. I punch in the access code, and the door slides open with a hum.

"This code," I explain, turning to them, "is customized. Only the five of you should know it. Don't share it with anyone."

I don't add that every staff member like me already does.

"There's a curfew," I continue as we step inside the small hall. "Strict. Weekends are extended, but don't confuse that with flexibility. Being late is... discouraged." I glanced pointedly at Whitmore. "As you already know."

He rolls his eyes so hard I'm surprised they don't get stuck. A few of the others laugh, quick, sharp bursts, like they surprised themselves by finding something funny.

Then the broad boy, the one with the intensity, cuts in.

"Look," he says, voice low but firm. "I don't know what you think this is, but this isn't some stay in hotel we all chose to come to. I want to speak to my dad. Now."

I sigh. Not annoyed. Just tired.

"I understand your frustration, Mr. Deveraux," I say gently. "But that's not possible at the moment.

His nostrils flared.

"Which reminds me," I add, reaching into my cart. "Your student educational devices."

I hand each of them a sleek, unfamiliar object, part phone, part tablet, part something else entirely. No visible buttons. No brand markings.

"These are strictly for school use," I explain. "Study applications, camera access, internal communication. You may contact security, medical, or schedule therapy sessions."

I paused and smiled. "Those calls must be legitimate. False dialing a guard or nurse will result in corrective punishment. For your own... sanity, I wouldn't fiddle with it."

I look directly at Whitmore and the loud, blonde one.

Mr. Deveraux's jaw tightens. "Can I call my dad on this thing?"

"And my mother?" the curly haired girl adds quickly.

Blondie snorts. "Yeah, c'mon. Little princess here wants her mommy." He grins at her. "And you seem like a very giving lunch lady... in more ways than one." He winks.

I blink. Then I smile wider, so he's *that* one of the group.

"How charming of you."

My voice drops, not loud enough for cameras to care, but clear enough that every one of them hears me.

"But let me tell you something I won't repeat. None of you will be seeing your parents. Don't ask again. And if you truly want to improve here, don't bring it up to any other faculty member."

The air shifts. They look at each other, then back at me. *Good.* That's the feeling settling in.

"Now," I say brightly, clapping my hands once, "into your rooms. Get settled. Since it's your first day, you're off. No classes."

Mr. Deveraux lets out a humorless laugh. "Wow. One actual humane thing you people have done in this fucked up place."

"Hell yeah!" Blondie says.

I tilt my head. "Don't get used to it. This is your only holiday."

I turn toward the exit. "Supper will be served in your rooms tonight. Starting tomorrow, you'll see me every time you eat." I wave as I walk away.

"Excuse me," one of the girls calls suddenly. The dark headed. Polite. *Brave.* "What's your name? We only know you as the cafeteria lady."

I stop and meet her gaze.

"That's all you need to know me as," I say. We have rules in this place, no attachments and no emotions. But something inside me fails that consistency. Then, softer, almost kind, I add, "But my name's Wendy."

I give them a chipper smile, the kind that looks harmless if you don't know better and step out of the sector. The sector door slides shut behind me. Five children alone. And I must get back to work.

Chapter 3

Not doing the whole best friend thing.

Angeline.

The door slides shut behind Wendy with a sound that's way too final for my liking.

I stood there for a second, staring at it, half expecting it to open again so she could pop her head back in and say, 'just kidding, this was all a joke!' It doesn't. Of course it doesn't.

"Well," I say, forcing brightness into my voice, "guess this is home."

The girls' dorm is... *fine*. That's the nicest word I can find.

Two beds. Perfectly made. Identical gray blankets tucked so tightly they look concrete-sealed. Plain walls with plain lights. White everything, no posters, no mirrors, except one small rectangle over the sink, of what looks to be an even smaller bathroom. It smells like detergent and something sharper underneath, like plastic that's been overheated.

I have this fuzzy, aching sense that my room used to be better. Softer. Pinker. Bigger. I can almost see it if I squint;

pillows, fairy lights, a vanity but the image slides away before I can grab it, like trying to remember a dream five seconds after waking up.

I hate that feeling.

The other girl, with dark hair and somber eyes, sets her device carefully on the bed closest to the window.

"So," I say, because silence makes my skin crawl. "I guess we should... do the 'name' thing now?"

She nods, small and stiff.

"I'm Angeline Solarae," I say, smoothing my curls over my shoulder out of habit. "But everyone calls me Angie. You can too. If you want."

She hesitates, then says, "Dahlia. Dahlia Moretti."

Her voice is quiet, but not weak. Thoughtful. Like she measures every word before letting it out.

"Nice to meet you," I add quickly, *I mean I need to make some effort, we are sharing a room after all.*

"Yeah," she says, darting her eyes away from mine, turning her back completely away from me. "You too."

Another pause. Okay. So, we're not doing the whole best friend thing. That's fine. *Totally fine.* I don't even care. Definitely *not.*

We sit on our opposite beds, not looking at each other, both pretending to be very interested in the extremely thrilling gray walls ahead of us.

When dinner arrives, it's delivered on the floor of the door, like we're in some kind of fancy prison and I don't hesitate. I dug in immediately. My hands move before my brain can start yelling at me.

Dahlia notices. I can feel her eyes flick over as I eat fast, mechanically, barely tasting anything. The food is bland but warm. Pasta. Bread. Something green I ignore. But I need something, anything that will satisfy my craving for food.

"You're... hungry," she says carefully.

I stiffen hard like a board, "Yeah? So?"

"I just meant," she stops, frowns slightly. "You don't have to rush."

"I'm not rushing," I snap, even though I absolutely am. "Why do you care?"

She looks startled. "I don't. I was just..."

"Look," I cut in, heat crawling up my neck, "you've already made it clear you don't want to make friends right now, *remember*? So maybe don't comment on how I eat."

That shuts her up. *Good.*

I finish quickly, brush crumbs off the blanket, then grab a small handheld vacuum sitting neatly under the bed. I run it over the fabric with more force than necessary, erasing every stupid, little trace.

"Bathroom," I mutter, already walking away. I lock the door behind me.

The bathroom is even worse than the bedroom, tight and confined with white tile and there is nowhere to hide. I grip the edge of the sink and stare at my reflection. My curls are a mess. My deep amber eyes look too big. My cheeks feel wrong.

Everything does. Turning, I met an old friend. The toilet. Kneeling, I lose track of time.

What am I doing? Why do I feel this way? For some reason I can't stop myself.

When I finally hear a soft knock on the door, my heart jumps.

"Angie?" Dahlia's voice, muffled. Hesitant. "You've been in there a while. I... I heard something."

I swallow, panic flashing hot and sharp, my hair an absolute mess. *Shit! How long have I been? What does she think I've been doing in here... Did she hear me? No, no she couldn't, right?*

Quickly to stop suspicion, I let out, "I'm fine."

"Do you want me to call a nurse?" she asks gently. "Just in case?"

"I said I'm *fine*," I shout, my voice cracks. "Go away!"

Silence. Then her footsteps retreat.

I sink down against the door, breathing hard, the hum of the lights buzzing above me. Feeling like the weight of the world is sinking against my chest.

Chapter 4

Awkward.

Dahlia.

I stand outside the bathroom door for a moment after Angie snaps at me, my hand hovering like I might knock again. I don't. Instead, I sigh, quietly so she won't hear and tell myself not to take it personally. People lash out when they're scared. I know that. I've always known that. It's easier to give others grace than to expect it back.

I turn away and head toward my bed, but halfway there I notice a door that I didn't before. That's when I hear voices. Male voices. My stomach tightens.

I open it to find some kind of shared study room sitting between the girls' and boys' dorms, all glass walls inside, but unseen on the outside, long desks like the school expects us to be collaborative but not comfortable. I step inside slowly and find the three boys from the capsules standing there, looking just as unsure of what to do with themselves as I feel.

No one speaks at first. The silence stretches, awkward and heavy, until the boy with black hair and true-blue eyes exhales and rubs the back of his neck.

"Okay," he says. "This is getting unbearable." He turns toward me, offering a small, surprisingly polite smile. "I'm Wes. Hi."

"Oh," I say quickly, nerves firing. "Hi. I'm Dahlia. Dahlia Moretti."

My voice comes out softer than I intended. I clasp my hands together, so they won't shake.

The loud blonde one, the one with the grin and restless energy tilts his head. "Dahlia, huh?" He repeats it like he's testing the sound. "That's pretty. But I have to be honest, you look like a Dolly." He grins wider. "Dolly. Yeah. That's got a nice ring to it."

"I," I blink, caught off guard. "I don't,"

He laughs. "I'm kidding. Mostly. I'm Freddie."

Wes shoots him a look. "You can't just rename people."

"Sure I can," Freddie says. "I just did."

I smile despite myself. Just a little. My eyes drift to the third boy.

He's standing near one of the cupboards, back completely turned to us, arms rugged, posture rigid. He doesn't move. Doesn't acknowledge me at all. I don't understand why, did I have something on my face? Did I accidentally do something that was rude? How could I, in only the couple of hours we've been in this place for.

What a dick.

"That's... uh," Wes says, gesturing vaguely toward him. "That's Nick."

Freddie nudges the guy's shoulder. "Hey, man. Say hi."

Nick doesn't turn around. Doesn't even react.

I feel heat creeping up my neck. Rude. But also, I guess we're all scared and confused in this place.

I nod once, more to myself than them. "It's fine," I say. "You don't have to."

Nick huffs quietly like that proves some kind of point and shifts his weight further away.

Seriously what is this guy's problem?

Freddie raises his brows at me. "So, where's the princess?"

"Angeline?" I ask. "She's... in the bathroom."

That's all I say. My eyes drift around the room, trying not to stare at Nick's back, and that's when my eyes catch a small round mirror hanging on the cupboard, just about head height. It's crooked, slightly scratched.

And in it... Nick's eyes. Dark. Sharp. Watching me.

I freeze.

For half a second, we're locked like that, my reflection and his gaze colliding in the glass. Then he scoffs under his breath and turns away sharply, repositioning himself so the mirror no longer catches him. My heart thuds painfully. Before I can process it, my dorm door opens. Angie steps out.

She looks... better. Or at least more put together. Her curls fall perfectly into place like before, expression brightening the second she notices the boys.

"Well," she says, hands on her hips. "This is the welcoming committee?"

Freddie laughs. "There she is. Feeling better, princess?"

She rolls her eyes. "Please. You wish."

Freddie responds extremely formally, like he thinks he's in royal presence, "Frederick, madam. Kidding, it's Freddie sweetheart." Finishing with a quick wink.

Angie stares back, blinking a few times then looks at Wes. "Hi, I'm Angeline. Angie."

Wes smiles back. "Wes."

She even manages a polite nod in Nick's direction. "And you are?"

Nick finally turns.

"Nick." he says flatly.

That's it. I'm not spending one more second in the presence of someone who doesn't even want to notice mine.

I don't stay long enough to hear more. I slip back into our room, sitting on my bed just as Angie follows me in, closing the door to the study behind her with a soft click. On the other side of the wall, I hear the boys moving, checking the study room, their bathroom, then their dorm. Doors opening. Closing. Settling in.

I lay back on my pillow, staring at the ceiling. We're all here now. May as well get used to it.

Chapter 5

What did I just claim?

Freddie.

People always say first impressions matter.

Which is hilarious, because my first impression of this place is that it wants to kill me politely.

The boys' dorm is big and oddly spacious, which in a place like this, you'd expect a jail cell overlooking a *lakeside mountain*. Three beds form a lazy half–semi-circle facing the door. Desks line the walls. Lockers. Shelves. Everything is identical. Everything grey.

Three duffels at the foot of each bed. Already packed full of our clothes and stuff. Like someone knew exactly what to bring and did it without asking.

Creepy? *Yes.* Convenient? *Also, yes.*

I'm the first one through the door after Wendy's ever so bittersweet departure, and I don't hesitate. I sprint and launch myself onto the middle bed.

"Mine. Claimed." I announce.

Mr. Intensity barely looks at me. "Like I care."

The pale guy snorts. "Oh, so you won't mind if I take the bed furthest from the door, near the window?"

Mr. Intensity pauses. Slowly turning and looking at the bed. Then back at him.

"No," he says flatly. "Uh... no. That's my bed."

From what I can see, it didn't look like much of a lakeside view, I couldn't see anything but terrifyingly tall, dark gates surrounding the building. Nothing after that, but I grin at him, wide and innocent.

His jaw tightens. He noticed my satisfied look immediately. He knows.

He bends down, scooping up my school blazer off the floor, and hurls it straight at my chest.

"Oh, shut up."

"Ow, easy!" I grunt dramatically, clutching my heart. "I'm fragile!"

I sat up, still smiling. "By the way, Frederick Kensington." I stick out my hand. "But just Freddie."

He just stares at it like it might bite him. Sighing, he then shakes it once, firm and annoyed. "Nickolas Deveraux."

My smile sharpens. "Sooo... Nickie."

He locks eyes with me. Dark. Dead serious.

"Absolutely not. Nick is fine."

I flop back onto the bed. "Alright, whatever you want."

Nick exhales and looks at the last guy standing. "What about you?"

He straightens a little. "I'm Wesley Whitmore but you guys should already know me."

He says it like it's obvious. Like we missed something. Nick and I exchange a confused look.

I squinted at him. "Uh... how? We all just met."

Wes's face falls, staring down at the floor. "Actually... yeah. I don't know why you would." He rubs his temple. "Why did I say that?"

Wow, you can really cut the awkwardness with a knife. Wes reaches back and slowly closes the dorm door. The click sounds louder than it should, definite. I don't like that.

When he turns around, the joking edge is gone.

"Okay," he says. "So seriously what the fuck is this place?"

I sit up. "None of us know." I pause, irritation crawling up my spine as the headmistress's voice echoes in my head.

'Your parents have sent you.' "But apparently our parents do."

Wes shakes his head immediately. "That's ridiculous. I don't know about your parents, but mine would never do this to me."

Nick cuts in, voice low, direct. "I don't need to hear about your parents. We're not friends. We don't even know each other. We're all just here because of some inconvenient coincidence."

That lands heavier than I expect.

Wes and I glance at each other, reality settling in. He's right. We aren't friends. We're just... stuck.

Nick crosses his arms. "But one thing I know?" He points toward the door. "I do not like that security guy from assembly. Something about him is off."

I nod slowly. "Yeah. Agreed."

Wes, leaning back into his pillows, whispers "All I gather is that the three of us and those two chicks are in the same boat. So, let's keep our heads down and try not to fuck with these crazy pricks. Cuz frankly, the smiley bitches give me the creeps."

Nick nods. No argument there.

We break apart after that. Start unpacking. Folding clothes that don't feel like ours into drawers we didn't choose, in a room that already smells like people pretending this is normal. I lay back for a second, staring at the ceiling. Right now, that's the only thing that will keep me sane.

Chapter 6

When life gives you apples... RUN AWAY.

Angeline.

I've been here for days, though it feels longer. Long enough for the monotony to seep into my bones and long enough to notice the sharp edges of this place weren't just in the rules, they were in the people, the walls, the very air.

I slipped into class quietly, careful not to draw attention. Wes was already there, sitting two rows ahead, scribbling in a notebook with that sarcastic tilt to his lips I hated and liked at the same time.

"Hey," I whispered as I slid into my seat.

He glanced back, just for a second. "Hey," he murmured, and went back to whatever he was writing.

I hate pretending that we're friends. I mean, we give each other the time of day but no one in our sector really knows each other.

The teacher's voice cut through the low hum of the room like a blade. "We will resume where we left off last time but first, rise for the pledge."

I felt my stomach twist. I'd said those words a hundred times now but hearing them now, today, felt different.

"Why are you here?"

"To be improved."

"Does improvement require consent?"

"No."

Our voices echo around the room.

As we continue, I drift my eyes anywhere to avoid this dreadful excuse for a class. My eyes eventually landed on a girl, maybe a year younger than me, at the far end of the hall. She has dark hair and fox eyes, which are darting around quickly. Her breathing starts to quicken- then suddenly she starts to scream. Tears stream down her face.

"Please! I can't! I want to go home!" Her voice cracked. She lunged toward our door, but two guards were already on her in seconds, dragging her away.

The teacher's lips curved into the calmest, sweetest smile. "Continue the pledge," she said softly. "Louder."

My throat tightened, *what the hell was that?* I repeated the words, my voice barely above a whisper. The air seemed to thicken around us.

"Who leaves unchanged?"

"No one."

"And if improvement takes time?"

"We will remain."

I saw him then. In the reflection of the monitor, one of the guards, standing just out of sight of the others, pressed a long needle into the girl's neck. Her struggle stopped almost immediately. She went completely *limp*.

My heart felt like it was trying to punch its way out of my chest. I wanted to scream, to do something, anything but no one else reacted. No one. Just more pledges, louder, like it was some sick ritual.

The rest of the class passed in a haze. As soon as I heard the bell, I grabbed Wes as we left the room. "Did you see that?" I hissed, pulling him slightly into the hallway.

He shrugged, expression unreadable. "See what?"

"The girl. The guard. The needle,"

He held up a hand. "I didn't see anything. Don't."

I stared at him, my chest heaving. "You can't just act like it didn't happen. She's, she's..."

He shook his head, eyes sharp. "You think you saw something. Forget it. This isn't something we fix. Not us. This place scares the hell out of me, so just... blend, for your own sake man."

What is this school doing to its students?
I wanted to argue, to tell him it was wrong, but I swallowed, nodding, feeling the weight of it settle in my stomach.

That night, rumors say the girl didn't return to her dorm.

Lunch the next day was a nightmare. I was last in line, the trays almost empty by the time I got to the counter. A sliver of chicken, half a scoop of mashed potatoes, a tiny roll. Wendy's empathetic expression stared at me. "I'm sorry love, I tried to save you some. But that's all I could do."

"Don't be sorry Wendy, the fact you tried at all is more then I can say for anyone else in this place." Looking at Wendy's kind nature, with her light brown hair that had grey highlights purring through, her rosy cheeks peeking from within, I wanted her to know that I didn't take her gesture for granted. "This school needs more people like you Wendy." I say as she matches my smile.

"Now quickly sit down Miss Solarae, you don't want your chicken to get cold!"

I sat down at a table in the corner, shoving the empty calories in faster than I probably should have. Still, it wasn't enough. My hands shook as I chewed.

Until a shadow fell over me. I looked up to see a girl sitting beside me, red hair pulled into a tight ponytail, toned arms visible even under her uniform. She smiled, nudging an apple toward me.

"Here. Take it. I'm Alyssa. Alyssa Quinn."

Relief flooded me. "Thanks..." I whispered, taking it gratefully.

I didn't even get a chance to take a bite before a nurse's sharp voice cut through. "You. Stop. What are you doing?"

I freeze, looking up at the short woman standing in front of me. "I... I'm..."

Alyssa's grin turned sly, her grey eyes menacing. "She snatched it up. Don't worry about it."

"Is that so?" the nurse snapped, stepping closer, turning her attention back to me. "Did you take something not on your tray?"

I shook my head frantically. "No! I didn't!"

Before things could escalate, Dahlia suddenly appeared beside me, her gentle eyes calm but firm. "I saw," she said quietly, voice carrying just enough for the nurse to hear. "She didn't take it. I saw her at the table."

The nurse glared, mouth a thin line. "Do not lie for her! You know the rules. Exchanging food is forbidden." She pointed at me. "Isolated detention. Consider yourself lucky you were seen, or it would have been double! Now give it back to Miss Quinn."

"Oh, please keep it, I don't want it after it's been in...your hands. Also, she looks like she's just...dying for it."

That red headed bitch.

Dahlia backed down, and I saw her mouthing, "I'm sorry," as she sat back down.

Alyssa's expression flickered between amusement and something sharper, but she didn't push it. I sank back into my seat, defeated, slightly humiliated and definitely not hungry anymore.

Chapter 7

Spying? Never been a fan.

Dahlia.

The door clicked behind us, and since lunch, the dorm felt almost like a safe space. Angie plopped down onto her bed, still holding that apple like it was a trophy.

"You know," she said quietly, "I'm glad you... you know, stood up for me back there. But why? Why did you defend me?"

My eyes lit up surprisingly. "Well... I couldn't just watch them do that to you."

Angie smiled, scanning my face up and down, causing my nerves to creep back up. "What?" I ask blankly.

Angie looks down, trying to find the words to say whatever it was she was thinking. "So does this mean you want to be my friend now?"

"I wouldn't mind it. I actually would really like that." I responded. And it was true. I weirdly felt connected to this girl. She made me feel safe and comfortable, unlike anyone else in this *mental institute*.

I don't know what changed. Maybe being here for days has opened my eyes to the fact that I'm really trapped. Having someone to lean on couldn't hurt. I just couldn't help but push her and the others away. A deep dark voice sits in my head, telling me I've always been alone.

"I'm glad... No more awkwardness then!" Angie gushed, fixing her hair. "Also, Lia, did you save anything from lunch that you don't want?" she asked while looking in the bathroom mirror.

I blinked, surprised. "Lia?"

"Yeah!" she said, "The ending of your name Dah-Lia, it's adorable. I like it, can I call you that?"

I hesitated, then let a small smile slip through. "Sure. Lia's fine. My mom used to call me that." My mom. Why can't I remember more? *Like remembering that she called me Lia will help me get out of this hell hole.*

"Perfect," she chirped, grinning. "Officially calling you Lia from now on."

I laughed softly. Maybe this whole place wasn't entirely hopeless. I couldn't help but want to know more about this girl, seeing as we're now *friends.*

"So..." I start, "Do you throw up a lot?" I knew it was harsh and out there, but after what happened at lunch, I really wanted to know. To know that she was okay. I could tell something was wrong.

Angie pauses, looks at me, hesitant to answer but sighs, "So, you heard me that first day?" She responded.

I nod awkwardly.

"I -uh, I have been doing it for as long as I can remember." Angie mumbles.

This shocks me. *As long as she can remember... And* the fact that she *answered* me.

"So, you remember your life before this?" I question.

"No. No, I just remember it always being a big part of my life. Like something or someone expected me to do it." Angie replied annoyed, with a slight touch of timidness.

That's awful. To be expected to do that.

"Your secret is safe with me. It's not my business to tell. Cross my heart." I reassure her.

I could tell that meant something to her but could also see that she didn't fully trust me. *Smart.* I mean I don't fully trust her or anything in this place either.

We settled into a quiet rhythm, nibbling on my leftovers from lunch and talking in hushed voices about the redheaded girl.

"So... Alyssa," I said, "she's... what, a little bit of a bully?"

"Bully? More like Bitch," she said, rolling the apple between her palms. "She's got that look, like she wants to assert herself. But she's also... trying to see how far she can push people. She's pathetic."

We lapsed into a brief silence, causing me to shift the conversation. "The boys," I murmured. "Have you noticed... uh... you and that Freddie guy? You two-"

Angie waved her hand, coughing at the mention of his name, "No! No! There's nothing. We're just... bantering. That's all."

"Uh-huh," I said skeptically, smirking. "Bantering. Sure."

She gave me a friendly frown, attempting to throw a crumb at my face, "Shut up! Anyway, Wes and Nick seem nice. Cool."

I frowned. "Wes, yeah. But Nick... I don't know. There's something off about him."

"What do you mean?" Angie asked, tilting her head.

"He's... weirdly cold, but just to me. No one else. And when he's around me, things get super tense. I can't explain it."

Angie's brows rose but as she was about to open her mouth to say something, we heard a chuckle. Coming from the study room.

"Wait." Angie demanded, skeptically walking toward the shared study room, bursting the door open.

Inside, Nick and Freddie, sitting at the table.

"Knew it." Angie mumbled while shaking her head. "They were listening!"

"Again, with the stalking?" Freddie's voice rang out, teasing. "There's a door right there... you do realize we can hear you through that thin piece of wood."

Nick rolled his eyes, silent except for a faint, dismissive scoff. His dark eyes scanned the room, finally catching mine as I appeared in the doorway.

I froze. Something in his gaze was sharp, calculating, and... uncomfortable.

He stood up abruptly, giving me a death stare, the air shifting with him, and walked back toward the boys' dorm without another word. It was like he was angry that I was just standing, like my presence was an inconvenience to him. *He really is that much of a dismissive jerk.*

Wes came in just after him, a small frown on his face as he glanced between us and the study room.

"Everything okay?" he asked, though his voice carried that same half-sarcastic, half-serious edge.

"Yeah," I muttered, "Just... him." closing the study room door behind me, with Angie following.

Angie flopped back onto her bed with a sigh. "Ugh, I swear, these guys. Can't they just... not?"

It felt like we were slowly carving out a tiny space for ourselves in this place. But Nick... that boy made it obvious we weren't in the clear yet.

Chapter 8

Isolated detention… What a joke.

Freddie.

Walking from class to class had somehow become the dullest part of my life, well besides the food, the uniforms, the creepy smiles, and the constant, low grade threat of isolation. I shoved my hands in my pockets, weaving through the halls, trying to keep my head down.

Until I saw someone talking with a red-headed girl.

Nick. Leaning against the lockers. She was laughing, one hand grazing his shoulder in some fake friendly gesture. He jerked away immediately, and the smile dropped from her face like a mask falling to the floor.

I smirked to myself. Classic Nick never letting anyone get too close, not even an obvious impish brat. I almost called out to him, just to see if he'd acknowledge me, but figured discretion might be the better part of valor.

I started walking past them when a teacher suddenly stepped in front of me, arms crossed, eyes like icy daggers.

"Frederick Kensington," she said sharply. "Recite the pledge."

I stopped, blinked. "Uh... excuse me?"

"The pledge is to be recited on command at any time. Now," she repeated, voice low but dripping authority.

I raised an eyebrow. "You mean the one I've been reciting every ten seconds since I arrived here?"

"Yes. Immediately."

I let out a slow exhale and crossed my arms. "Listen, I don't know if you've noticed, but I've got a bit of a memory problem. Or maybe it's selective hearing. Yeah... selective hearing. And apparently, it's really, really bad right now."

She blinked, expression tightening. "This is not optional, Mr. Kensington."

"Oh, really?" I shot back, smirking now. "Because last I checked, threatening detention was optional for teachers too. I mean, don't get me wrong, I love a good punishment. Isolation, who wouldn't? From what I've heard it seems great! Cozy little room, quiet, time to think... But maybe I'll pass this time."

The corners of her mouth twitched like she wanted to bite back, but she stayed rigid. "You are insubordinate. Isolated detention."

I arched an eyebrow. "Wow. That's... fast. I mean, efficiency is nice. I like efficiency. But could we maybe... schedule it? Like a little heads-up? A warning? A little thing called courtesy?"

She just stayed still, only letting the corners of her mouth tilt into a smile. "Enough."

I sighed dramatically, letting my hands drop to my sides. "Fine, fine. You win, teacher lady. Isolated detention, coming right up. But just so you know, I'll be talking about this later. Not complaining. Just... analytical observations for the record."

She turned and walked away, expression unreadable, leaving me with a smirk and a shake of my head. *Isolation.* The place couldn't sound more surreal if it tried.

I glanced back toward Nick, still talking, oblivious to the chaos around him. I shook my head. "Some people just get all the fun," I muttered.

And with that, I started heading toward class, curiously waiting for when and whatever little punishment they had lined up for me. Bring it on Montclair, do your *worst*.

Chapter 9

Red's never been my color.

Angeline.

I've learned how to disappear here. Although disappearing has never been my forte. I can't exactly remember why, but I can feel it. It's just not me; I'm not one to shield myself from others.

My heels click softly against the hallway floor, each sound too loud in my ears, like I'm announcing my existence to a place that would very much prefer I didn't have one.

Detention. I hug my arms around myself as I walk, eyes fixed on the ground. I don't look at other students anymore. I don't want to see the way they watch, blank, curious, relieved they're not going where I am.

I turn the corner. And stop.

She's waiting at the end of the hallway like she planned it. Weight settled on one hip, arms crossed, red hair cascading over her shoulder as she flicked it back deliberately. Alyssa smiles when she sees me.

"Angeline," she calls, dragging my name out like it's something sweet she wants to savor.

Behind her, one of her friends, one of the girls who always trails her like a shadow, steps into the light.

I sigh.

Slowly, I turn around, heels clicking faster now, my pace shifting into something sharper, more frantic. I make it three steps before another figure moves. A second girl steps out at the other end of the hallway, blocking my exit. My stomach drops.

"You've got to be kidding me," I mutter, turning back toward Alyssa. "I don't have time for this. I'm already late."

Alyssa tilts her head. "Always running, huh?"

Her eyes flick down, too fast, too knowing and my skin prickles.

We trade words back and forth, sharp and quiet, the kind of argument meant to cut without drawing attention. My heart is racing, panic buzzing just under my skin.

Then...

"HEY!"

The shout cracks through the hallway. Everything freezes.

One of Alyssa's girls stumbles back, losing her footing, and suddenly she's on the ground. Someone emerges from the shadows, standing above the helpless girl. His chest is heaving.

Wes.

He looks up, fire in his eyes as he turns to Alyssa. "Don't you have something better to do? She clearly has detention. If you keep holding her up, she'll get another one."

Alyssa scoffs, unimpressed. She steps closer, voice low and cruel.

"Aw. Little miss Angie needs big boy Wes to stand up for her."

Her eyes flick to me again, as she spits, "You're weak, Angeline. Maybe it's because you skipped breakfast today, hm?"

My heart stops. *Where did she get that from? How... How does she know?* She steps in front of Wes like she owns the space.

"I... I need to go," I whisper.

I don't wait for permission. I don't wait for anyone to say anything else. I turn and walk... no, bolt away.

I slam my dorm door shut behind me, chest heaving. I throw my things onto my bed, as I feel my skin breaking into a sweat, my breath hyperventilating.

Dahlia is sitting on her bed; she looks up instantly.

"Hey, what's wrong-"

I snap.

"What's wrong?" My voice shakes with anger and something worse underneath it. "What's wrong, Lia, is that you told Alyssa about my problem! How could you do that?"

She stands up so fast the bed creaks. "What? No, Angie, I... I promise I didn't. I would never. I don't know how she knows!"

I shake my head, tears blurring my vision. "I thought we were becoming real friends..."

The words fall between us, heavy and broken. I don't wait for her to answer. I turn and leave the room, walking anywhere that isn't here, that isn't her, that isn't the place where everyone seems to know my weakest parts.

I don't know who told. I don't know who to trust. I do know that I am 100% late for isolated detention.

Chapter 10

Again... Why am I used to that?

Angeline.

I wake up to brightness.

Not the soft kind, or the comforting kind. The kind that hurts your eyes and forces you to squint.

The room is empty except it isn't, because the walls curve, bending and stretching back at me, my reflection fractured into a hundred wrong versions. Funny house mirrors. Made to amuse but only warps bodies until they become untrue. I sit up too fast and the world tilts. My head throbs, and my throat is scratchy when I swallow.

The floor is cold beneath my palms. When I open my eyes fully, I spot it in the exact center of the room:

A toilet. A single cookie on the floor, perfectly placed. And a plain toothbrush, white plastic, no toothpaste.

My stomach drops. This isn't accidental. This is a lesson.

"Hello? Is anyone there? Please, please let me out! You... you can't keep me here!" I plead as I bang my fists against the mirrored walls.

My chest tightens as memory rushes in fragments, guards' hands gripping my arms, their fingers bruising even through fabric. My shoe's scraping against the tiles. My desperate cry's simply ignored. *Isolated detention*. For stealing food. I didn't even steal it. I just... held it too long. I looked at it. I *wanted* it.

The mirrors catch me as I timidly look around.

One making me too wide. Too narrow. Another makes me too tall. Too skeletal.

Each step shifts my body into something new and worse. I turn sideways, then forward, then lift my shirt slightly to inspect my stomach. The mirrors exaggerate every curve, every flaw.

Disgust coils tight inside. My eyes flick back to the cookie. Chocolate chip. Soft and Innocent. Cruel.

My hands shake as I pick it up. It feels heavier than it should, like it carries consequence instead of calories. I hesitate, heart racing, then bring it to my mouth.

I eat it quickly, like I'm afraid it will disappear if I don't. The sweetness hits my tongue, and something breaks inside me. Shame, relief, Fear and comfort. All at once.

The mirrors don't let me forget. They watch. They warp me larger with every chew, louder with every swallow.

My breath becomes shallow. I turn to the toilet without fully deciding to.

Kneeling feels familiar in a way that makes my stomach twist harder. My hands grip porcelain. My fingers embrace my throat before my mind can catch up.

I glance at the ceiling, my eyes finding a sly camera. I turn to it, making sure they know they won.

"I did it. Are you happy? Did you get what you wanted!" I whimper.

When it's over, I sit back on my heels, shaking. Empty.

I scrub my mouth with the toothbrush until my gums sting, until my tongue feels raw, until I can pretend for just a second that it never happened.

I look back.

The mirrors are worse now.

I lean closer, inspecting myself like an enemy. Pulling at skin. Turning side to side. Searching for proof that I've failed. That I'm disgusting. That I deserve this room.

A flicker.

Bright lights. Cameras. A woman's voice, sharp and controlled. "Again."

Hands pressing on my shoulders. Fingers tight in my hair. The sound of retching echoing too loudly. Flashing bulbs. Applause somewhere far away.

Smile after.

My breath catches violently and the image vanishes as fast as it came, leaving me trembling, confused and cold.

I don't understand why my chest hurts so badly. I don't understand who the woman in my mind was, why her presence was so chillingly familiar.

I curl up on the floor, surrounded by distorted reflections, the toilet still in front of me like an accusation.

The cookie is gone. My hunger isn't. The last clear glimpse, a nurse, a guard and a tray of needles.

Chapter 11

The damsel *not* in distress?

Freddie.

The halls were quiet now, the last echoes of the day fading with every step. The sound of busy students stabbing my ears as I made my way back to the sector. Classes were done, meals were eaten, rules were followed... *mostly*.

I was ready for nothing more than collapsing on my bed and pretending the day hadn't been half as absurd as it was.
That's when I saw her. I'd recognize her curly locks anywhere. *Princess.*

Her heels weren't gliding; they barely made a sound. Her shoulders were slumped, head down like she was carrying a storm inside her chest. I caught up to her quickly.

"Hey," I said, jogging a little to match her pace. "Where has her majesty been?" That's when I see the expression on her face. "You, okay?"

She flinched slightly at my voice but didn't turn to look at me. "I'm... fine," she said, her voice tight, like she was trying to keep everything bottled up. I could tell.

I grabbed her arm gently. "No. Not fine. Come on, what's going on?"

She sighed, pulling her arm back, but there was no anger in it. Just exhaustion. "It's nothing," she said. "I was just in this... white room. For the day. Barely anything to eat, barely anything to do... not clean. That's all. It's... nothing."

I stopped in the hallway, and my gut twisted. "What? They just... left you there? For a whole day? That's fucking, that's sick."

She shook her head quickly, trying to force a smile. "It's fine. Really. Don't worry about it."

Before I could push further, a voice cut sharply through the hall.

"It was just a nightmare. Come inside and stop telling people about it, you're frightening them!" a voice chipped.

Princess stiffened, then turned and followed a slumped, dirty blonde rat down a side corridor, followed by guards.

My stomach churned. I wanted to storm in after her, tell them to leave her alone, to explain that no one should be treated like that, but she was out of sight before I could even move.

I shook my head, muttering under my breath. "Unbelievable."

I trudged back to the sector still thinking about her as I punched in the entry code, when Nick came following behind me. His dark eyes scanned our room, landing on mine, and a smirk tugged at his lips.

"Still sulking about Barbie?" he asked, leaning against the doorframe, taking off his shoes.

I rolled my eyes. "You think that's funny?"

He shrugged. "I'm just saying... she's lucky to have someone checking on her. Not that it's my business but come on."

I sat down lightly on the edge of my bed, wiggling my eyebrows at him. "Duh. Who could resist this charm and face?" I nodded toward myself, exaggerating the gestures.

Nick snorted, shaking his head. "You're ridiculous. Seriously. But yeah... I get it. She's... something else."

I frowned, "Something else? Nick, you've seen her. She's... she's... you know, she's tough, even when she's scared out of her mind. And she hides it so well, it's insane."

Nick's eyes glinted, unreadable, but there was a small nod. "Yeah. I noticed. Don't know why you care so much, though."

I leaned back, grinning despite myself. "Because someone has to. And I like seeing her smile, just as much as I like riling her up. You should try a smile sometime, it works wonders."

He rolled his eyes, muttering something under his breath that I didn't catch, plopping down in the chair at his desk. "You're hopeless."

"Maybe," I admitted with a chuckle. "But at least I'm charming while being hopeless. Unlike some people I know."

He didn't answer. Just leaned back, arms crossed and stared at the ceiling. And I couldn't help but notice... the corner of his mouth twitched like he almost wanted to smile.

I shook my head, chuckling. "Yeah, this place is messed up. But hey, we've all got issues right?"

Nick grunted. "Speak for yourself. The only issue I have is this conversation."

I huffed and flopped fully onto my bed, still thinking about Princess somewhere. Hoping she's okay.

Chapter 12

Who hired that wacko?

Angeline.

"Welcome, Miss Solarae."

I stare blankly across the room at my *supposed* therapist, I'm told. A blond lady, with her hair chopped to her chin. She is wearing a soft pink knitted sweatshirt, with a white button up underneath. A dark blue, similar to the headmistress, knee length skirt hugs her hips, with pale tights covering her thighs.

The guards had guided me into this cold and unfamiliar room just moments after she interrupted my conversation with Freddie. I should be glad; the conversation was awkward enough.

However, this one takes the cake.

The room smells like honey and roses, bright and unnecessary colors in every corner of the room. A bright pink couch sat across from a yellow armchair and a small, round table in the middle. It was barbie purple, with a red flower vase. From afar you couldn't tell the roses were fake. Until you got closer.

My eyes ran her up and down. Her eyes don't drop from me once. I'm silently begging for a guard to come running in, or even for a blink so I get a moment of relief from her glossy green balls of judgement.

"So, Angie, my name is Dr Matilda, but you can call me Tilly!" she introduces. That smile still doesn't move. I can see her hand quiver, deciding whether she should attempt to reach out and shake mine. I'm surprised she can pronounce a whole sentence with that fake smile plastered on lips. Her red lipstick is precise, not a smudge off her lips.

I shove my hands to the side of me and sigh.

"Great. My name is Angeline. Not Angie. Not to *you*." I say bluntly.

"Right. Okay then *Angeline*." She pronounces my name in a way that is borderline to mocking. "We're just going to run through some boundaries and rules before we start. Now Angie, Oh... I mean, Angeline, if you are to attempt to get physical with me, I will push this little red button here and guards will have to come in and restrain you." Her smile twitches slightly and she points to a tiny red button on the side of the flower vase.

My frown just deepens.

She wouldn't be able to reach it if I tackled her down.

Something I'm seriously considering, if she says even one thing that will set me off.

"You look young for a therapist. New job?" I ask with a fake smile.

She just blinks at me. "The headmistress believes that the closer in age to the students, the more comfortable they'll feel."

I let out a quiet breath through my nose, glancing her over, really looking this time.

"Right... except none of the other nurses look like you." My head tilts slightly. "You look like you should still be in college, halfway through your degree."

She doesn't reply.

I let the silence stretch a beat too long before adding, softer now, almost thoughtful–

"Tell me... what exactly did you have to do to get this job, hm?"

She just tightens her interlocked hands and purses her lips tight enough to show she's not going to say anything else. Doesn't need to.

Her eyes say enough.

To me, they say *'I don't get paid enough to deal with you, but I'll judge you for free anyway.'*

"Second rule. You may not lie. Honesty is very important for a healthy relationship, and I want you to trust me. There is no need to lie in this room!" the topic switches like the lights flicking on and off.

Rude. What therapist can't even answer questions.

I peek at the cat shape clock to my left. It ticks back at me; the tail swinging left to right.

"Before I start the questions, I just wanted to ask you. Do you feel safe here in this room, Angeline?"

"You just asked a question." I replied. She blinks slowly at me.

"Let me rephrase it then. Before I start the most *important* questions. Do you feel safe here in this room, Angeline?"

I look around. "I mean I can't say no can I... that would be *lying*."

She just stares at me. I start to fidget under her stares, and my eyes look anywhere but hers.

"Wonderful. I heard you had your first isolated detention this morning. What were you feeling throughout your time there?"

I don't want to talk about this, but something tells me she'll push, so I just shrug, peeking at the floor. "Oh, you know, the usual just,".

"Elaborate for me please. Was there anything you were expecting to happen?" she interrupts. I look up at her, hesitant to answer.

"Well, as I was trying to say, I felt like I normally do. Hungry. I wasn't expecting anything to happen, no."

She just sighs and looks at me for a minute before pushing me harder. "Did anything make you feel afraid?"

I grinned. "Afraid? Yeah, afraid I'd fall asleep and miss the excitement of the circus mirrors you guys set up for me."

Freddie would have loved that one.

"I understand you stole food for breakfast. Do you understand why following the rules is important?" Dr Matilda bluntly asks me, dropping her previous smiley act now.

My eyes squint slightly, "Excuse me, I didn't steal,"

"Answer the question."

"Oh, yes. Because this school's rules are *completely* balanced."

"Answer me Angie, are you willing to improve your behavior?"

I scowled. "Depends. Will improvement include not being embarrassed or left to starve in a windowless room? And I told you, you can call me Angeline and that's it."

"One of my colleagues mentioned to me you struggle with your eating. Do you feel guilt or fear when you eat?"

That question takes me back. My stomach flutters and I shuffle in my seat. "Um..." I hesitate.

Do I feel guilty? "No."

She starts scribbling on a tablet I didn't notice before.

"Right. Do you eat when you're stressed?"

Heat rises in my cheeks. These questions have gotten very personal. "If this is what you're wondering, I eat fine okay?"

"Do you feel embarrassed knowing what I'm asking is true? Because you know you need help but are too scared to ask?" her grin is slowly creeping back.

"Are you finding enjoyment in this *Tilly*? Creepy women like you finding entertainment from a young girl who seems to be struggling? You're not very professional." I spit out at her. I expect a reaction, even for her to get angry. Instead, she just sits there.

"Wonderful Angeline, it's a big step for you to admit you need help. I have just the thing for you." She reaches forward and pulls out a journal.

"This is one of our mental health journals, only for students who need it. In it, there is some information on the school. I want you to document what you eat, when and the portion."

I scoff and just look at her hand holding the black, hardcover book my way. "As if, you think I can remember all that. But that's what you want isn't it? You want me to struggle with my memory! How can I write that information if I can't remember it!" I lash out.

She frowns. "Take the book Angeline." her tone becomes harder and sharper. I flinch and suddenly feel shame for doing so. I reached out and snatched it.

The book has a golden logo of the school on the front cover.

"Now Angeline, do you believe your body is yours, or ours?" she asks and patiently waits for my response.

My stomach turns and bile rises in my throat, "It's mine you weird fuck. I don't know what you mean by that." my foot starts tapping.

She hums, "I understand. Now I need you to understand that food refusal will be documented."

"No, it won't," I scoff "Because this school doesn't care about us."

She nods silently. "Angeline, I am proud of you for being so open about your feelings to me. Now I know you expect me to get mad at you, however deliberately resisting compliance is just another way of trying to gain control over your body. Which means you're anxious, you don't understand your feelings. Is it because no one has brought this up to you before?"

I just stay silent and peek at the door again, refusing to entertain her.

"I see." she says softly. She is pretending to care. She doesn't. No one in this school does. Yet I find a tear slipping down my cheek anyway. I wipe it away quickly. Stupid emotions.

Stop it, Angeline! Pull yourself together!

"What was your first thought when you saw that toilet and cookie Angeline?" she asks.

I flinch again and curse myself for it. I look at her. "I thought that I'd suddenly lost my appetite... and possibly my faith in humanity."

She grins. "Yet you still ate the cookie."

"What are you, my therapist or my biggest critic?" I growl at her and turn away.

I flip open and skim through the pages of the dairy, not taking in anything but wanting to escape this never-ending battle with this bitch.

Welcome to Montclair Academy. You are here to be
improved.

Progress is measured through behavior, emotional
stability, and compliance with academy procedures.

Daily Routine:

- Wake at 06:00am

- Breakfast served according to performance
  level

- Classes begin at 07:45

- Lunch at 11:00

- Study hall at 13:00

- Showers and tidying 15:00

- 30-minute stretch break. Free to walk the
  grounds.

- Head back to dorms 15:30

- Dinner 17:00

- Free time 18:00

- Lights out 20:30

Behavioral Guidelines:

- Follow the pledge at all times.

- Keep journals accurate; missing or unhelpful
  entries will be corrected.

- Observe, do not disrupt, report only factual
  events.

- If asked, you must recite the pledge.

Progress Monitoring:

- Colored boards display improvement status - Located in the main entry's hall.

- Scores updated daily; failure to maintain progress will result in reassignment or reflection.

Important:

- Trust in the academy is paramount.

- Individual emotional distress is an opportunity for growth.

- All instructions must be followed, even if the reason is unclear.

Remember:

- Improvement requires no consent.

Then the clock chimes loudly three times.

"Great, Angeline, you made it through the whole session. Well, done! Please, take a cookie on the way out." Dr Matilda stands and offers. As I stand up, I look at the cookies but walk away. I attempt to rip the door open, but it won't budge.

"Oh Angeline, please. Take a cookie. I won't allow them to open the door, until you do." Her voice echoes around the room.

Screw you.

I turn around and walk close to the hot plate of cookies. I take the top one, the smallest with the least chocolate chips. I take a nibble out of the side and put it back down, rolling my eyes at her inhumane expression.

"Good." She then presses a button under the table, and the door clicks open.

"I will see you next time, Angeline and remember, improvement requires no consent. I will be checking your diary next time for any improvements."

As the door opens, I see her reflection in the shiny wall in front of me on my way out. She grins and waves.

Who hired that wacko?

Dear diary,

Having to sit myself down and devote time in my day to write in this journal is ridiculous if you ask me. But I guess my opinion doesn't matter, because here I am. Writing in a stupid journal. I got told by Dr Matilda that I needed to document my food intake here, and I told her basically to get lost. There's no way I can even remember the portion size of what I ate this morning.

But we made a deal - okay, a one-sided deal that she doesn't know about. I'll only write what I eat and skip that other crap. That's the only way they can get information about the situation.

On a side note, the nurses and teachers here creep me out... the headmistress must be superrr specific in what she is looking for when she hires people because they all have the same smile, the same tone and even the same shade of teeth.

I only got here the other day, and I think I'm hiding in the crowd pretty well - oh except for that annoying red head who couldn't hide if she wanted to. You can guess what I mean. Or is it her mean horns floating around her head as she walks- stinking out the hallway with her minions.

I just physically gagged.

When she first sat down next to me, I thought she would be like... a nice girl with just a resting bitch face. Actually, scratch the resting part. I think she pulls that face 24/7 on PURPOSE. Seriously, who does she think she is?? I'm sure she has been here longer than me and therefore knows the stupid food rule. In my defense, I didn't know about it. She's like one of those popular bullies in those cheesy movies - that say stuff like 'I'm gonna give you a knuckle sandwich in a minute if you don't dunk your head in the toilet willingly!!'

I don't know what to do. I don't know how she knew about my... control issue in edible form. I'm telling you; it must have been Dahlia. Although I can't see Dahlia getting along with the red headed rat... but Dahlia is the only one who currently knows about the silly little side quest I do after every meal. So, it must have been her.

Right? Xoxo, Angie.

Chapter 13

Strangers are friends you haven't met yet.

Freddie.

The door to my dorm creaks like it's 1000 years old, which for a *"school that's for the rich and elite"*, is pretty ridiculous, the headmistress's words still haunting the back of my head.

"Dude," I mutter, shoving it wider with my shoulder. "I swear, one day I'm gonna WD-40 you whether you consent or not. Hah, *'Improvement requires no consent'*."

I see Wes, sitting on his bed when I walk in, elbows on his knees, staring at the floor. That alone kills my joke momentum.

I dropped my bag anyway. Attempting to break the silence.

"Yo," I say carefully. "You look like you just failed to... you know...." gesturing down there.

He snorts, but it's weak. "Sure, something like that."

I kick off my shoes and flop onto my bed, springs protesting under my weight. "Okay. You gonna explain or should I start guessing wildly? Because my first guess involves whatever's going wrong with your dick."

Wes exhaled, scrubbing a hand down his face. "It was Alyssa. And Angie."

My stomach tightens, even though I don't totally get why yet. "That escalated fast."

"I can't stop thinking about it, she cornered her. With her friends." His jaw clenches. "They were saying stuff. About... about Angie not eating. About breakfast. Like it was a joke."

I blink. Once. Twice.

"...What?"

Wes looks up at me then. "Yeah."

I sit up. The goof drains out of me like someone pulled a plug I didn't know I had.

"Why would Alyssa say that?" I ask. "Angie doesn't eat breakfast. Is that, is that like a skinny joke girls have? Like, 'Oh my god, I only drink iced coffee and vibes'?"

Wes huffs. "Freddie."

"I'm serious," I insist. "I mean, I'm not serious-serious, but I don't get it. People skip breakfast all the time."

"She wasn't joking," he says quietly. "And Angie didn't take it as a joke."

Something ugly curls in my chest. "That's messed up."

"Yeah." Wes stands grabbing his hoodie. "I told them to back off. Angie ran off, she already had isolated detention, she was already going to be late. So, I didn't follow her."

I nod slowly. I don't blame him. There wasn't really a right move there.

"Well," I say, forcing some air back into my voice, "if Alyssa was trying to win 'Most Punchable Personality,' she's really committing to the bit."

Wes almost smiles at that.

"I'll see you around," I add, standing. "Try not to insult any chicks with your disabled disadvantage before dinner."

"No promises. And my dick is fine!" He calls out.

I leave before he can say anything else, my mood souring with every step down the hall. People pass me, laughing, talking, existing like nothing in their precious lives have cracked sideways.

Then I saw Dahlia.

She's turning the corner ahead of me, dark straight hair swinging, shoulders tense like she's carrying something heavy she didn't ask for.

"Hey–!" I jog forward. "Hey, Dolly, wait up!"

She pauses, turning slowly. Her smile flickers when she sees me. Not fake, but I can tell she's tired.

"Hey, Freddie."

I fell into step beside her. "So. Hypothetical question."

She raises a brow.

"Okay, less hypothetical." I rub the back of my neck. "Do you know what's going on with Princess?"

Her mouth tightens just a little. "Angie?"

"Yeah. I heard some stuff. Not details. Just… stuff." I grimace. "Bad stuff."

Dahlia keeps walking, not making eye contact with me anymore. "She's not really talking to me right now. So no, I don't know anything."

That's when I know she's lying. Not a big lie. A protective one. The kind you tell when the truth would hurt someone who isn't ready. I turn directly in front of her, slowing my pace so she has to either slow down or ditch me. She slows.

"Dolly," I say gently. "I'm not asking to pry. I'm asking because I care."

She sighs, stopping completely now. The hallway feels too quiet.

"She ran into the bathroom," she says finally. "The first day. When we arrived."
She looks around, hesitant to continue. I nodded her on.

"She was shaking," she continues. "Like... like she'd felt something awful. Or thought she had." Her voice drops. "I think she got sick, I tried to offer help, but she shooed me away."

My chest tightens. "Just you?"
She nods. "I wasn't sure at first, but I sort of worked it out later when we talked, what was going on."

"And that is?" I ask softly.

Dahlia hugs her arms around herself, shaking her head. "No, look, I don't know everything Freddie and I'm not going to tell you more. It's not my story to tell."

"That's fair. I get that," I say quickly. And I do. "I just... Alyssa clearly knew something. I don't like it."

Dahlia's eyes flash. "I don't like it too." She hesitates, then adds, "Angie doesn't... she struggles, I can tell. With food. With control. That's all I'm saying."

Wow. I really want to pretend I didn't hear that. I can't explain why it bothers me to hear that she struggles. I don't even know her and something inside me snaps, learning that there is something going on with her, that I don't know about.

I nod slowly. "Okay."

"I don't know how Alyssa found out," Dahlia says. "I swear. I never told anyone."

"I believe you."

She looked relieved, but only a little. "Please don't confront Angie. Not yet."

"I won't," I promise. "Scout's honor."

She snorts. "Were you even ever a scout?"

"No," *I think.* "But I would've been great at the snacks part."

That earns me a real smile. As she walks away, I stand there for a moment, hands in my pockets, staring at the floor like Wes did earlier.

Princess.

Whatever Alyssa thought she was doing, she crossed a line. And goofy or not, I don't let people mess with my friends. Even the ones who don't know they're my friends yet.

Chapter 14

A free haircut.

Freddie.

Nick is sharpening a pencil, weirdly very intimately. Intimate like he wants to *kill* that pencil.

I watch from my bed; hands laced behind my head. "You know," I say, "statistically speaking, that pencil has done nothing to deserve this level of hostility."

Nick doesn't look up. "It snapped earlier."

"Ah," I nod solemnly, throwing up my fist in the air. "Then by all means. Vengeance."

He finally snorts, which for Nick is basically a belly laugh. "You ever notice this place smells like, out of date disinfectant and... I don't fucking know, regret?"

"Every day," I say. "I miss air that doesn't feel like it's judging me."

Nick sets the pencil down and leans back in his chair, running his abnormally large hands through his dark brunette hair. "I hate it here."

"Same," I reply instantly. "The walls are too clear. Like they're trying to convince us we're clean or something."

"Or empty," he mutters.

Silence settles between us, but it's not awkward. Nick and I don't do awkward. We do mutual sardonic and strategic quiet.

"I'm going for a run." He says, standing, changing into a sleek black shirt. "Field's empty this time of day."

"Try not to outrun your demons." I tell him.

He pauses at the door. "They're faster than me anyway."

Then he's gone.

I roll to my desk chair and spin once, just because I can. The room feels bigger without him. I face the desk, tapping my pen, trying to pretend I care about the worksheet in front of me.

What the fuck. How am I meant to even answer this question...

Something slams into the back of my neck. Hard.

It's not painful at first, more like my body forgets what it's supposed to do. My breath vanishes. The room tilts. My hands slide off the desk as everything goes dark.

Light. Too much of it. My eyes blink, burning, trying to adjust. The ceiling above me is white. Not dorm white. Sterile white. *Endless* white. "Oh," I whisper hoarsely. "That's... not good."

The White Room. We meet at last.

My head throbs as I push myself upright. The air smells sharp and chemical. I touch my neck instinctively, fingers shaking as I trace the lines tattooed into my skin. Footsteps click softly. A nurse walks in. Pale dress. Pale smile. Eyes that don't blink enough.

"Well," the woman croons. "You make things difficult, don't you?"

I glare at her, catching my breath. "I prefer the term *nonconformist*."

She laughs lightly, like I've complimented her. She steps closer, reaching out, fingers brushing through my soft hair. My body reacts before my brain does as I swatted her hand away.

"Don't touch me," I snap.

Her smile vanishes.

"How dare you," she says coolly. "Guards."

The doors slide open. Two of them appear, a black mask making them faceless. They grab my arms, hauling me to my feet. As they drag me down the hall, something flickered in my mind.

My mother.

Her fingers gentle, humming softly as she brushed my hair in the mornings. Always careful. Always proud.

"You've got beautiful hair, Freddie," she'd say. "Don't ever let anyone tell you it doesn't matter." Another flash, my father's voice, sharp, dismissive.

"Hairdressing is a waste. Grow up." Yelling echoed throughout the hallway. But it was not coming from her.

The memory slips away as the guards shove me into a chair. Cold metal presses against my scalp.

"Wait, what?" I say, pulse spiking. "What are you doing?"

The woman steps into view again, holding an electric razor. It buzzes to life with a low, hungry sound.

"Punishment," she says sweetly. "For refusal. For disrespect."

"I just didn't say the pledge," I protest. "That's- that's not-"

She tilts her head. "You will learn."

The razor touches my head. Hair falls. I freeze, breath shallow, watching my blonde strands hit the white floor. Something twists in my chest, sharp and wrong, but I don't understand why. It just feels like something is being taken that I didn't agree to give.

Finally, it's over, she steps back, satisfied.

"Take him," she says.

As they pull me away, I catch my reflection in the glass. Bare. Stripped, *I've been violated...* but the confusion disappears, as I feel a fuzzy feeling catching my eyes. It's gone. My hair, the image, everything is unclear.

Chapter 15

The rainbow room.

Freddie.

The guards guided me into a sickeningly colorful room. *A rainbow room.* I gasp jokingly and pretend to look around fascinated.

When I turn around, a blond young lady appears in front of me. *The same bat that interrupted Princess and me.*

"Why hello, Freddie. I can call you Freddie, can't I?" she says lightly. The room around us looks like a big bowl of sprinkles. Pink on one wall, yellow on the other.

Oh, and I can't forget the inviting, colorful chairs in the middle of the room.

Are those fake flowers?

"Sure, whatever. It's what everyone calls me." I respond vaguely.

"Great, I hope you feel comfortable. You know I decorated my office myself. Picked out all the colors."

"On purpose?" I mutter. *Like I give a shit about the color of her room?* "Yeah so" I continue, "look I don't reallly want to be here, so as short as we could make this would be fantastic." I say, picking a chair to sit on.

Right as I landed on the pink cushions, the smile on her face flicked upside down.

"That one's mine. Up." she clicks and demands.

I scoff, "Uh- okay? Didn't realize you were emotionally attached to that couch... some real hard moments must have come out over there." I sit down again, this time on the small yellow armchair. I just fit in the chair's width. I shuffle around, the sides of the chair pressing into me.

Damn, I should have brought a chair from our dorm.

"Right. What's on the agenda today..." I squint to read her name badge, "Tilly. What questions do you have for me?" I cross my arms over.

"Well Freddie, a little kitty told me recently that you just had your first isolated detention. So that's what we're gonna be talking about today."

"Wait, I thought the saying was a little 'birdie'?" I interrupt. "I mean, don't quote me but..."

"Oh no, for some it is, but as you can see, I just love cats!" she points to the tiniest, little sticker next to her name badge.

I just stared at her. *Is she genuinely... okay?*

"First, I need to run through some rules and boundaries just so you understand and don't attempt to get physical. That's the first rule, getting physical will result in those two guards outside having to come in. I'll leave it to your own imagination what will happen after that!" she hums, her bony finger guiding my eyes to the door.

I nodded, slowly turning my head back to her. *Fuck, I didn't realize therapy meant sitting in a real-life bowl of lucky charms.*

"Second rule. You may not lie. Honesty is very important for a healthy relationship, and I want you to trust me. There is no need to lie in this room!" Her tone says she is dead serious, but her grin says otherwise. She said that sentence so quickly it sounded rehearsed. Like she has said it many times before.

"Righto, no lying got it. Hey, do you ever stop smiling? My cheeks hurt just looking at you,"

"Let me make another personal rule just for us Freddie. No talking about me!" she giggles awkwardly. It sounds like she takes a breath between every 'he-he'. I have to squeeze my mouth shut, since my mind is saying; *what the actual fuck?*

I wonder if this school has any priest's available because she needs a blessing and an exorcism. Mainly for that laugh.

I'm sure she would make another personal rule for us if I said that out loud.

"How are you feeling right now?" she asks.

I hesitate. "Oh, fantastic. You know, I feel like this weight has been lifted off my shoulders since I got my head shaved. Well, more like lifted of my head if you know what..."

"You're using humor to keep distance." She interrupts my joke. "That usually means something hurts. Would you like to tell me more how you felt after looking in the mirror for the first time?"

I frown at her and look down at my hands to realize my fingers are tightly squeezed into fists. I take a breath and push down the anger bubbling inside me. She's getting in my head. *Freddie, stop being a pussy and man up. One blond crackhead lady won't make you crack.*

"Well, honestly, I thought to myself, I'm just thrilled I get to rock this military chic look. Very in Season. You know."

She starts scribbling on a pink tablet. "You're more upset than you're letting on." she softly replies.

"And I think you're more dramatic than you seem. It was a free haircut. I'll survive. It's not something that has emotionally fucked me up."

"Surviving isn't the same as being okay. You know that." she peeks up at me now.

"You know what," I start, pushing myself out of the seat that's pulling me deeper in. "I don't give you permission to assume that I'm fucked up in the head, and that I'm some depressed monkey now because my hair is gone. Okay?" my jaw clenches. I hate all these feeling talks. I don't need her fake empathy and *for what?* It's just hair.

"Mr. Kensington, I don't require your permission. I will speak freely about what I need to. You don't need to act tough."

I smirk, "What? I thought I would look tougher with no hair!" I joke, almost letting a laugh slip through. *She cannot be for real.*

"You don't look tough." she immediately replies. "You look smaller."

My smile drops. "Well, so much for a fun experience in this room. You are in *such* a mood to kill Tilly."

I can see I'm getting under her skin. She smiles harder, taking a deep breath.

"Do you think your punishment was justified?"

"Absolutely. I always wanted a closer relationship with my reflection and the cold breeze. Thanks, guys." I yell loudly at the guards outside.

"Right. You're not funny because this is funny Frederick. You're funny because being serious here feels unsafe." Her shoulders dropped after saying that, like she released some tension.

And passed it to me. My breath hitches and I squeeze my jaw from saying anything back to her.

"Freddie, do you know why we chose to get rid of your hair?"

I shrug. Maybe they make Voo-doo dolls with this shit? *How was I supposed to know that?*

"It wasn't about the audience or power it would give you around campus." She stays silent, like she's waiting for me to say something back. I don't answer.

"It was about you knowing we can do it again. Whatever we want. Anything to successfully reform you." she hums, satisfied. *Does she know how insane that sounds? This bitch is crazy!*

"I have one more question for you. When you were getting your hair shaved, did you think of anyone in particular? Maybe someone close to you or even related. Maybe even Angie?" Tilly asks, her voice clean as day.

Fuck no. Not in this world, you cat loving freak.

I point directly in her face, warning her, "You have no right to call her Angie. Her name is Angeline. And even if I did think of someone, I wouldn't tell you. I have a right to stay silent." I lean back into my chair.

"You may think you do Frederick, but in this room, silence isn't an option. You know, some things get taken from us before we even know how much they matter."

That same unsettling feeling rises in my stomach. My chest tightens, and goosebumps prick across my arm. Suddenly, I can feel something warm brush across my scalp. I reach my hand up.

"I'm going to be a hairdresser one day Fred's."

Her voice echoes around me and my breathing hitches. But when my hand touches my head, the feeling goes away.

"Do you remember her, Freddie?" Tilly's voice brings my mind back to the session.

"Who? Remember who? I don't know what you're talking about." I mentally reach for the memory to come back, but

I'm left with only the sweet thoughts of the princess. I smiled to myself wondering what she's doing right now. Maybe brushing her golden locks, or batting those long, dark lashes at someone. Hopefully not another guy. I internally groan at my own thoughts.

Suddenly, a cat starts meowing over and over again. She grins. "Wonderful Freddie, you made it to the end of the session! Now, when you go out, I don't want you to think any more about why it was a punishment. I just want you to process it instead. Okay?"

I just blink at her before nodding. Then when my back's turned and the doors opened and I finally rolled my eyes.

"Don't roll your eyes at me, Kensington."

What a creep. I hope to never see her face again, or the rainbow room.

Chapter 16

A fun fact about me is…

Wes.

They've shoved us into this room like we're loose screws, they finally got tired of tripping over. No windows. Circular table. Too many chairs. The kind of place that smells like forced cooperation and bad decisions.

A woman I don't recognize, with a tight bun and tighter smile, stands at the front with her hands clasped like she's praying for our souls.

"You have not been behaving appropriately." she says. "You were placed together as a group for a reason. Your inability to get along is unacceptable."

Inability to get along? I'm confused, I mean I'm fine with everyone. Freddie's easy, the girls are…girls and Nick. Nick… yeah, I'm done. *Who could possibly not be getting along?*

Nick scoffs immediately. Loud. On purpose.

I glanced at him. "Careful, man. She looks like the type who feeds people to basements."

He doesn't respond, but the corner of his mouth twitches.

The woman continues, unfazed. "You will remain in this room until you learn how to function as a group. Like you were told on the first day, you will be evaluated as individuals *and* as a unit. As do all students in their sectors. We do not like repeating ourselves. Failure to do so will have consequences."

I hate when adults say consequences, where the hell are their consequences? She leaves without another word. The door locks and the silence drops like a bad punchline.

Angie shifts in her chair first, fingers twisting through her tight curly locks. Dahlia, Lia to us, sits stiffly beside her, eyes fixed on the table.

I clear my throat. "Well. Anyone want to start with their problems or should I go first?"

"Wes." Dahlia says softly.

"Too soon?" I grin. "Yeah. Fair."

Angie exhales, then turns to Dahlia. "I'm sorry." That gets everyone's attention.

"I shouldn't have snapped at you. You didn't deserve that. I realize you wouldn't tell Alyssa anything."

Dahlia finally looks up. Her eyes are glossy, but she smiles anyway. "I'm sorry too. I should've said something instead of shutting down."

Angie reaches for her hand. Dahlia takes it. *Okay. That's... good. Unexpectedly wholesome. I mean yay girl power.*

Freddie leans back in his chair. "Wow. Emotional growth. Love that for us."

Nick snorts. "Don't get used to it."

I glance around the table. "So," I say, "can we talk about the elephant in the room?"

Freddie tilts his head. "Which one? The emotional repression or the fact that I look like a boiled egg?" That's when I really look at him. His hair's gone. Completely vanished.

"What the fuck?" I blurt. "Freddie, did you lose a bet with God?"

He shrugs. "Didn't say the pledge. Apparently, my follicles were too rebellious."

Angie's face twists immediately. "That's it?" she snaps. "That was your punishment?"

Freddie blinks at her. "Uh. Yeah?"

"That's not fair," she says, jaw tight. "That's nothing."

My stomach drops a little. "Angie... what happened to you?"

She freezes. Then laughs too quickly. "Nothing. Just a nightmare."

Nick's eyes flick to her, almost with an ounce of concern. But he doesn't push or dare to show us he cares. Smart. We sit there for a moment, the weight of unsaid things piling up like dirty laundry.

I lean forward, elbows on the table. *Well, if we're airing things out, I might as well go.*

"Speaking of nightmares, I keep having this recurring one and it's driving me insane." I mutter.

"Not my problem." Nick spits as he looks around the room for any kind of escape."

"You are such an asshole." Lia shot back.

"Oh yeah, me I'm the asshole? Why, because I don't want to sit here and listen to you guys bitch!"

"Would you both just stop it! Whatever issues you two have, get over it! They're probably watching us! So just shut up and let Wes finish, so we can get the hell out of this tiny, stuffy room!" Angie ordered, pointing at Lia and Nick.

Nick sighs, his fist tensing up instead of hitting something as Lia just directs her body fully onto me, blocking Nick completely from her tunnel of vision.

"Thank you, Angie." I grin.

"Well, what do you see man?" Freddie asks.

"It's the same every night. I'm in bed, sleeping, when I suddenly see a nurse injecting me with some needle. And I can't stop her! I'm strapped with restraints, in a dark, empty room. I can't move. Then my mind starts to feel numb and I'm out of it again. By the time I wake up, it's morning and the breakfast call is made. I don't know how many times it's happened. I think I've forgotten them a few times."

"What?" Nick whispers.

"Yeah, I know. It's just a nightmare, probably,"

"No. I've seen that too." Nick responds.

Okay. What the hell is going on.

"I... I have too." Lia says, slightly shaking.

I look at Freddie and Angie, who are already staring at each other. They broke and both nodded at me.

"So, we've all had the same dream?" I ask.

"But in mine, I'm alone. You guys aren't there." Angie explains.

"You know what. Enough. It's this place. Okay, it's getting to us. There is nothing more than this, we don't share nightmares. So, let's just drop it. The way I take it, we pass the year with the 'reform trials', and we can go home. So just... chill." Freddie rushes, smacking his hand on the table.

"Look, all of us just don't mesh. For different reasons. But clearly the school wants us to play house." I respond.

"Hard pass." Nick mutters while flashing his judgmental brown eyes.

"Yeah, yeah," I say. "But unless we burn this place down, we're stuck."

Freddie nods. "And I don't burn places down unless everyone agrees. Democracy."

Lia smiles faintly while Angie looks at the ceiling giggling. However, takes it back when she sees the amusement it brings Freddie.

Angie squeezes Lia's hand. "I don't want us fighting anymore."

Nick says nothing. Doesn't even look at Dahlia. She doesn't look at him either. It's like there's an invisible wall between them, thick and deliberate. I clock it. Don't comment. Nope. I am *not* getting in the middle of that.

"Fine," I say. "Truce. Temporarily, until we get out. Then we never have to see each other again."

"That was implied." Freddie says.

Chapter 17

Who is the man in the air?

Dahlia.

I hate assembly. Shoes scuff the floor in uneven rhythms, voices kept just a little too quiet, like the walls might lean in if we're not careful.

Angie walks beside me, her arm brushing mine every few steps. She smells like something floral, sweet and comforting.

A guard passes us, boots heavy, posture stiff. Angie waits until he's out of earshot.

"Do you think he practices walking in the mirror?" she asks.

I bit my lip, then lost the battle immediately. "Absolutely. 'Intimidating but approachable.'"

Angie straightens her shoulders and starts marching, face blank, arms stiff and exaggerated.

I wheeze, grabbing her sleeve. "Stop. You're gonna get us killed."

"Worth it."

I shake my head, still smiling, and for a moment it feels almost normal. Like we're just girls walking to an assembly, not pieces being moved around a board we didn't agree to play on.

The doors to the assembly hall open, swallowing us into noise and light.

The boys are already there, Freddie slouched like chairs were invented to inconvenience him, Wes next to him, sitting upright, eyes scanning the room, Nick is a few seats down, rigid and distant. I pause before sitting.

I don't know why I look at him. I just do. He's such a jerk, but there's something about him that fascinates me. I'm just drawn to...

No! No Dahlia, snap out of it! You can't stand him!

He doesn't fidget. Doesn't talk. Doesn't scan the room like Wes or slouch like Freddie. He sits with his hands clasped loosely, gaze forward, jaw set, not angry exactly, just... guarded. Like whatever he's holding inside is sharper than what's around him.

I wonder what it takes to make someone build walls that thick. What he's afraid would happen if he let them down. The thought is heavier than I expected. I look away before he can notice.

Angie and I took our seats. I end up next to Wes. The room fills fast. Too fast.

Voices rise, layer upon layer, until it's all one swelling sound. A laugh bursts somewhere behind me, high and sudden and my breath stutters in response.

I lace my fingers together in my lap.

In. Out.

The lights dim slightly. A staff member steps onto the stage, voice amplified, words crisp and sharp. I try to focus, but the sound spreads, presses in.

"And now," the voice announces, "for our outstanding achievement award–"

The name is called. The room erupts.

Applause slams into me all at once. Clapping. Hard and rapid, relentless. Cheers echo, whistle sharp and piercing. The sound isn't just loud; it's *everywhere*.

My chest tightens violently. I don't clap. I can't.

The noise twists, stretches into something else entirely.

A door slamming. Hands coming together once. Why does this bother me? Am I really that pathetic that I can't handle some loud claps at a school assembly?

"Stand up straight. Keep your eyes straight. This will toughen you up." A harsh and almost demonic voice screeches through both my ears. What is going on? The applause has faded and there is no one left on stage... Who said that? Who's speaking? Just as I start to make out a man's face in literal thin air.

Someone says my name. Once. Twice.

"Lia?"

Wes. I don't look at him. I don't think I can without everything spilling over. My hands are shaking now, fingers numb. The cheering comes back, keeps going. Then, quiet.

It drops suddenly, like someone cuts the cord. The noise recedes enough for the room to snap back into focus. I suck in a breath that feels like it's the first one I've taken in minutes. I finally turned my head.

Wes is watching me, brows drawn together, not panicked, not demanding. His hand had been resting near mine on the armrest without me even noticing. Now he pulls it back, slow and deliberate, giving me space.

He gives a small nod. *You're okay. I see you.* I nodded back.

Not gratitude. Not embarrassing. With acknowledgement. The assembly moves on. Names, applause, order restored. But my pulse stays loud for a while longer. Still, I sit there. Breathing. Present. And that feels like enough.

Chapter 18

School pledge, my ass.

Nick.

I'm staring at the math board, trying to make sense of some meaningless numbers, when I feel it. A folded note slides onto my desk.

The fuck?

Alyssa, of course. That bitch is grinning like she's won some twisted prize. Out of everyone in the class, I had to be seated next to her. I open it.

"Hey, Mr. Moody 😊 Looks like someone needs tutoring... maybe I can help you after class? Or maybe during? 😭"

I scowl, ignoring it. Not gonna dignify this shit.

Another note lands. She's leaning closer this time, brushing my arm. Winking. Flirting. The note reads:

"You look tense. I could fix that under the desk if you stopped pretending you don't want me. 🐱"

I slam my hand down. No. Fucking. Way.

I take a glance at her, hoping my glare will scare her away. One finger is fiddling with her hair. She bats her lashes at me and playfully bites her bottom lip. Her cheeks are a hot red.

Then, she reaches her spare hand over, sliding it up my thigh. That's it. Rage explodes like a fuse I didn't know was lit. I grab her hand and shove it as hard as I can. It bangs against the desk.

"Ow!" she gasps, like I just ruined her whole day.

I want to punch something. "Are you fucking kidding me?!" I snap, voice loud enough to make the class turn. "Get your hand the fuck off me, you psychotic bitch!"

Everyone's eyes are on me now. *Perfect.*

The nurse walks over to me, wearing the same grin she was an hour ago. Then I feel a guard's gun tapping the back of my shoulder.

"Outside. Now."

I stand up, nearly sending the table across the room. I have no choice but to follow the guard, jaw tight, fists still itching. He stops me by the door. Arms crossed. "Recite the last line of the pledge."

I groan, muttering under my breath, "Fucking really?" I try to dredge it up from the dark, brain-dead recesses of my mind.

"Nickolas," he says, voice hard. "Recite it, or detention."

I grit my teeth. I can't remember it. I sigh, thinking about this morning's assembly. My mind flicks from the headmistress, suddenly to Dahlia. She is sitting in her chair next to Wes, her soft facial features glancing at the stage. I couldn't remember anything about the assembly because my stupid eyes kept flicking to the exact seat she was in. I can feel my shoulders dropping, and I let out a breath.

Nick, pull it together. She's the reason you can't remember right now. And she's about to be the reason you get detention. *God, I hate this.*

Here I am stuck, and she just has to make every situation so much harder. Angie at least tries to keep her head down, but Dahlia, she's just so irritating, like she's asking for trouble.

Oh, what am I saying. She hasn't done anything.

But I can't explain it. She just gets under my skin, like I should hate her. Maybe the back of my mind is thinking of a reason why. Almost *remembering* a reason why...

Jesus Christ, Nick. That's ridiculous. Focus!

Then I remembered.

"Does improvement require consent? No."

The guard scowls. "One minute to lunch. You can start leaving,"

I turn around walking off. My footsteps carry the halls as I stomp away. Of course, he can't just let it go. "Nickolas, be aware, any sort of intimacy between students is not allowed–"

I spin, sarcasm dripping from every word. "Oh, just perfect, harassment is fine, intimacy is banned, and consent is a joke! Got it, school pledge, you useless sack of shit!"

I storm down the hall, past three classrooms with doors wide open. And then I hear it. Teachers finish each other's sentences, word for word, like some sick, hypnotic recording:

"...the curriculum must ensure that..."

"...that every student follows the rules without exception..."

"...without exception, at all times..."

I stop mid-step, muttering, "What the actual fuck... is this place?"

My stomach twists in disbelief, but my blood is still on fire from Alyssa. The notes. The hand. The *audacity.* Should I tell the others? *Nah, fuck the others and their stupid emotions. Then I'll just be forced to talk about mine.*

After a few blocks of walking, I finally made it to the doors of the cafeteria to see Wendy's smiling face.

Chapter 19

Dry cereal, a carrot and saltwater?

Nick.

I'm first in line. Hunger does that, it makes you impatient, mean around the edges. Wendy slides my tray forward, already reaching for the oatmeal ladle, then freezes.

She sighs. Long and Tired.

"Nick," she says, "you need to up your performance. I just watched your performance color go from yellow to red." She grimaces. "Sorry, kid. Dry cereal and salt water today."

She drops the tray in front of me with a dull clatter.

I stared at it. Then at her. "Performance color?" I ask. "What the hell is that?"

Wendy rolls her eyes and looks straight up at the ceiling like she's appealing to a higher power. "You kids don't know? Ugh. Your teachers were supposed to explain it on day one. Jeez, are my coworkers useless or what?" She looks back at me. "The school evaluates you with performance colors. Green means you're complying. Reform trials are going well.

93

Yellow means you're slipping. Red means you're failing." Her mouth tightens. "Rewards and consequences come with each level."

Her eyes flick down to my tray.

It sinks in.

"So, this," I say slowly, nudging the bowl of dry cereal, "This is a consequence?"

"Yes."

"Well, how do I keep track of my color?" I ask. "How do I check?"

"There's a performance board on floor one," she says. "Front entrance. Your barcode shows your photo, name and color."

I groaned. "Amazing. So, I get a carrot that looks like it's seen war."

She snorts and waves me along. "Eat or don't."

I took my tray and sat down. Dahlia joins me a moment later, soft rolls of bread steaming in front of her. I scowl at my food.

"You're grouchier than usual." she says.

"Didn't realize I had a baseline." I mutter

She gives me a look. The kind that says don't lie to me. I don't answer. She sighs. *Why is she so interested in what I do? Why is she so, so…*

We exchange a few quiet glances, nothing heavy, just… loaded. She looks like she wants to say something. I'm bracing for it when–

SLAM.

Wes drops his tray onto the table and slides in next to Dahlia like a human jump scare. *Thank God. Sitting here like this was making my insides curl.* He's grinning, all brazen and loud, trying to inject life into the dead air.

"So! How's everyone surviving the culinary nightmare today?"

No one answers. I glare at him. Hard.

His grin falters. "...Okay. Tough crowd."

Freddie and Angie join us. Freddie's talking about something ridiculous from his class, Angie nodding along. I half-listen, then mutter, "I almost got detention today."

I know I wasn't going to bother them, but my blood's still boiling. I have to get this off my chest to someone, anyone.

"Alyssa." I add flatly.

Angie makes a face and pretends to gag. "Ew. Don't even say her name."

"She crossed a line," I say. I won't go into detail. I don't have to. "Touched me. Wouldn't stop."

There's a pause.

Dahlia's jaw tightens. She takes a long, loud sip from her drink. It's *empty.* Everyone looks at her.

"What?" she snaps. "Can't a girl enjoy a... uh..." She squints at the label. "Swampy apple pop."

Freddie laughs. Wes groans. "That sounds illegal."

"At least you got something decent for going green on the mood ring of doom," Wes mutters, poking at his oatmeal. "I dropped back to yellow."

"What does that mean?" Dahlia asks.

"There's a performance board," I cut in. "Tracks how obedient we are. I dropped to red today."

I shove my tray forward.

"This is it," I say. "I'm guessing the salt's to 'hydrate' me, so I don't get too thirsty."

Freddie scoffs. "That's not how hydration works."

Before I can respond, I feel it.

Dahlia isn't listening anymore. She's staring. Daggers. Pure, murderous focus across the cafeteria.

Alyssa.

She's laughing with her little group, hair perfect, posture smug. Dahlia doesn't break once. Then Alyssa notices. She whispers something to her friends. They snicker as Alyssa rises to her feet.

My stomach drops. "Dahlia–" I start to say and reach over to grab her wrist. When my hand touches her, I practically get zapped. I pull my hand back quickly, my fingers tingling. My eyes scan over her. Alyssa starts to walk over, hips swinging like the showoff she is. Only to stop right at our table.

"What the hell are you looking at?" she snaps at Dahlia.

Dahlia doesn't answer.

Alyssa turns to me, smiling curly. "Hey, Nickie, offer's still up."

Something hot and violent twists in my chest.

"Just fuck off, Alyssa," I say, gesturing my hand to shoo her off.

That's when Dahlia stands. The chair screeches back. Everyone nearby freezes.

"DO NOT call him Nickie, you asshole," she yells. Her voice cuts straight through the cafeteria. "You touched him without consent and you're standing here acting cute about it?"

Alyssa scoffs. "Relax–"

"SHUT UP," Dahlia snaps. "You don't get to relax after what you did."

Freddie moves fast, stepping between them, "Ladies, ladies, please let's just sort this out like soul sisters or some shit!"

Angie scuffs, causing Freddie to throw his hands up in the air, not knowing how she would handle the situation just as a guard approaches.

"That's enough" the guard barks. "Both of you."

Alyssa folds her arms, rolling her eyes. "She started it."

The guard turns to her. "Recite the pledge."

Her face drains. She hesitates.

"Now," he snaps.

She stumbles through it, voice shaking, cheeks burning. The cafeteria watches every word. When it's over, she storms off with her friends, furious. The guard lingers a second, then walks away.

Dahlia's still breathing hard. Angie looks impressed. Wes looks stunned. Freddie exhales like he was holding his breath the whole time.

I glanced at Dahlia. She doesn't look at me. Not yet.

Why would she do that, I mean it's clear we're like oil and water. *Why help me?*

Now I feel a bit shitty. Maybe that reason in the back of my mind was wrong.

I don't know anything anymore... and yeah, my heart's still racing.

Chapter 20

Silence is survival.

Dahlia.

The clock says **11:10 a.m.** I stare at it longer than I should. The second hand ticks. My stomach tightens, a thin thread pulling inward. That's not right.

I could swear- *I know*- the clock in my first class this morning said the same thing. Same numbers. Same spacing between the digits. Same faint scratch on the glass just above the ten.

11:10. *Maybe I'm seeing things...*

I blink hard and look back down at my notebook, half-expecting the page to have changed while I wasn't looking. It hasn't. My handwriting looks like mine. Soft curves. Careful lines.

You're fine, I tell myself. *You're just tired.*

The teacher's voice drifts through the room, words blending like they don't want to be understood. A student two rows up taps their pen- *tap, tap, tap.*

My shoulders inch higher. Then the alarm sounds. It's sudden. Piercing. Not just loud- *commanding.*

"LOCKDOWN. THIS IS A PRACTICE DRILL."

The words echo through the speakers, distorted, metallic.

Chairs scrape. Someone yelps. Another student laughs nervously, too high-pitched, already unraveling. The teacher shouts instructions, their voice raised and urgent.

"Everyone against the wall, now! Quiet!"

The sound hits me like a fist. My breath disappears and the room tilts. The edges blur. My hands lock around the edge of the desk, knuckles whitening as something old and buried claws its way up my spine. The door slams.

"Stand still."

A voice, deep and cold, cuts through the memory like it never left.

"Don't cry. Tears are weakness."

My heart slams against my ribs, frantic. I can't move. I know I should, everyone else is, but my body won't listen. The noise stacks, piles on itself.

Someone screams. Someone knocks something over. My vision tunnels.

"Again", the voice says in my head. *"Watch"*.

I smell something sharp. Metal. I taste it at the back of my throat. My hands start shaking, uncontrollable, like they belong to someone else.

"Dahlia?" someone whispers near me.

I don't answer. I can't. The alarm keeps screaming.

And then... nothing. The world skips.

I'm walking down a hallway. No, being guided. A hand at my elbow, firm but not unkind. The noise is gone now, replaced by a low hum that makes my teeth ache.

"Just a routine evaluation," a nurse says calmly. "You did the right thing."

I nod automatically. My head feels too light, like it might float away if I don't keep it down. The door opens.

The room is small and white, with a padded chair in the middle. Clean surfaces. No corners to hide in. The air smells sterile, empty of anything human.

"Sit," she says.

I do.

Headphones are placed over my ears. They're heavier than they look, pressing down just enough to make me aware of my own skull.

"This is Level One," she says. "Just listen. Answer when prompted."

The sound starts low. Almost nothing. A hum beneath the silence. I close my eyes. At first, it's harmless. Just static and soft tones. A voice asks easy questions.

"Do you feel safe?"

"Yes." I whisper.

"Do you trust authority?"

I hesitate. "Yes."

Something shifts. The sounds change, not louder, just... *different*. Tiny clicks beneath the tones. Rhythms that don't quite line up. Words that almost sound like they're coming from far away.

"Obey. Still. Quiet".

My fingers curl into my palms. Another question.

"What do you do when you are afraid?"

My throat closes. A flash– *hands on my shoulders, squeezing too tight. A room dark, the smell of death. A body on the floor that doesn't move.*

"You will learn," the voice says in my memory. *"Or you will break."*

"I– I stay calm," I say instead. *Lie. I do not stay calm.*

"Good," the woman's voice says faintly, somewhere beyond the headphones. "Very good."

The hum continues, the sound's layering. Sliding under my thoughts like fingers testing for cracks. I don't know how long it will last. When the headphones come off, my ears ring. The room feels farther away than it should, like I'm watching it through thick glass.

"Evaluation complete," she says. "But before you go, here." She gently grabs my arm, meeting it with a small needle. "For the pain." She continued. "You may return to class."

I nodded. My legs wobble, but I don't fall. I don't ask questions. I don't say anything. As I walk back, a sudden fuzzy feeling spreads from my chest to my mind, all within a split second.

Where was I going again? Oh, right class...

Chapter 21

Broken walls are breaking us.

Nick.

We sit where the staff can see us. That's the rule now. Unspoken, but enforced. Tables closest to the raised platform, backs straight, movements minimal. Like we're exhibits instead of students. Freddie's across from me, stabbing at something that might've once been chicken. Angie's beside him, peeling the label off her water bottle with surgical focus.

I hate this place.

"I swear," Freddie mutters, leaning in slightly, "if they keep watching us like this, I'm gonna start charging for the show."

Angie snorts. "Please. You'd love the attention."

"True," he says easily. "But not from *them*."

I don't say anything. I keep my eyes forward, jaw tight. You survive places like this by giving them nothing. Wes drops into the seat beside Freddie a moment later, tray trembling

104

just enough to notice. He looks... off. Paler than usual. Tired in a way sleep doesn't fix.

"You hear about the punishments?" Angie asks quietly. "People are getting pulled left and right."

"Yeah," Wes says. "Like they're bored or something."

Freddie frowns. "Where's Dolly? We've been here like ten minutes."

My stomach tightens before I can stop it. My dark brown eyes scanned the cafeteria despite myself.

Then Angie points. "There."

She's walking toward us from the far side of the room.

Dahlia.

She's pale. Not her usual soft olive, but drained, like someone turned the saturation down. Her long dark chocolate hair embracing her face, fitting her perfectly. Her hands shake just slightly as she balances her tray. Her steps are careful. Measured. Like she's bracing for impact. The only open seat is next to me.

Like a reflex, I sigh and shove my chair over an inch. "Lucky me."

She doesn't respond. Just drops her tray onto the table a little harder than necessary and sinks into the chair like her bones forgot how to hold her up. I watch her without meaning too.

The way she keeps her shoulders tight. The way her fingers curl around the edge of the table like she needs the pressure. The way she avoids looking at anyone.

"You look like you had a fight with a ghost," I say quietly. "Ghost win?"

Her head snaps toward me. The look she gives me could kill a lesser man however I feel myself almost smile.

She opens her mouth, probably to rip my head off, but Wes cuts in first.

"Can we–" his voice low. "Back to the punishments…"

Freddie straightens instantly. Angie's teasing expression vanishes.

"Yeah," Freddie says carefully. "What'd everyone get?"

Silence stretches. I wait. Count breaths. I know the signs. Wes doesn't want to talk. But he will.

"I'll go last," he says quickly.

"Nope," Freddie replies. "That's never how that works."

Angie nods. "Start with you, Wes."

He swallows. Hard. "I was late," he says. "First day."

My grip tightens my fork.

"Yeah, we know?" Freddie asks. "Wait, I thought they were kidding that day? You got isolated detention for being late?"

The cafeteria noise fades. Or maybe I stop hearing it.

"They put me in this white room," Wes continues, eyes fixed on the table. "Strapped my head back. Metal prongs held my eyes open."

Angie's hand flies to her mouth. Freddie's face drains of color.

"They made me count seconds," Wes says quietly. "Out loud. For minutes. Hours. I don't know."

I feel my stomach squirm.

"They gave me meds," he adds. "To make me sleepy. Every time I messed up, every time I lost count, they reset it." His voice shakes now.

"And they whipped me. With a belt. To keep me awake."

The table is dead silent. Dahlia's breathing is uneven beside me. I can feel it. Her aggressive inhales. Like she's fighting something of her own.

"That's-" Freddie's voice breaks. "That's torture."

Wes shrugs like the movement costs him something. "Guess I should've worn a watch."

Angie reaches across the table without thinking, gripping his hand. "Don't joke."

"I'm not," he whispers.

Something ugly twists in my gut. I've been hurt before. I've seen this shit like this done. I can't remember exactly why but this feels familiar, like when something goes against a plan, I know to expect things like this.

But Wes? He's smart. Cool. He tries to help. He didn't deserve that. None of them do.

"Hey," Freddie says softly. "You don't have to talk about it anymore."

Wes nods. Doesn't look up. We don't push it. No jokes. Just a quiet understanding settling over the table like a heavy blanket. I glanced sideways. Dahlia's staring at Wes, eyes glossy, lips pressed tight. Her hands are clenched in her lap.

For once, I don't say anything. Loathing or not, whatever this is between us, I don't think either of us is breathing quite right. I realize something worse than fear is happening. They're breaking us. One by one. And I don't know how much longer any of us can pretend we're fine.

I kick my chair back, it bounces off the floor to almost an entire wall because of the impact I made as I mutter, "Fuck this."

Chapter 22

Her.

Nick.

Assembly feels different today. Louder. Restless. Like everyone's sitting on a coiled spring.

The headmistress stands at the podium, hands folded, face carved into that permanent look of authority. "This weekend marks the first free weekend of the semester," she announces. A ripple moves through the hall. "Students may choose to remain within school grounds without supervision, or-" she pauses, letting it land, "-head into town with a guard."

A few people murmur. Someone cheers and gets shushed.

I peeked sideways. Wes is already grinning. Freddie looks like he's planning something illegal while glancing sideway looks towards bouncing blondie over there. Angie can't sit still in her seat. My eyes drag slightly passed everyone else though, and latch onto Dahlia... she's staring forward, unreadable. That familiar tightness pulls at my chest. Her eyes are glossy as she watches the stage closely. She seems almost absent. Angie suddenly grabs her hand squeezing tight as she squeals into her ear. Then a soft smile grows onto Dahlia's face.

"You are now dismissed." The headmistress calls out, and cheers and exited chatter lift the hollow spirit of the assembly hall.

Back in the dorms, drawers slam, towels get thrown, swimsuits appearing like magic. I can hear Angie all the way through the study room to her dorm, she's narrating everything she packs like she's hosting a reality show.

"If I drown," she says, "tell my story."

"You'll drown because you won't shut up," Freddie calls out, yanking his shirt over his head.

Wes snorts. "Yeah, and she'll probably scare the lake away with her personality before she gets in."

I can hear her, Dahlia laughs, quick, bright. It does something stupid to me. Makes me look out to their dorm. I hate that I look.

We head out together, sun blazing overhead, heat soaking into my skin. The walk down to the lake feels unreal. The trees open and there it is... water stretched wide and glittering, sunlight scattered across the surface like shattered glass. It's beautiful. I don't say that. I just shove my hands into my pockets. I'm finally out of that place. I look around, trying to take notice of my surroundings to see if I can work out where I am. Hell, I don't even know if I'm still in Florida. But nothing sticks out, it's all too...perfect, like it was purposefully made, like we're in some simulation. *What the fuck have my thoughts come to?*

Freddie doesn't even hesitate; he grabs Angie and throws her straight into the water.

She screams. Then resurfaces, spluttering. "I WILL END YOU."

We all lose it. Wes throws off his shirt next, and that's when the mood shifts. The scars catch the light.

Long. Thick. Angry lines crossing his back and shoulders, some faded, some still darker than the rest of his skin. *Belt marks.* No mistaking it.

The air goes quiet. Wes notices. Of course he does. He rolls his shoulders like it's nothing. "What? You guys have never seen abstract art before?"

Angie swallows hard. Freddie looks away. I clenched my jaw.

Dahlia steps closer to him. Gentle. "Does it still hurt?"

Wes shrugs. "Only when it rains. Or when I think about it. Or when I breathe." Then he grins. "So yeah. Totally fine."

I want to say something. Anything. But the words stick.

Then Dahlia softly touches his shoulder, looking closer at the scars. I *swear* I see Wes's cheeks go pink.

I turned to Freddie, looking for backup. He's... smacking his forehead, too busy watching Angie glide around, floating in the water. I smack him lightly anyway.

"Help me, idiot," I mutter, but he doesn't even look at me.

Then he finally peeks my way, and shrugs. "What?"

"He is blushing." I mutter at him. He just shakes his head.

"No, he's not, I think somebody is jealous!" He laughs as I shove him.

"Seriously?" I ask him, pointing at Angie.

"Relax. It's a strategic swim," he says, grinning.

Suddenly, Wes is running up the hill and reaching for a long strand of rope. Next thing I know he is launching himself off the rope swing, backflipping clean into the lake. The splash breaks the spell of my fury. Freddie whoops and dives in after him. Angie swims over to retaliate. Laughter comes back, tentative at first, then real.

Then I see Dahlia stripping down into her bikini.

Holy fuck. She's stripping down, slow, deliberate, every curve exaggerated by the sun bouncing off her skin, and I'm losing my mind. I feel like my entire chest and stomach just got replaced with screaming sirens.

FUCK, stop staring, Nick, stop.

And of course I don't, I can't, I'm memorizing everything, every sway, every line, and it's killing me from the inside.

I hate it. Hate. It. My stomach twists, my brain tries to fire a warning. Stay composed. But I can't look away. She's moving with this ease, this confidence, and my chest tightens. Walls up.

I peel my shirt off, toss it aside, and step into the water. It's cold enough to steal my breath. Dahlia notices my glare. She smirks. I hate that smirk too.

I waded toward Dahlia. She's already in, hair slicked back, eyes glinting in the sun.

I can't stop staring. She's moving gracefully, tossing water from her hands, her laugh bubbling over the lake. I hate how it makes my stomach do flips. My eyes rake over her olive skin, the drops of water sliding off her arms. Her chest rises and falls with laughter as she bobs around in the water.

Something shifts under the water, her foot slips on the rocks. She goes under with a sharp gasp.

I don't think. I grab her, haul her up, and one arm around her waist. She coughs, fingers clutching my shoulders. Water slips off her skin. My hand presses flat against her stomach for balance.

Shit. Shitshitshit.

My gaze flicks down. She's wet. Shivering. Perfect. My hand tingles, feels... wrong. I pulled it back like it burned me.

"You, okay?" I manage, putting her back down. Keep it calm Nick.

She nods, eyes searching my face. "Yeah. Thanks."

I step back, shove my hair out of my eyes. "Watch yourself." I say cold and short, starting to walk off.

Her smile fades. Just a flicker. She covers it fast. "Right."

Freddie's back at it. "Hey, I think Nick just saved a damsel! Did you see that, Angie?"

Angie squeals, dramatically flailing. "Is this a love story? Do I need a popcorn machine?!"

I glare. Dahlia just narrows her eyes at me, like she can read everything. It's... terrifying.

Wes climbs onto the dock, backflips again. Angie mocking. Freddie jumps in, yelling something obscene about form and grace. The chaos is ridiculous, and I feel a tiny smile tug at the corner of my mouth.

Angie claps, bringing her hands to her mouth, to exaggerate the volume of her voice, as she yells to Freddie and Wes, "Show-offs!"

The sun hangs low now, light turning gold, the lake glowing. Everyone's laughing again. Other students talking over each other. For a moment, it feels like something close to normal.

Angie's back to bantering with Freddie. He's trying to dunk her again. He grabs her ankle mid-splash. She shrieks. I swear, their laughter carries across the lake. It's loud. Infectious. Heartwarming.

Then Wes walks toward me. "Walls are falling, Nick," he taunts softly. My gaze flickers over his scars as he walks past. My chest tightens again. Poor bastard.

I catch myself staring at Dahlia again. The way she laughs. The way she tilts her head when she listens. It makes me nervous. Makes my skin buzz.

I hate that.

She reminds me of something I don't remember clearly, just shapes. Feelings. Negativity clinging to warmth. I don't trust it. So, I harden. Put the walls back up. She notices. Of course she does. And the worst part? I want to tear them down.

Chapter 23

Caught in 4K?

Angeline.

I barely made it out of the lake, dripping and shivering, when Nurse, whatever *her name is,* appeared like a shadow. Her smile was too wide, too bright, and her eyes had that sharp glint that made my stomach tighten.

"Miss Solarae, your swimsuit," she cooed, tilting her head like she was admiring a rare bird. "It's... quite... provocative."

I froze, then whipped my head around.

"Excuse me? Provocative? I'm literally wearing a two - piece, not a... a pole-dancing outfit!"

Freddie stepped up beside me immediately, his jaw clenching. "Provocative? Her tits aren't even showing!"

I whirled to him, eyebrows shooting up. "Freddie, were you looking at my tits?"

He went red, tomato-level red. His stammering was adorable and mortifying at the same time. "I-I mean... I-"

"Relax, Freddie," I snapped, trying not to laugh. "Not that it's any of your business, apparently."

The nurse's smile widened, almost stretching impossibly across her face.

"Boys," she said, her voice silky but with a hint of menace, "perhaps you would like to step back. Or you'll all be... disciplined."

Meanwhile, Nick was leaning against a tall rock, arms crossed. "This is absurd," he muttered under his breath, mostly to himself. "Absolutely ridiculous."

I glanced at him. "Nick, are you doing anything helpful, or just brooding in your corner?"

"Brooding." he said flatly, giving Dahlia, who seemed to be too annoyed by the nurse to even notice, a side-eye. Dahlia was in fact standing to the side, covering her bikini with her arm. Her jaw was practically on the ground.

Until I see Nick slip her his white oversized shirt. She hides behind him and then pops back out covered up.

It's practically a dress on her.

"Miss Moretti, don't think I didn't see your bikini either." The nurse grins over to Dahlia and Nick.

Nick's glare just deepens, and Dahlia shrinks into his shadow.

Before Freddie could even breathe, Wes jumped in, hands flailing like a slightly panicked diplomat. "Uh... Nurse, what if we... you know... made this go away? Maybe we can... uh, compensate? There's... lunch in it?"

The nurse's eyes glittered. "Compensation, hm? You think that would... sway me?" Her smile flickered to something almost hungry. "Detention is still on the table."

I crossed my arms, refusing to back down.

"Look, lady, I'm not here to argue about my bikini. Maybe try... not being a nightmare?"

She tilted her head slowly, and the smile stayed fixed, but colder now. "I do enjoy a good challenge, Angeline. But rules are rules. You... and your friends... to your dorms. Now."

We all groaned, but we shuffled obediently back toward the school campus with the guards. Freddie was muttering something about how "stupid" it all was, and Wes was still whispering bribes under his breath.

When we finally slammed the door to our study room, Dahlia was leaning against the table, eyebrows arched.

"Wow. That's... intense."

I flopped onto a seat in front of her, rolling my eyes. "Intense? That's this whole school for you. It's like the nurses are... happy piranha's with a clipboard."

Freddie plopped beside me, still flushed. "I, uh– I just... you can't let her talk to you like that. Not ever."

I smirked. "Thanks, Freddie. I appreciate the... hyper-protective weirdness."

Wes, not to be outdone, muttered from the corner, "Next time, I'll just slip her Mary Jane, or something. Works on everyone, right?"

Dahlia laughed softly. "You three are ridiculous. But... I kind of love it."

I turned my body, facing everyone, finally feeling a little less embarrassed. I hated the way she noticed my body, more that she brought everyone else's attention to it.

"Yeah... ridiculous, but I'm not dealing with her alone ever again."

Nick just groaned. "Really Wes? Marijuana?" I see a small crack in his frown though, like he's preventing a grin from cracking through, retrieving his massive wet t-shirt from a small Dahlia that he stands over, walking away.

Chapter 24

Resistance to reform. Fuck reform.

Wes.

Dr. Matilda insists I call her **Tilly**.

"Less clinical," she says, smiling like she's doing me a favor. "More approachable."

Bullshit.

Her office is warm in a way that feels fake. Soft lighting. Bright colors that irritate my already sensitive blue eyes. Made more vulnerable from my punishment. If that's what I should call it anyway. The chair im sitting on is angled just slightly lower than hers.

Power move.

"So," she says, folding her hands in her lap. "Let's talk about your isolated detention."

My jaw tightens. "I'd rather talk about literally anything else."

She chuckles. "Deflection is very common in boys like you."

Boys like you.

I lean back, crossing my arms. "You don't know shit about me."

Her smile doesn't falter. "That's why we're here." She taps her tablet. "Tell me how it made you feel."

The room blurs for a second. Pressure at my temples.

"Like shit," I snap. "Like I was being punished for existing."

"Language," she says gently. "Anger suggests guilt."

My vision flickers. Counting *One... two... three...*

My throat tightens. "Or" I say, voice sharp, "anger suggests you put me in a fucking torture chair."

She tilts her head, studying me. "You were late."

The words land wrong.

"You embarrassed us." "Do you have any idea what you've done?"

My father's voice bleeds in, uninvited.

"You think being late means–" I stop, breath hitching. "You drugged me. You kept me awake. You hurt me."

Tilly's eyes soften. Calculated. "Pain is a powerful teacher, Wesley."

I flinch. "Don't call me that."

She notes something down. "Interesting reaction."

Another flash– cameras. Flashing lights. A hand gripping my shoulder too tight. *Smile. Say nothing.*

"I counted until I couldn't tell if I was awake anymore," I say through clenched teeth. "I messed up once and you reset it. Over and over."

"And yet," she says calmly, "you're punctual now."

Something snapped.

"You don't get to rebrand fucking *abuse* as growth," I hiss. "You don't get to pretend this place is helping."

Her smile finally sharpens. "Careful."

I laugh. It came out wrong. "What are you gonna do, Tilly? Strap my eyes open again?"

Silence stretches. She stands, slowly.

"Your hostility indicates resistance to reform."

"Fuck your reform."

She doesn't react. I have a feeling that's worse.

"Report back to your dorm," she says coolly. "We'll continue when you're ready to cooperate."

I shoved out of the chair. My hands are shaking, adrenaline buzzing under my skin.

As I leave, she adds softly, "Your parents would be very disappointed in this behavior."

That one hits deep.

Fuck that wannabe therapist, and that stupid colorful room.

The dorm is empty when I get back. No Freddie running his mouth. No Nick brooding in the corner. No background noise to drown out my thoughts.

I grab a clean shirt from my drawer. The fabric brushes my knuckles and I'm not here anymore. I'm standing in my childhood living room. Cameras just outside the door. My father pacing, tie loosened, jaw rigid.

"Do you have any idea what you've done?" he demands.

"I told the truth," I say. Younger. Louder. Dumber.

"You made us look weak."

"I'm not a prop!"

He slams his fist into the table.

"You are whatever I need you to be."

My throat burns.

"You sent me away," I whisper to the empty room now, fighting the tears. "Because I didn't smile right."

The memory finishes snapping into place like a lock clicking shut. The speeches. The pressure. The expectation to be perfect.

Re-election season. Reform.

I dropped the shirt onto my bed and sit heavily beside it. I remember everything. And I decide, right then, I'm not telling a single soul. Not Freddie. Not Angie. Not Nick. Not Lia. Because if they know who my father is, what I did, I'll never just be Wes again. I'll be headlined. And I've had enough of those to last a lifetime.

Chapter 25

On the big screen.

Freddie.

The assembly hall is our graveyard.

We're all herded here like a bunch of corpses, rotting. Rows of chairs, too straight, and quiet. Everyone facing forward like good behavior can be drilled into us if we sit still long enough.

I rest my elbows on my knees and stare at the stage, already tired before anything's even started.

A staff member steps up to the podium. Smiling. Calm. The kind of smile that never actually reaches their eyes.

"Today students," he says, "we'll be discussing eating habits and self-control."

My throat tightens. I don't know why just yet. I just know it does. He talks for a while. About discipline and about choices. About responsibility. Words that sound clean and harmless until you realize how sharp they are when pointed at the wrong person.

Then the screen behind them flickers.

I don't even process what I'm looking at first. It's shaky. White tiles. A school bathroom. I recognized her instantly.

Princess.

She's bent over, one hand braced against the toilet seat, the other tangled in her hair. It's filmed on a student device. I can tell. The sound hits a second later, and something in my chest caves so hard I forget how to breathe.

The room doesn't react right away.

No gasps. No staff members rushed to stop it. No "*this is inappropriate*" or "*we'll investigate who filmed this.*"

Nothing. They let it play.

"This," the staff member says calmly over the video, "Is what poor choices look like. Repeated behavior. Lack of control. It is this kind of rebelliousness that will compromise the reform trials and prove to society what we as a school already know, that you, young people need to be disciplined into correction and control."

Repeated? Poor choices? My hands curled into fists so tight my nails bite into my palms. I turn my head slowly, like I already know what I'm going to see but can't stop myself anyway.

Angie is sitting a few rows ahead of me. She's not moving.

Not crying loudly. Not covering her face. Just... still. Like her body has shut down to survive what her mind can't. Tears slide silently down her cheeks, one after another, catching the harsh assembly lights before dripping off her jaw.

The staff keep talking. Like she's not even there. Like this is some helpful lesson instead of public execution. They make it sound like she does this all the time. Like this is who she is. Not someone struggling. Not someone hurting. Just a problem to be displayed. I feel sick.

Anger burns so hot behind my eyes it scares me. My heart is pounding, loud and uneven, like it's trying to break its way out of my chest and do something, anything, to make this stop.

She didn't choose this moment. She didn't choose to be filmed. She didn't choose to have it thrown back at her in front of everyone like a warning sign.

I don't care what she's done. I don't care what rules she's broken. She doesn't deserve this. The video ends, the screen goes blank and I look at Angie again. She's wiping her face now, fast and embarrassed, like she's apologizing just for crying. Like she's the one who's done something wrong by being human.

Something in me cracks. Not loudly. Not dramatic. Just a quiet, devastating break. I feel disappointed, not in her, never in her but in this place. In the adults. On the way they watched a girl drown and called it discipline.

And maybe... a little in myself. Because I stayed seated. Because I didn't stand up. Because I didn't scream. Because all I did was sit there, shaking, and hope she couldn't feel how furious and helpless I was behind her, but I knew that if I did,

I'd get punished, maybe they'd punish her too. I couldn't risk it.

When the staff member finally dismisses us, Angie stands alone. So small. They didn't punish her to help her *'behavior'* or *'for correction'*. They punished her by exposing her. And I don't know how I'm supposed to survive in a place that thinks that's okay.

Chapter 26

In the girls bathroom?

Angeline.

I slammed the bathroom door behind me and sank to the floor, trying to hide my face from the mirror. Hot tears burned my cheeks and ran unchecked, and I felt... small. The kind of small that makes the world feel enormous and terrifying. I was desperate.

A soft knock on the door startled me. "Angeline?"

I choked back a sob. "Go away..."

The door cracked open, and there he was... Nick.

He wasn't grumpy or sarcastic. He looked calm. His expression was softer than I'd ever seen. He crouched down to my level, leaning against the doorframe.

"Hey... hey, it's okay. I've got you."

I couldn't stop the tears anymore. His presence felt like sunlight breaking through storm clouds. "I... I just..." My voice trembled, breaking.

"Shh," he murmured. He didn't lecture, didn't pry. He just sat there, letting me cry, letting me exist in my own storm. Slowly, I felt my chest loosen a little.

After a long silence, he finally asked, "Why... Why didn't you tell me, Ange? About... the eating...?" His voice cracked slightly, a rare vulnerability slipping through his usual walls. "I'm here. I could have helped you."

Something about the way he said it made my chest ache. I sniffled, blinking up at him.

"I... I didn't know if I could... I didn't want to bother you. It's like you said about all of us, we're not friends. And you are the first one in this group to leave when issues are mentioned."

"You never bother me," he said firmly, eyes soft. "I care... more than you think. I walk away, and I'm guarded because... that's my only way of protecting myself."

I laughed, shakily, a little through tears. "You're... being... nice. Weird."

He smirked faintly. "Maybe. But it's true."

We sat like that for a few more minutes, the hallway outside fading away. Then, when I whispered a small, shaky,

"Thank you."

His expression hardened back into his usual mask, the walls going up again.

"Don't mention it," he muttered, already turning away. Just like that, the warmth left the space between us, but a little ember of it stayed with me.

Classes rolled on. The school's slogan across the board: "Reform, Correction, Excellence." Somehow, it felt heavier today.

Then, a surprise test. My heart plummeted as the teacher handed out papers, and I glanced up. Nurses. Standing behind each row of students, pens and notebooks in hand, eyes sharp.

"This test," the teacher said, voice calm, "is to evaluate how you handle pressure. Identical pens for everyone. The clock reads 11:10. Begin."

Almost immediately, the room erupted in a chorus of clicks. Every student pressed their pen down in perfect unison. I clicked mine... a second late.

The teacher's gaze locked on me. I squirmed, trying to shrink in my chair.

A student to my left suddenly started muttering the pledge under stress, mumbling it like a lifeline. Behind him, the nurse scribbled notes rapidly while chatting to another staff member. Every click, every scribble, every quiet cough felt amplified, like the room was shrinking and I was the only thing too *big* for it.

I forced myself to focus on the words on the page, but my hands trembled. I felt their eyes on me assessing, analyzing. My heartbeat was deafening.

What sort of reform trials are we preparing for in this confined facility?

Chapter 27

A different wacko?

Angeline.

The moment I walked in, I knew something was wrong. Same room, pink couch, yellow armchair. The same purple table sitting between us like a polite lie.

Different woman.

She was already sitting down in the yellow armchair. Her pen moved before I even closed the door, dark hair pulled back too tight, posture rigid. No warm smile. No fake softness. Just eyes that flicked up once, assessing me, and moved back to the page.

I hesitated. "Uh... you're not-"

"Sit," she said flatly, not looking up.

I sat. Slowly. My confusion curdled into irritation. They hadn't told me they were switching therapists. No warning. No explanation.

"Um... I normally sit in that chair." I said softly.

"Not today you don't." she replied quickly. I frowned. "Alright, Angelica," she said, finally meeting my eyes.

"It's Angeline," I corrected immediately.

She paused, her pen hovering. Then smiled faintly. "No, it isn't."

My stomach dropped. "You literally just said–"

"I didn't," she interrupted calmly, already writing again.

Is she trying to manipulate me into thinking I don't even know my own name?

"We won't waste time on imaginary errors."

Is this idiot high? Heat flooded my chest.

"That's not imaginary."

She leaned back, studying me like a puzzle with missing pieces. "You're feeling emotionally volatile after the video," she said. "That's normal. Rage distorts perception."

I clenched my jaw. Rage doesn't make me forget my own name.

"Speaking of rage," she continued smoothly, "let's talk about your eating disorder. Your book. Any progress?"

I laughed, sharply and ugly. "Progress? You mean the pages I write so you can catalogue how broken I am?"

Her pen scratched harder. "Careful," she said lightly. "Sarcasm won't protect you here."

I leaned forward. "You don't scare me."

She smiled then. Not wide. Not friendly. Precise. "Everyone says that at first." Silence pressed in. Heavy and intentional.

"And the video?" she asked. "How did it make you feel?"

"Like smashing something," I snapped. "Like screaming until my throat bleeds."

She nodded, satisfied. "Good. Anger is useful. But uncontrolled anger leads to... consequences."

My pulse spiked. "Is that a threat?"

She tilted her head. "It's a fact."

I shrank back onto the couch, rage still burning, but now edged with something colder. Fear. She wasn't here to understand me. She was here to own the narrative.

Therapist: Nurse Calder (aka Satan's Intern)

Date: 12/03/2037

<u>Dear Diary,</u>

Met my new therapist today. Surprise! Because apparently informed consent is optional now. She got my name wrong, denied it, and then implied my anger made me hallucinate. Fun start. Strong vibes of "smile politely or else."

Video aftermath: rage. Still there. Eating disorder: still annoying. Me: still breathing, unfortunately for them.

She said anger leads to consequences. I say, so does gaslighting teenagers. Guess we'll see who wins.

Angeline

P.S. If she calls me Angelica again, I might actually prove her point about rage.

Chapter 28
The boxing ring.

Dahlia.

Free time feels fake. Like the school hands it to you with a warning label and expects it back untouched.

Angie and I kick our shoes off and head for the grass, weaving through students sprawled in lazy clumps. I scan faces automatically, searching.

"Where are the boys?" Angie asks.

"They said five minutes," I say. "Which in boy-time is-"

The noise hits us before I can finish. Yelling. A crowd has formed near the outer fence, thick and restless, bodies pressed shoulder to shoulder.

My stomach sinks. We break into a jog, catching up to the crowd.

"Excuse me- sorry- move," Angie says, elbowing gently, then not so gently. I follow, ducking under arms, catching flashes of red faces and clenched jaws. The air smells like adrenaline and dust.

"Oh no."

Freddie is on the ground.

Not losing exactly, just very, very horizontal. He's flat on his back with a guy easily ten times his size straddling him like a collapsing building. His arms are up, fists tight, and chin tucked perfectly.

He *knows* what he's doing.

"LEFT, YOU IDIOT," He yells, snapping a punch up into the guy's ribs. "NO, YOUR OTHER LEFT! FUCK, YOU'RE HUGE AND STILL BAD AT THIS."

The guy grunts, trying to pin him harder. Freddie slips, rolls his shoulder just enough to avoid a full hit, pops another sharp jab into the guy's jaw.

Wes is nearby, already swinging like he's enjoying this far too much.

And then I see Nick.

He's off to the side of the chaos, arms crossed, watching like this is a delayed train and not a fistfight.

Freddie sees him.

"OH, COME ON," Freddie yells, breathless but still somehow sarcastic. "NOW WOULD BE A GREAT TIME, NICK. I'M LITERALLY FLATTENED. THIS IS A CRY FOR HELP."

Nick exhales slowly. Looks at the ground, looks back at Freddie. He shifts his weight, like he's standing at the edge of a cliff deciding whether the fall is worth it.

I feel panic spike sharp and sudden.

"Nick- DON'T!" I shout.

He doesn't hear me. The big guy rears back for a heavier hit, and something in Nick snaps. He moves.

It's not dramatic at first. No yelling or running. He just steps in, grabs the guy by the back of the collar, and yanks him off Freddie like he weighs nothing.

Freddie rolls away instantly, scrambling to his feet. "THANK YOU," he pants. "I HAD IT, BUT STILL-"

Nick doesn't answer.

The second guy swings Nick's head. Nick ducks, pivots, drives his shoulder into the guy's chest and slams him back. A punch lands. The crowd goes dead quiet.

Wes stares like he's just watched a magic trick. Freddie adjusts his stance automatically, eyes sharp, ready to jump back in then pauses.

"Oh," Freddie says faintly. "Okay. You're... doing that."

One of the guys stumbles away. The other hits the ground and stays there. Nick stands still, breathing hard, knuckles red. For a second he looked almost startled, like his body betrayed him. Guard's whistles shrieks in the distance. Students scatter. The noise dissolves into chaos again.

As I'm watching, something in my mind snaps. I know I've never liked violence, realistically I don't know why I'm standing here watching this. But for some reason this violence doesn't bother me. Was I watching for my *friends?* Was I watching for *him?* Or was I watching because this sort of violence *disturbingly awakened something in me that I can't exactly remember...*

Nick finally looks up. Our eyes meet. Something tightens in my chest. Not fear. Not relief. Shock. He turns away like nothing happened.

Angie grabs my wrist. "Did Nick just?"

"Yeah," I say.

Freddie jogs past us, grinning despite the blood on his lip.

"For the record," he says proudly, "I was winning."

I'm not sure if any of us believe that.

Chapter 29

Any day now!

Freddie.

I knew this was going to be a problem the second Angie's name came out of his mouth like a punchline he was proud of.

There are three of them. Typical. Big mouths, bigger shoulders, and absolutely nothing going on behind the brain. They're leaning against the fence like they own oxygen, talking loudly about girls who aren't there to hear it.

Which is brave. *Stupid.* But brave.

"Yeah," one of them snorted, "From that video at assembly, all I'm wondering is if Angie has a good gag reflex."

Wes stops walking.

That's it. His jaw tightens; shoulders square. I feel the air change.

I sigh. "Oh no."

Nick exhales beside me, already annoyed. "Don't."

"I'm not doing anything," I say automatically.

Wes turns slowly, a smile creeping across his face but it's not friendly. It's the kind of smile that promises regret.

"Say that again," he murmurs.

The biggest guy laughs, a bark of disbelief. "Relax, pretty boy. We're just talking."

"About girls you don't even get to look at," Nick says flatly, eyes cold, coming from across the grass.

"And about girls who could snap you in half emotionally," I add, nodding. "Which is honestly worse."

Something clicks in Wes and Nick at the same time. Their stances widen, fists clenching without them even thinking.

"Try me," Wes says softly, voice low, deadly calm. "Say one more word."

Nick tilts his head, eyes narrowing at the three idiots, "Go ahead. Test it."

One of the guys smirks at Wes, leaning in like he owns the world. "Bet she'd choke on it all if I made her, I'd enjoy every second of it, just like the little slut she is."

What. The. Actual. **FUCK**. My Eyes Darken.

I don't even get a chance to ball my fist up to shut up the first fucker when his friend makes another comment, "Bet that little gag reflex of hers turns her on more than she'd admit."

That's when Wes moves.

I don't even get to throw my punch when I'm tackled by Mount Idiot himself. We hit the ground hard, and- okay- he is huge. Like if buildings could punch.

Still. I know how to box. I tuck my chin, bring my fists up, and start working the ribs. "FUCK," he yells.

"WHAT DID YOU THINK THIS WAS," I grunt, landing another jab. "A DISCUSSION?"

Out of the corner of my eye, I see Nick. Standing. Watching. Hands in his pockets. Looking like this is deeply inconvenient.

"Oh, YOU'VE GOT TO BE KIDDING ME," I yell. "NICK. HELP. I AM BEING CRUSHED."

Nothing. I jab again. He wheezes. I'm winning spiritually.

"NICK," I shout again, louder. "IF I DIE, TELL ANGIE I DIED HOT."

That gets it. Nick snorts.

Still, he doesn't move but laughs before catching himself. He scans the crowd, eyes flicking over heads. I can tell he's looking for the girls. They're not here yet, but he's checking anyway. Like muscle memory.

I grin through the pain. "OH GREAT," I say. "YOU'RE DOING A HEADCOUNT WHILE I'M A GODDAMN PANCAKE."

He just watches still. I hesitate for a moment before attempting to shove the prick off me. I grunt. He doesn't budge.

"OH, COME ON," I yell, breathless. "NOW WOULD BE A GREAT TIME, NICK. I'M LITERALLY FLATTENED."

Nothing. He just stands there.

Then Nick's expression changes. It's subtle. The kind of shift you only notice when you know someone too well now. His eyes lift, not to me, not to Wes, not even to the guy actively attempting to turn me into pavement but past us.

Over the crowd. Toward the edge. I follow his gaze and see them pushing through Dolly's hair first, then Angie's face, both pale and wide-eyed.

Oh. *Ohhh.* That explains it.

The big guy raises his fist again, and I don't even bother yelling this time. Because Nick's already moving. Dahlia's voice cuts through the quiet. Sharp. Panicked.

"Nick, DON'T!"

He steps in fast, grabs my attacker by the collar, and hauls him off me like he weighs nothing. I roll free and scramble up just as Nick turns on the second guy. It's not flashy. It's not loud. It's efficient in the scariest way possible. One punch. A dodge. Another hit. The refrigerator that was previously on top of me goes down and stays there.

The crowd goes silent. I stand there panting, adrenaline buzzing, blood on my lip. Next to Nick, for half a second, he just stands there, fists clenched, chest heaving.

Then he looks up. Straight at her. *Dolly.* Nick freezes. Something passes over his face, shock, guilt, something almost like, *oh no.* Like he didn't mean for her to see that part of him as he turns to walk away from our ugly scene.

I jog past him towards the girls, still buzzing, and mutter, "For the record I was winning."

Chapter 30

Basements? Watch a horror movie.

Dahlia.

Angie and I are heading back to class after the grass incident, swinging our joined arms slightly.

"If today's another drill, I'm screaming," she says. "I don't care who hears."

"You say that every day," I reply softly.

"And one day I'll mean it."

We turn the corner toward our classes, when I see the boys. Freddie. Wes. Nick. They're standing near the wall, a nurse speaking to them in low tones. Freddie's joking, of course he is, hands moving animatedly. Wes looks tense, nodding like he's forcing himself to listen.

Nick doesn't move. He lifts his head. And looks straight at me.

It hits me low in my stomach. A flutter. Sharp and sudden, like my body noticed him before my mind did. His gaze is dark, steady, too intent to be accidental. Every time our eyes lock, I can't help but want to sprint at him and ask him, *what*

he wants from me? Why is it like this between us? I keep walking.
I don't look back.

But I *feel* him.

Angie leans in, practically buzzing. "Oh my god. Nick is
totally staring at you."

I scoff too quickly. "No, he's not."

"Yes, he is. Lia, he looks like he's trying to solve you."
Angie squeals in my ear.

I risk a glance over my shoulder. Nick's still watching. My
breath stutters.

I turn forward immediately, heat creeping up my neck.
"You're imagining things."

Angie grins. "Sure. And I imagine my reflection too."

I don't answer. My heart is beating too fast for that.

In class, I try to focus. I really do but at this point, my mind
is anywhere but learning.

Paper rustles. Scissors snip. The teacher's voice floats
somewhere above us, distant and unimportant. I'm cutting
shapes from a sheet of paper, neat and careful at first. But my
thoughts drift.

A man's face flickers in my mind. I don't know why. I try
to make it out.

Strong jaw. Shadowed eyes. A presence that fills a room without raising its voice.

My chest tightens, an ache blooming where something should be.

I blink and the scissors slip. A sharp sting blooms across my palm making me gasp softly. Red dots the paper. Then more. Drops sliding, staining the white.

"Miss Moretti?"

I look up. The nurse is crouched in front of me, concern etched into her face like she's practiced it. "You're hurt."

I stared at my hand. Blood seeps from a thin cut, deeper than it should be. The scissors lie on the desk, rusted and dull.

"I– I didn't mean to," I whisper.

She stands. "Come with me."

Two guards appeared at the door like they were waiting. Of course they were.

I'm sitting in the nurse's office on Floor 1, back against the wall, knees pulled to my chest on the patient bed. My hand throbs, wrapped loosely in gauze that's already tinged pink.

The silence presses in, thick and uncomfortable. The nurse steps out of a door inside of the room, mumbling something about supplies. The door doesn't close all the way. It catches on something.

Minutes pass. Five, at least. The clock keeps ticking. No footsteps. No voices. Just the door the nurse left in, slightly open, stuck because I can see it's broken. A descending staircase beyond it.

They really need to fix the infrastructure of this school, and why haven't they? It's greatly funded right.

I stand before I can talk myself out of it. The stairs are narrow, concrete, lit by a single buzzing light. The air changes immediately, cooler, and damper. It smells like dust and something metallic.

"Hello?" I call softly.

My voice echoes back wrong. Warped. The steps keep going. Down.

My pulse quickens as I realize, this isn't another floor. It's some kind of basement. The light flickers.

"Hello?" I tried again, louder. Nothing.

I step off the stairs and into a hallway that shouldn't exist. Pipes run along the ceiling. The walls are unfinished, grey with marks that almost look like scratches. Doors line the corridor, some ajar, some sealed shut.

I choose the first open one. Inside, a curtain hangs crookedly, swaying slightly but there's no breeze. As I push it open, filing cabinets crowd the walls, drawers yanked open, papers spilled onto the floor like discarded secrets.

My eyes run over them, I see names. Dates.

My hands shake, but just as I choose to investigate, I feel something *moving* behind me. I gasp and bolt, heart slamming, running back into the hall, my cut hand stinging as I clutch it to my chest. I just run. Up the stairs. Out of the dark. Away from whatever that place is.

By the time I reach the light again, my breath is ragged, my head spinning. The door to the camouflaged basement swings shut behind me. *Perfectly*. Like it was never stuck at all.

Chapter 31

Weakness? Someone swallow me whole.

Dahlia.

The sector lights feel too bright when I get back.

Then again, I did just come back from the darkest place in the school. That I know of...

Why would they hide a basement? Why not just say we can't go down there for safety reasons or some other bullshit they come up with. The halls are empty, I can't even here anyone talking anywhere.

Angie is the first one I see. She's pacing, actual pacing around our study room. Wes stands near the wall, arms crossed, jaw tight like he's holding himself together with pure will.

"There you are," Angie blurts the second she spots me. "Where did you *go*? You've been gone for ages."

"I..." My voice catches. I swallow. "The nurse left. The door was open. I went downstairs."

Wes's eyes sharpen immediately. "Okay, slow down. A nurse, why were you with a nurse? Downstairs where?"

Really? 'I need to slow down'.

"The basement."

Angie's face drains. "There's no,"

"There is," I say quietly. "I saw it. I saw files and cabinets full of them. Names..."

Wes steps closer. "Did anyone see you?"

"I don't think so."

That's when he reaches for my hand.

"Wait–" I start, but he's already turned it palm up.

Blood. The cut looks worse now, angrier, like it's pulsing in time with my heart.

"What the hell, Lia," Wes mutters. "You're bleeding."

"It's nothing."

"It's not." He's already moving. "Don't move."

He jogs off toward his dorm, leaving Angie staring at my hand, her eyes shivering with empathy.

"A basement," she mutters. "Bleeding. Great. Fantastic. Anything else this school wants to throw at us?

Before I could respond, voices echoed towards us.

"What happened?" Freddie demands, stepping from his room, "What's all the commotion? Why is everyone freaking out?"

Nick is right behind him. My chest folds, I turn my face from him, for some reason I feel embarrassed. I don't want him to see me like this. *Hurt. Weak.*

Why does it always feel like I can't seem weak in front of others? Where did I learn that?

I can feel his gaze lock onto me like a hook. Focused. Deep. I glance to see if he's moved on from me. *His gaze hasn't.* It slides from my face to my hand and something dangerous flickers there. Anger maybe, or something worse because I can see it's building.

"What did you do?" he asks, flat.

I bristle. "Excuse me?"

"You're hurt," he says. "So. What happened?"

"I cut my hand."

"In class?" His eyes narrow.

"In the basement," I snap before I can stop myself. "...well, I did cut myself in class yes."

Freddie freezes. "The what?"

Nick's jaw clenches. "You went down there?"

Angie throws her hands up. "She followed a nurse!" Nick doesn't look at her. He doesn't look at anyone except me.

"Are you trying to get yourself killed?" he asked cruelly. His words sting.

"I didn't ask for your concern."

He tilts his head as his mouth twitches. "That's funny. Because you're bleeding on our floor."

Before I can fire back, Wes reappears, holding a bandage triumphantly.

"Okay," he says, breathless. "Got it. Sit."

He reaches for my hand again, when...

"What the," Wes splutters. "Dude?"

Nick snatches the supplies off Wes and plops himself Infront of me. He completely ignores Wes. He takes my wrist, firm, warm and infuriating, and presses the bandage to my cut with careful precision. Every thought in my head evaporates. His thumb brushes my skin.

I forgot what I was going to say. My breath stutters. Part of me wants to recoil, to say *get off*, to reclaim ground. The other part of me... flutters. Traitorously. Nick's expression is unreadable, but his grip softens just slightly, like he's aware of the effect and refusing to acknowledge it.

"Hold still," he murmurs.

Wes blinks. "Uh- rude?"

Nick finally looks at him. "You were taking too long."

"I was literally gone for thirty seconds."

"Too long."

Angie watches the exchange like she's courtside at a championship match. "Wow," she says. "Okay. That's... a thing."

Nick releases my hand like it burned him. I miss the warmth it brought me immediately.

Freddie clears his throat. "So. Nurses. Since we're sharing."

Angie points at them. "Yeah. What happened?"

"We got warned," Freddie says. "Apparently fighting shows signs of failing to *reform*."

Wes scoffs. "Figures."

"They put us back to red," Freddie continues. "Temporary."

"And Nick?" Angie prompts.

Nick doesn't look at me when he answers. "Supervised. All day."

Suddenly, a knock at our sector door alarms all of us. We follow in line behind Nick, out to our hall and open our sector door.

A guard is waiting right on cue, arms crossed.

"Let's go Deveraux."

I glance at Nick before I can stop myself. "You okay with this?"

His eyes flick to mine. His eyes dashing to my mouth, then back up locking his brown eyes with my watercolor eyes. Just for a split second.

"I've had worse." he says.

The tension hums between us, unspoken, dangerous, alive. As I watch him strut his broad shoulders and muscular arms away followed by the guard, there's a part of me that wants to grab him by the hand and touch his neck, wishing I could break through his walls he puts up. Wanting to tell him that it's okay to be scared in a shit hole like this place or even to be a little happy, finding people, friends like us...

Friends, right. That's what we are. Maybe?

Chapter 32
I'm not crazy.

Angeline.

My head is down as usual, my heels echoing the halls. A group of girls turn the corner, see me and instantly look at each other. They don't even attempt to hide the aimed giggles. My cheeks flush, so I grip my books harder and walk faster.

"Oh honey, I believe the girls' bathroom is that way!" A dark, green eyed athletic girl points.

I just scowl. Her friends all erupted into loud laughter as I shoved past.

I turn the hall and start jogging away. The laughter doesn't stop; it echoes in my head.

They can see the cookies you ate this morning, Angeline. Quick, the bathroom is just down that hall.

The memory is over just as quickly as it entered. I take a deep breath and peek behind me to make sure the girls are gone.

"Angie?" A familiar voice calls out.

I turn to see Dr Matilda standing outside her door. *Great.*

"...Angeline." I corrected for what must be the 100th time.

"Is everything okay? I heard you running down the hall." she points out, slipping the door wider open like she's attempting to guide me in. I just stand there.

"Um... yeah no, everything's fine. Hey, the other day I thought I had a session scheduled to be with you. I didn't realize the school had another therapist." I ask her, rubbing my neck and feeling that stupid tattoo I was branded with day one. When I get out of here, the first thing I'm doing is getting this thing removed.

Please don't ask about my journal. Please don't ask about my journal. Please don't ask–

"Angeline, I'm the only therapist here, I have been for three years now. Now how is your journal going? Do you have it with you?" she asks precisely, her voice carrying the halls.

I frown. "But I had a session with someone else? I remember because she got my name wrong... and when I corrected her, she acted like I was crazy!" My tone getting angrier now.

I'm not crazy. I know I'm not. It's this school.

She just takes a deep sigh, before fixing her smile. "Well, Angeline. I did hear about your... video incident the other day. My colleagues said the rest of the day you were 'angry and disrespectful'. Extreme emotional states, especially anger, can trigger perceptual distortions, hallucinations, vivid dreams, or even false memories. It's your mind trying to cope with the intensity."

"... Did you not see the same video I did?"

I'm a step closer now. She shrinks the tiniest bit, like she's bracing to jump back into the room if she has to. "Of course I was filled with anger. What, did your stupid colleagues expect me to run around all happy that my 'secret issue' is out now?" I spit out at her.

Her smile wavers. "Angeline please. I don't appreciate your tone. Why don't you come inside so we can talk more? Something is clearly affecting your ability to let it go, and I think saying it out loud might help.

"Let it... go?" I repeat. I just laugh. Nothing else comes out of me except uncontrolled laughter.

"Angeline, may I see your journal?" she asks again. I shake my head.

"NO! Because I didn't bring it with me, okay? Now if you would, I have to get to class." I hurry and walk straight past her. Suddenly her boney hand reaches out and grabs my shoulder.

"Angeline–"

"DONT! Don't you DARE touch me!" I almost yelled. I get close to her. My eyes dared hers to look away. "If you touch me again, I will make sure that button on the flower vase is out of reach. No one will be able to help you." I threaten.

She isn't smiling. She just stares, before recomposing herself.

"I will be documenting this interaction, Angeline. You're free to go."

I hold myself back from ripping her apart as I walk off. However, I decided the basic turn and hair flip will do, considering she is going to 'document' my behavior. Although I can't work out if she's threatening me or if she means it. But don't worry, *Tilly...* I will also be documenting this interaction.

14/05/2037

Today was... something else. I saw Dr. Matilda in the hall. She called me "Angie" like she always does, but I corrected her anyway. (Of course.)

When I asked her about my previous session with the other therapist, SHE SAID THERE WAS NO OTHER THERAPIST. No nurse. No session. Like I'm crazy. I'm not crazy. I remember it. I remember her getting my name wrong. I remember correcting her. I remember her denying it.

Then she started talking about my anger, like it makes me hallucinate or invent things. Hallucinations. False memories. Vivid dreams. Basically, saying my brain is lying to me because I'm angry.

I swear, if she thinks I'm going to just nod along to that... no.

Of course, I snapped. I told her she didn't see the video. I told her it's ridiculous to expect me to walk around smiling because everyone now knows my "secret issue."

She didn't like that.

She asked me to see my journal. I didn't let her. NO. I'm not letting her in.

Then she grabbed my shoulder. Grabbed. My. Shoulder. I told her not to. I threatened her. I probably went a little far with the flower vase comment... but she was touching me. I can't have that.

She stared at me, didn't smile, then said she'd be documenting it. Well, congratulations, touché. Bitch.

I don't know if she's threatening me, or if she's trying to scare me into believing her manipulative nonsense. Either way, I'm keeping track. Evidence. My own memory. I will not forget.

Angie♡

Chapter 33

Final curtain call... The performance
is starting.

Dahlia.

It's been months and yet another bland, routine day that makes my head want to explode.

I walk beside Angie on our way to the cafeteria from floor 1, our steps slower than usual. As we headed in the direction of the stairs, I felt my feet drawn toward the performance board. Angie's eyes dart just as fast as my feet take me, but neither of us wants to be the first to see what the board says. My fingers keep twisting the hem of my sleeve. I hadn't even realized I was doing it until Angie gently nudges my arm.

"Hey," she says. "Breathe."

I nodded, even though my lungs don't listen.

The Performance Board looms at the entrance, big, bright, merciless. Names neatly displayed. Colors carefully coded. Green. Yellow. Red. My eyes find my picture, barcode and name instantly.

The world tilts.

"What?" My voice comes out thin. "I was yellow. I was *yellow* yesterday."

Angie leans in, reading it twice like it might change. "Okay. Okay. Don't panic."

My heart is already sprinting. I rapidly stare from the board into Angie's eyes, then back to the board then back to Angie then to the board then around the floor.

"Do you think they know?" I whisper. "About the basement. About the room. What if they,"

"Hey," she interrupts firmly, turning me toward her. "No spiraling. Not yet."

But the thought sinks its claws in any way. Once it's in, it can't escape. The files. The stairs. The way the door closed behind me like it had been waiting to see whether I would dare go down or not.

"Oh my gosh..." Angie mutters, stepping closer to the board. She points at a student's picture and barcode on the screen. "This is the girl who got injected that first week, during class. Her name was ...Grace."

I read the board out. "It says she has been successfully reformed... huh. Good for her, I guess. At least she's free." I mutter.

My mind keeps flicking back to worrying thoughts about my own color. What if red isn't punishment? What if it's a warning?

"Dolly!" a voice calls.

Freddie pops around the corner like he's been launched, his blond shaved head catching the fluorescent lights. He grins when he sees us, hands shoved into his pockets.

"Why are you guys down here on floor 1?" He asks surprised, "Breakfast is about to start!"

"Why are you down here on floor 1?" Angie quickly mocked him.

"I, your highness, had to pick up a flier for a therapy session. My math teacher saw I didn't have one yesterday and practically forced me here this morning. Said I should have one, if I wanted to re-schedule one." Freddie explained.

"Do. Not. Recommend. Do you know how much I have been seeing her? She's around every fucking corner I turn, with that creepy smile of hers. I mean seriously if she's going to smile that much, she needs to learn to brush her teeth or invest in a really good teeth whitener!"

Just as Freddie lets out his orangutan laugh, replying how he wasn't interested in seeing Dr Matilda's face either, his laugh falls short, turning to Angie, "Yeah. About that... Why do you have so many–"

Angie cuts him off, directing the subject into something they often banter about. Or at least that's what I assume. I can't hear them. Or maybe I'm choosing not to. I haven't excelled. My father must have sent me here; I mean that's what the headmistress said on day one. *'Your parents sent you here.'* And there was no way my mother could have. I shiver. But why? Why can't I remember her? All I see is him. I finally remembered the face I saw in the air that day of my panic attack. It was him, my father. He sent me here and I haven't done what he wanted. I've lost. I haven't *performed* well enough, and the beaming red is the perfect indicator of that.

"Hey-" Freddie waves his hand in front of my face, attempting to bring me back into reality, not knowing he's helping me escape from my self-destroying thoughts. "Hey, Dolly, Hello? Why are you staring off into some abyss? Are you high? Is she high?", he turns, asking Angie excitingly. "Can I have some of whatever you've got?!"

Angie slaps Freddie on the arm, "Oh, please! Get a hold of yourself!"

I can feel Freddie's green light eyes follow my gaze.

"Oh. The board."

I swallow. "I dropped."

He squints at it. "Huh."

"That's it?" Angie snaps. "*Huh?*"

Freddie shrugs easily, "Don' worry about it Dolly, I've heard lots of people get put on red. It so happens that I've been threatened with it three times this week!"

"I wonder why..." Angie chuckles. Freddie forces a fake laugh, communicating how Angie gets under his skin.

I want to believe him. I really do. He flashes me with a reassuring smile, the kind that usually works. It helps, just a little.

"C'mon," he says. "Breakfast before the oatmeal solidifies into concrete."

"Oatmeal for you," I mutter. "Dry cereal for me."

Inside, the cafeteria hums softly. Trays slide. Cutlery clinks. For a brief, blessed moment, it almost feels like a normal school. Wendy is at the counter. Her hair is tucked neatly under her cap, eyes kind in a way that makes my breathing settle. She brightens when she sees us. A sign of slight relief, during this crap of a morning.

"Morning ladies... Blondie."

Freddie winks, as Angie and I say *hi* in unison.

"You lot are up early."

"Couldn't miss your cooking," Angie says sweetly.

Wendy chuckles. "Flattery before food. Smart."

She hands Angie a tray first, a warm roll of bread, steam curling into the air. A cookie nestled beside it. Something golden and soft smelling I don't recognize but instantly crave. Finally, it's my turn. *Here we go.*

Her smile falters. Just a little.

"Oh, honey," she murmurs, lowering her voice. "I'm sorry."

She sets my tray down gently. A Carrot, dry cereal and Saltwater.

The bowl looks sad. A single pale orange stick rolling around like it gave up halfway through existing. My throat tightens.

"It's okay," I say quickly, forcing a smile. "Rules are rules."

Wendy's eyes linger on me, full of something like an apology. "For the record, I have never agreed with the performance board."

I smile. It doesn't help me. It doesn't make me feel any better. It just proves how much of a push-over I am. How *weak* I am.

Freddie slides in beside me with his oatmeal, peering at my tray. "Wow. That's... aggressively healthy."

Angie glares at the bowl, almost gagging on my behalf. "This is cruel and unethical."

I laugh softly despite myself, though my hands shake as I pick up the spoon.

Red. The color bleeds into everything now, the room, the food, the quiet fear humming under my skin that was revealed the moment I was dumb enough to be impatient and curious. The moment I broke a rule. I take a bite anyway.

"This is what you deserve."

This is what I deserve.

"You couldn't perform how I wanted you to."

I couldn't perform how he-they wanted me to.

"You are MY daughter. I will own you. Always."

I am a student of this place. They will own me. Always.

Chapter 34

Who still watches Scooby-Doo?

Nick.

The alarm blared, a harsh wail that made my ears ring. A breach. A Lockdown. The guards had forced all students back into their sectors. *'Protocol'* at least we are out of class. The only problem? Us, stuck in the dorm. I groaned. Not exactly my idea of fun.

The girls were already gathered near their window, whispering like they'd been planning a covert mission, while Wes and Freddie flopped onto the floor like casualties of boredom. I leaned against the wall, arms crossed, feeling awkward and conspicuously useless.

"You think they even know how to fold a sheet properly?" Dahlia asked, holding up a crumpled corner.

Angie snorted. "If folding sheets is a life skill, they're screwed. But hey... at least they're cute while being idiots."

They giggled to themselves. I peeked over at Dahlia to catch just a peek at her smile. Her laugh echoed around when she threw her head back, her laughter coming straight from the heart. Genuine. I couldn't stop staring.

I don't know why the conversation on the sheets was so funny, but I hoped she would stay laughing for just a moment longer.

Fuck. She is driving me mental. Not in a good way either.

My mind started creating its own little images without my permission. Of her on the lake, her smile. My hand on her stomach, the way she held my shoulders. The sunlight beaming on her hair.

"No way... Wes look, Nick is smiling!" Freddie called out.

What? No, I'm not.

But when I went to frown deeper, I realized I was in fact smiling.

"Wow, Nickolas!" Angie teased. I quickly darted my eyes over at Dahlia again. Her cheeks had become rosy, and she was just staring at me. But when she realized I was holding her stare, she looked away, fiddling with the blanket.

"So... does anyone actually know what triggered the breach?" Freddie asked, scratching his head like the answer might magically appear there.

"Probably the security system doing its thing." Angie replied.

Dahlia was now sitting cross-legged on her bed, flipping through a textbook but sneaking glances at me. I ignored her. She deserved the cold shoulder for whatever reason my brain was obsessed with holding onto.

Then Wes stood and sat next to Dahlia on her bed. She giggled and shuffled over.

"Man, your beds are so much softer than ours!" he groaned. She put her hand on his shoulder accidently, letting out a small 'sorry'.

But I saw it. I saw the way his eyes peeked at her when she did it.

"Man, you're scowling again." Freddie murmured to me. I didn't take my eyes off them.

"He keeps looking at her." I muttered back. That warm, happy feeling I had before? It was burning in a red-hot flame.

Freddie scoffs. "He sees her as a sister, Nick. She's all yours bud!" he nudged my shoulder with his.

"She better be." I groaned.

"What?" Freddie looked at me smirking.

"I said, you better be done with whatever bullshit you're coming up with."

"So.... Ange. The other day, when Alyssa had you cornered and she mentioned something about you skipping breakfast... is it related to the um ...video?" Wes softly asks. I feel Freddie stiffen and then stare at Angie. He's waiting for a response.

Her cheeks flush and she readjusts her position. "Um... I mean if you're asking, I should be honest..." She looks at Dahlia for help. Dahlia just nods her on. Her expression is soft, filled with care. I can feel my walls softening slightly at her glossy eyes.

"Yes. Alyssa was being a right royal bitch to me, because she knows I'm mentally ill. I just know it was her who filmed me. I don't know why, or what's wrong with me. But recently... I keep having these flashes of memories, I think. Of my mom. What she has said to me previously. I think she would say these things like... '*Angie, I can see your stomach through that dress. Silk is for elegant people, who don't let their stomachs hang. There's a bathroom down the hall. Go now.*' I think she is the reason I act like this." Angie practically squeaked.

"No Princess, don't say that." Freddie quickly speaks up. "Don't call yourself mentally ill and hey all of our memories are fried, maybe it's not true, I'm sure your mom wouldn't do that to you. You're not alone in this."

Angie looks up at Freddie now. A tear threatening to fall. Then she cracks into a small smile. "Yeah, you're probably right... thanks Freddie."

"Angie, we are all here for you." Dahlia reassured.

Angie looks at me and I just nod.

"Wow... thanks guys. I guess I'm lucky I got put with the best people in the school, aren't I?" Angie looks around at everyone.

Wes opens his mouth to say something but gets interrupted by Dahlia smacking his chest and shaking her head.

He rolls his eyes with a grin. "I just wanted to say, whatever happens, this gang will always have each other."

Wes says within one breath, as quickly as he can. Dahlia whips her head around, and he raises his hands up to surrender.

"Ew, don't call us that! You're saying it like we're the Scooby doo gang..." Angie laughs.

Freddie laughs too. A part of me almost liked the fact that we were in this *shared proximity*. We were really like a *gang*. Wait, what the hell am I saying? This shit is the lamest thing I've ever heard.

"Well, I dibs being Scooby! How about it...Daphne?" Freddie turns, smirking at Angie.

She pretends to not giggle, asking, "Your name is literally Freddie, why not him?"

Make that the second lamest thing...

Chapter 35

Smile. You're on camera.

Dahlia.

Our dorm has started to feel homey. Not in the way that I'll ever call this place home but in a way that I feel personal with our sector. No matter what has happened throughout our shitty days, the five of us are able to come back to our sector and almost feel an ounce of peace.

Angie is sitting, feet interlinked on her bed, brushing out her hair while laughing at something I said, something stupid, probably, but she's laughing like it's the funniest thing in the world. The sound fills the room, warm and easy. I'm standing by the mirror, tugging on my sweater, watching us both like this moment might be fragile if I don't pay attention to it.

"I'm telling you," Angie says, grinning at our reflection, "if Freddie trips over his own feet one more time, I'm charging him hazard pay."

I snort. "He'd still find a way for us to owe *him* money."

She tosses a pillow at me. I catch it, laughing, the knot in my chest loosening for the first time in days. For a few minutes, I forget the board. The colors. The rules. I forget to be careful.

"Wait, let me grab my notebook and shut the door." I say, heading for the door.

My hand closes around the handle. And the world drops out from under me.

Photos. Dozens of them. Glossy, black-and-white stills plastered across the door from top to bottom. Crooked, overlapping, deliberately messy. Each one shows the same thing from different angles.

Me. In the basement. On the stairs. In the hallway. Standing in front of the filing cabinets. Frozen mid-turn, my cowardly eyes wide, hand hovering near the curtain. My breath leaves my body in one sharp, broken sound. Carved into the wood beneath the photos- deep, jagged, unmistakable-

WE KNOW WHAT YOU DID.

I don't remember screaming. I just know Angie is suddenly in front of me, hands on my shoulders, saying my name repeatedly while my legs give out beneath me.

"Lia- Dahlia, hey, look at me-"

"I didn't-" My teeth chatter uncontrollably. "I didn't think anyone saw. I didn't..."

Angie whirls around, fury blazing across her face. She starts ripping the photos down, tearing them in half, then quarters, then shoving the pieces into a shaking fist.

"Who did this," she snaps. "Who *did this?*"

I manage to get away from the carving, my back against a cold wall. My eyes stay locked on the words carved into the door, like if I look away, they'll burn themselves deeper into my mind.

They were watching. The whole time.

"Hey," Angie says, dropping down in front of me, gripping my face gently but firmly. "Listen to me. This is Alyssa. This has *Alyssa* written all over it."

I shake my head, barely breathing. "She couldn't have; these are camera shots. She wouldn't have access to..."

Footsteps pound down our sector hall. A nurse, sharp-eyed, slowly opens our door, stepping in looking at the mess in front of her, the torn photos littering the floor, the carving, my position on the ground. She doesn't look surprised. That scares me more than anything.

Angie looks confused, turning to the nurse, "How did *you* get in?"

"You kids left your sector door open, now what happened here?" she asks calmly.

Angie stands immediately. "Someone vandalized our door."

The nurse steps closer, examining the carving. Her fingers trace the letters lightly, like she's checking craftsmanship instead of a threat.

"This will be dealt with." she says evenly.

"That's it?" Angie demands. "Someone stalked her." Pointing down to me.

The nurse finally looks at me. Her gaze is cool. Measuring.

"Yes," she repeats. "It will be dealt with."

She turns and walks away without another word. The silence she leaves behind is louder than the scream that tore out of me minutes ago. Angie kneels beside me again, wrapping her arms around my shoulders.

"You're okay," she whispers. "You hear me? I've got you."

I nod because I don't trust my voice. But my thoughts are already spiraling. Because Alyssa might be cruel. But Alyssa doesn't carve warnings. And Alyssa doesn't have access to cameras.

Someone else knows. And whoever it is, wants me to know they're watching.

Chapter 36

Dear "Diary" (Psycho journal).

Angeline.

Yes, I'm back at it again. I don't like writing in this thing; it makes me feel like these terrible things that keep happening to us are real in a way that I don't always want. But tonight, if I don't get this out of my head, I think I might explode...

Lia screamed today.

Not her quiet gasp, not her startled flinch but an actual scream. The kind that comes from somewhere deep, somewhere scared. I don't think I'll forget that sound. Ever.

Someone plastered photos of her on our dorm door. Photos she didn't know existed. Photos that meant someone was watching her when she thought she was alone. And then they carved a message into the wood like this place isn't already terrifying enough.

We know what you did.

I ripped the pictures down. I would've ripped the door off if I could. I told her it was Alyssa because that made sense. Because it was easier. Because I needed her to stop shaking.

But the truth? I don't believe that for a second.

Alyssa is mean and calculated. But she wants reactions, not silence. Whoever did this wants control.

And that scares me.

Dahlia keeps apologizing, like this is somehow her fault. Like she deserves it. I don't know what happened to her before this place, but I know enough to know she shouldn't be carrying this alone.

I won't let her.

If someone thinks they can scare her into obedience, they picked the wrong girl to mess with.

I'm putting this diary under my bed tonight. Just in case. I don't know what "just in case" means yet- but something feels wrong here, and I don't want to forget how it started.

If anything happens, I want a record.

For Dahlia.

Angie♡

Chapter 37

PRI-VACY.

Wes.

I don't usually walk people back to their dorms.

Not because I don't care, because caring gets noticed here. And notice turns into leverage. But Lia's hands were still shaking when she told us what happened to the door, and when class ended, she didn't even hesitate before falling into step beside me. So, I walked her back. The hallway feels narrower than usual. Every sound echoes too long. Lia keeps her gaze forward, jaw set like if she looks anywhere else, she might splinter. Angie is dawdling behind us, her eyes scanning for Alyssa.

"You don't have to come in," she says quietly when we reach her dorm.

I already saw it. The door. It's not the same. The wood looks newer, lighter. Replaced. And it's open. Just enough to feel intentional.

"I'm not leaving," I say flatly. "I was coming to my dorm door anyway."

She swallows and steps closer anyway. The second we cross the threshold, my stomach drops. The room has been torn apart. Not messy, *searched*. Drawers pulled out and overturned. Clothes scattered across the floor. Angie's books dumped in a heap like someone rifled through them with practiced hands. The mattress on her bed is tipped up, frame exposed.

And there, right in the center of it all, a diary. Placed neatly. Perfectly. Like a display.

Lia freezes.

Angie steps out from behind us slowly, eyes scanning, breathing shallow. "Oh my god."

Taped to the diary is a note. White paper. Cheerful handwriting.

Make sure to keep this diary in obvious spots. Consider this as a warning from the nurses

My vision goes red. Freddie suddenly storms in behind Angie, takes one look, and rips the note clean in half.

"Oh, fuck *this*." he snaps.

Dahlia hasn't moved. She's staring at her bed. At the wall above it. Where the photos are. Again. Pieced back together. Every one of them smoothed flat, aligned carefully like someone took their time. Her in the basement. Her on the stairs. Her turning late.

She makes a sound I've never heard before. Not a scream, something smaller. Broken.

"Hey- hey," Freddie says instantly, stepping in front of her. He grabs the photos, tearing them down in quick, violent motions. "I've got this, Dolly. Don't worry. I'll deal with it."

He doesn't joke. Doesn't smile. Just blocks her view with his body like it's instinct. That's when Nick walks in. He stops dead.

"What the hell happened?" he demands.

Angie is already at the diary, flipping through pages with shaking hands. "They went through it."

Nick crosses the room in three long strides and snatches it from her. He flips faster. Harder. Then his face changes.

"What is this?" he snaps. He rips a page out and holds it up.

"This isn't mine," Angie says quickly, panic rising. "I swear, it's not my handwriting."

Nick reads aloud, voice tight with anger.

"*You think your little secrets are safe? You think writing makes you clever?*"

He tears the page clean in half.

"Why do you even have this stupid diary?" he explodes. "So, they can sneak around and see what we're doing? You're invading our privacy!"

Angie flinches. "No! Nick, they gave it to me. I *must* write in it. I didn't know they'd check it outside of my therapy sessions. I haven't written anything personal, I promise."

Her voice cracks. The room is dead silent. I look at Dahlia. She's pale as paper; arms wrapped around herself like she's trying to hold herself together. Her eyes aren't on the mess anymore. They're on *us*. Like she's afraid this is the moment we decide she's too much trouble. Something twists hard in my chest.

"This isn't on Angie." I say sharply. "And it's not on Dahlia."

Nick exhales through his nose, jaw clenched, but he doesn't argue. Freddie stuffs the torn photos into the back of his pants. "They don't get to scare us into silence," he says. "Not happening."

I wish I believed that was true.

Chapter 38

Singing in the rain.

Dahlia.

I'm in trouble. They don't say it outright, but I can tell the moment the nurse's eyes flick to my barcode.

"Front office," she says. "Now."

I don't argue.

The walk there is quiet. My stomach aches, not just from hunger, but from the familiar dread curling low in my chest. I already know this isn't going to be a warning. Warnings come before fear. This comes after. They don't make me sit. They make me stand in the center of the room while a man I've never seen before reads from a tablet like he's announcing the weather.

"You were documented in a restricted area." he says.

My throat tightens. "I didn't know it was-"

"That's irrelevant."

I scoff. *Of course it is.*

"Your punishment is ten laps around the oval. Maintain a speed of six miles per hour. If your pace drops, you will restart." He says, dry as ever.

My heart skips a beat, fluttering furiously. "Ten?"

He looks up at me for the first time. "Yes, and you'll be monitored," he adds, gesturing vaguely upward. "Through cameras and speakers. Begin immediately."

The oval is empty when I step onto it.

Gray clouds hang low overhead, heavy and swollen. The ground is damp beneath my shoes. I stretch my fingers once, twice, trying to ignore how weak I feel without food. A speaker crackles to life.

"Begin."

I started running.

Lap one burns in a way I expect. Lap two settles into my lungs. By lap three, my legs feel tight, like they're resisting me on purpose. I focus on my breathing. In. Out. Count steps. Don't think. By lap five, the sky opens. Rain pours down hard and suddenly, soaking my hair, plastering my clothes to my skin. Mud splashes up my calves. My shoes slip slightly with each step.

The speaker crackles again. "Maintain speed."

I grit my teeth and push harder.

My chest aches. My vision blurs at the edges. I don't know how many laps I have left, just that stopping means starting over, and I don't think I have that in me. Then, soft footsteps plod along beside me.

"Wow," Angie pants, matching my pace. "Rude of them to start a monsoon without warning."

I turned my head, shocked. "Angie, what are you doing?"

Wes appears on my other side, already soaked, hair stuck to his forehead. He grins. "Moral support. And cardio."

"You're not allowed–"

"Too late," Angie says brightly. "Also, I bet you five pushups I finish first."

Despite everything, a laugh bubbles out of me. "You're on."

We surge ahead, splashing through puddles like this is a game and not a punishment. Wes lags behind, laughing as we sprint past him.

"Hey!" He calls. "Unfair advantage!"

Rain pours down harder, but I don't feel it the same way anymore. My legs still burn, my lungs still scream, but something inside me feels lighter. We laugh as we run. Real laughter. Angie whoops when she pulls ahead, throwing a triumphant look over her shoulder.

"I win!" she shouts. "Five pushups!"

I cross the final lap seconds later, breathless and soaked, but smiling so hard my face hurts.

The speaker crackled one last time. "Detention complete."

We don't wait. We take off together, shoes squelching, clothes dripping, sprinting back toward the dorms like we've stolen something precious.

Chapter 39

Can I get a refund?

Freddie.

Nick was finishing his workout, all bulging muscles and perfect form, and I leaned against the mirror, idly running my fingers over what was left of my hair. Not that there was much. The stubble was short, sharp, alien somehow.

"What the fuck are you doing?" Nick asked without looking up, voice low, slightly annoyed. "You have no hair left."

"I... I don't know," I muttered. My fingers froze mid-run through the stubble. "Just... thinking."

"Thinking about what?" His tone was flat. Blunt. I could practically hear the I-don't-have-time-for-your-shit in it.

I shook my head. "Nothing. Just... weird feelings."

He finally glanced at me, raised brow. "Weird feelings. About what? Losing your hair?"

"Kind of." I exhaled, scuffing a foot against the floor. "The therapist... asked me this thing." My voice caught. "She said when I was getting it shaved did, I think of anyone in particular? Someone close... or even related. And... I don't... I don't remember thinking of anyone. But... there was... this tiniest flash of something. A face... someone warm. Maybe my mom... I don't know. I didn't... tell her. I didn't admit it. Didn't know if it counted."

Nick paused mid-stretch, still breathing heavily from whatever insane set he was doing, then gave me a look that was half annoyance, half... just watching me like he was figuring out some math problem.

"Huh. That's... fucked up," he said bluntly. "But also, I don't care. You're not *wrong*. You're just... thinking too hard."

I let out a short laugh that sounded hollow even to me. "Yeah... maybe. It feels like shit though. Like I should remember more, but I can't. And that... flash... makes it worse. Makes it feel wrong."

He stood, muscles flexing even without trying. "So, what? You want me to fix it?"

"No," I said quickly. "You can't. I just... feel... off." The words tasted bitter, like swallowing something I couldn't spit out. "I don't even remember why I was so attached to my hair. The therapist made it worse. I... I feel... off about it."

Nick's expression didn't change much. Not his usual slight grin, not his impatience, it was flat, dry, slightly grumpy. But it was steady, grounding. "Yeah. Okay. You feel off. That's... fine. Doesn't make you fucked up. You're still you. Hair doesn't matter."

I swallowed, forcing another laugh, shakier this time. "Thanks, Mr. Emotional-Controller."

He snorted. "Don't thank me. Just don't die while whining."

The girls and Wes burst in suddenly, arms full of clean, folded laundry.

"Laundry done!" Dahlia called, practically skipping in, and Angie added, "Fresh and warm. Don't even thank us yet."

I blinked, momentarily distracted from the gnawing weirdness in my chest. Nick grabbed a pile of shirts without a word, tossing them toward me with that same dry, no-nonsense efficiency.

"Uh... thanks?" I muttered, still trying to process the feeling I couldn't name. Part of me wanted to laugh, part of me still felt... wrong. But the warmth of everyone being here, the mundane comfort of folded clothes, Nick's steady presence helped a little.

"Try not to burn the building down folding it," Nick said, rolling his eyes as he went back to stretching.

I smirked faintly. "Yeah... yeah, I'll try. No promises."

Even with everything off inside me, I felt... lighter. Not completely okay but okay enough to breathe. To joke. To be here. With them. And with Nick, who didn't overdo anything, didn't coddle or lecture. Just... existed, and somehow that made it a little less fucked up.

I leaned back against the mirror again, fingers brushing my stubble. It still felt odd. Wrong, even. But maybe... maybe it was alright to not know everything.

Chapter 40

We can't win them all.

Wes.

I woke up to the weirdest, most "what-the-actual-fuck" scenario I've seen in this dorm. Well... technically I didn't wake up, but that was my first thought as I dragged myself back to the room after a long day.

The first thing that hit me? Suits. Neatly folded, crisp, absurdly formal, laid out on every bed. And on mine... a small piece of paper.

It read: 'Partner: Alyssa Quinn.' Alyssa. The bully. *The bitch.* My stomach churned. Before I could say anything, a chime rang through the dorm.

"Students," the headmistress announced, crisply, "as we have almost reached the middle of the year, a ball has been assigned tonight at 20:30 PM. Every student has been paired with a partner, and tailored outfits have been provided for your convenience. Take this as a polite reward for your progress in the reform trials. Please be prepared and arrive on time. Enjoy the evening responsibly."

I pinched the bridge of my nose. Randomly assigned partners, suits I didn't pick. Freddie stepped in behind me, peering at his own tux. He froze, eyes wide. He held the little white card up.

"Partner: Angie? Oh... fuck," he muttered under his breath, almost to himself. "Let's see what you've got for me, Princess. Fuck... she's gonna kill this night. Every damn eye in the room is gonna be on her. And... shit. I'm supposed to deal with it."

I blinked. He was pacing a little, tugging at his bow tie, and muttering like the room itself was about to combust. Not that he'd admit it but the awe in his voice was... real.

Nick, naturally, was leaning against the wall, grey suit laid out perfectly, cufflinks in place, expression bland as hell. He glanced at his note. 'Partner: Dahlia Moretti.' He didn't even twitch. Just folded his arms, dry as ever. "She'll glare at me if I take too long. That's all you need to know."

"Why do you guys get fine partners, and I end up with the bitch?" I ask, feeling absolutely set up.

Nick smirked, looking down, responding, "We can't win them all... And for your information, I'm not over the moon about my partner either."

Freddie gulped, muttered again, barely containing his tortured sarcasm. "This is perfect. This is just great"

Nick rolled his eyes, tugging on his blazer with all the enthusiasm of a cat being forced into a bath. "Stop whining. It's just a ball."

I sighed, tugging at my sleeves. Damn, Freddie freaking out, guess I'm screwed. Luck? Yeah... I was going to need a lot of it.

Chapter 41

Green is my favorite color.

Freddie.

We all met outside the dorms, awkwardly clustered in the hallway. Us boys were trying not to trip over our own feet, and the air smelled faintly of polished floors and nervous energy. Then I saw her.

Holy shit.

Angie. Emerald-green dress, perfectly fitted at the waist, flowing slightly at the bottom like she'd just stepped out of some fantasy I didn't deserve to be in. Her blonde curls forming down her back and arms, she was... breathtaking.

I muttered under my breath; barely aware I'd spoken aloud. "Emerald... fucking perfect."

Her brown eyes snapped to me, and I froze. She smirked. "Excuse me?"

"Oh... uh. Nothing. Forget I said anything," I stammered, pretending to adjust my cufflinks like they were suddenly extremely interesting.

"Sure, nothing," she said, raising an eyebrow, voice full of amusement. "Keep muttering to yourself. It's adorable."

I groaned. "Shut up."

I squared my shoulders. "So... you planning to blind everyone in the hallway with that... thing you're wearing?"

She smirked again. "Thing? Wow, harsh. This thing is going to make heads spin tonight."

"I'll need my game face ready." I muttered, more to myself than her, but she heard that too. Her smirk widened. "Noted. I expect nothing less than full glaring intensity from you, Frederick."

I cursed under my breath. "Goddammit. Why do you have to be so... perfect? I can't even talk properly."

"You're doing fine," she said. "For a human male. Barely."

I rolled my eyes, but I couldn't stop sneaking glances at her dress. Every time she moved, the fabric caught the light just enough to make it impossible to look away. She was... radiant. Gob smacked doesn't even cover it.

"So," I said, trying to recover my composure, "We... uh, waltzing in the hallway here, or are we just staring at each other awkwardly for the next ten minutes?"

"Depends," she said, stepping closer, "Are you planning to trip over your own feet or actually impress me?"

She really knows me too well.

I huffed, tugging at my tux. "Pftt, c'mon girl, I- I'll manage." *Of course I stumble over my words. Really bright Freddie.* "That sounded much smoother in my head." I chuckled, looking down to see the smile it brought to her gorgeous face.

She laughed softly, a little melodic sound that made my chest tighten. "Good. Keep that up. And seriously, don't faint before we even get to the ball."

"Absolutely flawless." I muttered again, just quiet enough that I thought it was for me, but she shot me another knowing smirk.

I groaned, staring at the floor. "I'm doomed."

Inside, I was a mess. Nervous, and already imagining the chaos of the ball. Every eye in the room would be on her. *Geez Freddie can you maybe act like it doesn't bother you anymore? I don't think the headmistress heard you.*

Chapter 42

Will my mind ever shut up?

Nick.

By the time I finished putting on my suit, Wes, Freddie and Ange were already gone. I stepped out of the dorm and froze. There she was. Dahlia.

Silk. Deep sapphire that shimmered just enough under the hallway lights, draping her body like it had been sculpted for her alone. The folds twisted and flowed in ways that made her look almost unreal, like she had walked straight out of a painting I wasn't supposed to see. My chest hitched, and suddenly the hallway, the polished floors, the other fucked up things in this place, they all vanished. It was just her.

Fuck.

I couldn't stop staring. Every strand of her hair, the curve of her neck, the faint dusting of freckles across her nose... I wanted to memorize it all, store it in my brain, and keep it forever. Every line, every shadow, every subtle detail. Ridiculous. Obsessive. And yet... completely necessary.

And the scent, her scent, soft, faint, like rich elegance, something untamed. I wanted to bottle it up. I knew I'd never forget it.

"Wow." I muttered, low and rough.

Her eyebrow quirked, a smirk tugging at her lips. "Wow? That's it? Just 'wow'?"

"Yeah. Wow. Just... wow," I said, voice tight.

She took a step back and slammed her back against the wall. My chest jumped, heat roaring through me. Too close. Too tempting.

"Careful there, Nick," she said, voice teasing. "You're staring like a total creep."

"Creep?" I asked, incredulously, tilting my head.

I swallowed, cursed, and took a tiny step closer. My hand brushed against her waist, not intentionally, but I felt it. *Shit.*

"Hmm. Careful," I whispered, letting my words skim her ear. "Don't push it."

Her smirk faltered for a fraction of a second before she leaned just enough to tease me. "Go ahead Nick, keep it up. Good luck. You're... hopeless."

"Hopeless?" I muttered, shaking my head, lips twitching. "Me?"

"Yes. Totally hopeless. And completely... distracted," she said, eyes glinting, sharp, testing me.

I exhaled, taking in every inch of her without meaning to. Her hair, her lashes, the subtle curve of her lips, the way the silk clung at her waist before twisting and flowing. God, I

could spend hours memorizing it all. And her freckles... damn it, those freckles.

"You look... ridiculous," I muttered, forcing some sarcasm into my voice, though my chest threatened to betray me.

"Right back at you," she said, smirking, eyes sparkling. "That suit isn't doing you any favors. You're still terrifying."

"Terrifying?" I asked, lips twitching. "I'm sophisticatedly terrifying."

"Oh, sure. You're... fine," she said, but with that faint curve of mischief that made my chest clench.

"I could say the same about you," I murmured, letting it hang there, teasing but dangerous.

Her smirk widened again, sharp and knowing. "Oh, I bet you could."

We froze for a heartbeat, just long enough for the tension to thicken. The accidental brush of my hand lingered in my mind, the warmth of her body pressed just slightly against the wall, the intoxicating scent of her...

Every step, every word, every glance was a gamble. And somehow, I wanted more. I wanted to see if she'd challenge again. Tease me. Let me see past the walls I built for her.

Not now. Not yet. But... oh, I wanted it.

Chapter 43

Prom night?

Wes.

The assembly hall was transformed. Strings of golden fairy lights crisscrossed the ceiling, casting a warm glow that made everything feel softer, magical even. A thin haze from the fog machine blurred the edges of the room, turning the dancers into shapes moving through liquid light. The bass thumped steadily through the polished wood floor, vibrating up through my shoes, a steady heartbeat syncing with the music.

Of course. Of course I get partnered with Alyssa. The queen of chaos herself, in a red dress that looked like it had been stitched out of fire and attitude. Every step she took was loud, deliberate, designed to make me uncomfortable. I stayed stiff, arms crossed, jaw tight, trying not to roll my eyes so hard I'd dislocate something.

She sidled up to me, brushing her hand along my arm like she owned the air around me. "Ready to survive the night, Wes?" she purred.

I gave her a tight-lipped smile.

"Survive you? Barely."

She ran her hand over the fake red rose that was pinned on my suit. I tried to focus on something else, anything else, and my gaze drifted around the room. Couples swayed together, some tentative, others like they had done this a hundred times before. I caught Nick and Dahlia a few feet away, dancing. Nick had his hands resting lightly on her waist, and Dahlia's hands were on his shoulders, a little unsure at first until, slowly, a wide grin broke across her face. Her laughter was quiet, delicate, and I felt a rare pang of warmth. She looked happy, free for once. It was strange to see her like that, radiant, not worried about anything, completely caught up in the music.

A few feet further, Freddie and Angie twirled with effortless rhythm. Angie's curls bounced, catching the lights, and Freddie spun her, her dress fanning out beautifully. Suddenly to my quiet disbelief, Freddie dipped her low, steadying her with that perfect mix of strength and gentleness, and she laughed like it was the only sound in the world. I watched them for a moment; they looked completely in sync.

I tried my best to sway in this waltz with Alyssa, but she was making it hard. She wasn't focusing. I noticed her lower lip quiver as she fought tears.

"Hey, what's going on?" I asked softly.

"I know everyone thinks I'm this heartless person. But it's not true. I'm just scared. I want to go home. I don't know why

I'm here and I can't trust anything, so my bitchiness, it's just a defense tactic."

This caught me off guard. *Completely*. I felt bad. I knew what it was like to be misunderstood.

"Oh god, why am I telling you this."

"Look, we're all scared. But you don't have to tear people down just because you don't trust them." I whisper.

"I know, I'm sorry. I just can't stand anyone here."

This triggered a chuckle. Nice to know she can't stand everyone in this place, including me. The guy she was waltzing with.

Just as we fell into a smoother rhythm, I felt Nick's gaze land on me, and before I could breathe, he was next to me leaning in, his voice dripping with sarcasm.

"Careful, Wes. Don't let her anywhere near you tonight, last thing we need is a repeat of... hands where they shouldn't be."

"Honestly, Nick... I could take you, teach you things your little prude virgin wouldn't even dream of," Alyssa said, eyes flicking toward Dahlia, who froze mid-step, shifting nervously beside Nick. "And trust me... I look even better on my knees. I bet she couldn't even handle it if I showed her." She giggled to herself, batting her lashes and licking her lips.

Time slowed. I felt my chest tighten, and Dahlia's wide eyes locked on Alyssa like she couldn't even breathe. Nick's face went from annoyed to absolute death in under a second.

"Shut the fuck up Alyssa." he barked, voice like thunder, echoing over the music.

I stepped forward, hands raised slightly. "Dude... calm down."

"Calm down?" Nick shouted back, stepping toward me, his face red, jaw tight. "Did you hear what she just said to Dahlia? *To Dahlia?*"

"I know, I know!" I snapped, voice rising. "But this isn't the way to go about it! You're being a dick, too aggressive, like always!"

Nick lunged. I shoved him back instinctively. The music, the swirling couples, the glittering lights, it all became a blur of color and sound. Nick and I were shouting, shoving, the kind of chaotic flailing that draws every pair of eyes in the room. I got a small glimpse of Dahlia, frozen in the spotlight. A deer in headlights.

Dahlia went pale, the light reflected off her dress, hands pressed to her chest, like the world had shrunk down to just us. I could see silent tears threatening, her body trembling. Freddie, quick as ever, dove in between us.

"Enough! Cut it out, both of you!" he yelled, arms flailing to keep us apart. "Dolly, are you okay? Dolly! Nick, stop it!"

Alyssa stood nearby, red dress glowing under the Red LED lights, a smirk on her face as if she'd choreographed this entire meltdown. Her hand toyed with the edge of her hair, enjoying every second.

Freddie ran to Dahlia, wrapping his blazer around her shoulders and brushing at her cheeks to wipe the silent tears streaming down. Her shaking only seemed to fuel Nick's anger further, and distracted, he swung another punch, this time connecting squarely with my jaw. Pain shot up my face, but I shoved him back, fists ready. *Really, so we're doing this?*

Chapter 44

20 minutes.

Dahlia.

Everything was too loud.

The music had stopped, but the noise hadn't. The shouting, the gasps, the echo of fists colliding. Wes and Nick were still fighting somewhere in front of me, but my body had already checked out. My hands were shaking so badly I couldn't feel my fingers anymore.

"Hey- hey, look at me," Freddie said softly, crouching in front of me. His jacket was around my shoulders now, heavy and grounding, but it wasn't enough. My chest burned. I couldn't get air in deep enough. Every breath felt wrong.

I nodded even though I wasn't sure I could hear him properly. The lights blurred. My vision tunneled. I was panicking.

My knees had buckled, and suddenly Freddie's hands were on my arms, steadying me. "You're okay. You're safe. I've got you," he kept repeating, like a lifeline.

Then everything exploded. Someone shouted. A body slammed into another. And then... silence. Not real silence. The kind where everyone knows something just ended.

Nick.

I barely registered how he got to me. One second, he was across the room, chest heaving, knuckles red and the next, he was there. Right in front of me. His eyes locked onto mine like nothing else existed.

"Dahlia," he said, and his voice cracked. I tried to speak. Nothing came out. He didn't hesitate. Nick scooped me up, bridal style, like it was instinct, like my weight meant nothing to him. The world tilted, and suddenly I was against his chest, my face pressed into his shoulder. His heartbeat was wild and fast under my ear.

People shouted. I heard a guard yell about protocol. I didn't care. All I knew was that Nick had me.

He carried me through the hallways, past doors and lights and everything that felt too bright. His arms were tight, protective, like he was afraid I might disappear if he loosened his grip.

"I've got you," he murmured. "You're okay. I won't drop you."

By the time we reached my room, my body felt hollow. He laid me down gently on my bed, like I was something fragile. His hands lingered for half a second too long before he pulled back.

I reached for his sleeve.

"Stay," I whispered.

He froze.

Nick didn't look at me right away. When he did, his expression was closed off, guarded, like walls snapping into place. "I shouldn't," he said quietly. "This doesn't mean anything. I don't want it to."

My chest ached. But he sat down anyway. He stayed.

He didn't touch me, just sat beside the bed, close enough that I could feel his warmth, close enough that I could breathe again. His presence anchored me. I don't know how long we stayed like that. Minutes blurred. My panic ebbed, replaced by exhaustion so heavily it dragged my eyelids down. Just before I slipped under, he leaned closer.

"You know," he said softly, voice low and rough, "if I ever let anyone that close... if I ever trusted someone like that, it would be you."

I drifted off, eyelids too heavy to hold open. When I woke up, the room was quiet. The bed beside me was empty, and the spot were Nick sat was empty.

I saw on the clock how soon he had left. I sat up slowly, the ache in my chest returning tenfold. The comfort he'd left behind had already faded, like he'd never been there at all. I pressed my hand to the sheets, swallowing hard. And for the first time being in Montclair, I cried myself to sleep.

Chapter 45

What. The. Fuck.

Nick.

Cold hits first. Not the sharp kind, worse. The slow, creeping kind that sinks into your bones and stays there. I wake up strapped to a chair; wrists submerged in metal basins filled with water so cold it doesn't even sting yet. It just exists. Waiting. One second, I was watching Dahlia sleep, the next I'm here.

My fingers are already stiff. Of course they start with my hands. I test the restraints instinctively. Tight. Too tight. Leather biting into my wrists. I try to flex my fingers. There's resistance, like my hands don't quite belong to me anymore. A voice comes from somewhere above. Calm and neutral. Almost bored.

"Cold water therapy," they say. "Designed to reduce aggressive impulses."

A scratchy laugh comes out of me.

"You people are idiots," I mutter. "You ever tried telling someone to calm down while freezing them?"

The water seeps deeper. My palms throb. Pins and needles explode up my arms, then fade into something worse, nothing.

I swear. A lot.

I don't even register half the words as they spill out of my mouth. Rage fills the gaps where feeling should be. Control is slipping, and I hate that more than the pain.

"Language" the voice warns.

"Go to hell," I snap.

There's movement behind me. A guard steps into view, holding a small white bar.

"No," I say immediately. "Don't you dare."

They force my head back anyway. Soap presses against my teeth. Something inside me snaps.

My chest tightens suddenly, breath hitching hard, and the room blurs, not with tears, but with memory. My father's face flashes in my mind. Red with anger. Veins in his neck bulging as he shouts words that don't even matter anymore. My fists slamming into something, someone. The sound of impact. The blood painting the floor.

Then my uncle's voice, smooth and quiet, cutting through it all.

"Are you telling me, that little brat gets everything! After all the shit, he's pulled over the years. He hasn't worked a day in his goddamn privileged life and I get NOTHING!" But the context fades.

Hands gripping my shoulders. Not here. Not now.

I can't breathe.

"Get off me!" I roar.

I twist hard, adrenaline surging. My chair scrapes violently against the floor as I wrench one arm free. My thumb makes a loud pop and instead of my hands feeling numb, I feel a surge off pain shoot through my left arm. I don't stop. I don't think. I continue to react. My elbow connects with someone's jaw. A shout. A body hitting the ground. Another guard rushes in. I swung blindly, catching him across the ribs. He gasps, stumbling back. The room erupts loudly, boots, yelling, alarms.

I'm out of the chair now, shaking, lungs burning, vision tunneling.

Too many hands grab me.

"Restrain him!"

I fight like an animal. Because that's what they want, right?

They overpower me eventually. They always do. They drag me down the hall, my boots barely touching the floor, past white walls that blur together. I'm thrown into another room, darker. Smaller. The door slams shut. A guard steps forward, rolling his shoulders like he's warming up.

"We didn't plan to punish you for the fight," he says evenly. "But we believe all fights should end fair."

My stomach turns while he smiles thinly.

"Whatever you gave us," he continues, "you get back. Twice."

I bare my teeth at him, heart pounding, fear and fury tangling so tightly I can't tell where one ends and the other begins.

"Do your worst." I spit.

Chapter 46
Blah, blah, blah.

Nick.

I don't look at her. I sit in her fucking ugly chair with my jaw locked so tight it aches; eyes fixed on the wall just to the left of her head. If I meet her gaze, she wins something. I don't know what yet but I know better than to give it. My hands won't stay still. Fingers flexing. Unflexing. Like they're still trying to remember what it felt like to move freely. My thumb is bruised all around, clicking whenever I move it.

"Good morning, Nick," Dr. Matilda says, voice smooth, practiced. "How are you feeling today?"

I say nothing. She doesn't seem bothered. She never is. That's the worst part. Silence doesn't unsettle her; it seems to invite her. She crosses one leg over the other, tablet resting neatly on her knee. "You were in isolated detention recently," she continues. "A rather intense experience, from what I understand."

My shoulders tense and I scowl, but quickly wince at the ache of pain across my face.

"Cold exposure," she adds lightly. "Physical restraint. Escalation."

I can still feel it. The numbness. The moment my hands stopped feeling like mine.

"Did it remind you of anything?" she asks.

That does it. I push up from the chair, anger snapping hot and fast through my chest.

"We're done." I take one step before a guard's hand clamps down on my arm and forces me back into the seat, my body still aching over the beating I took. The impact rattles my teeth.

Something dark flashes across my vision. I turn my head slowly towards her.

"Touch me again," I say quietly, dangerously calm, "and you'll be pulling *him* off the floor."

The guard hesitates, stepping back. Dr. Matilda watches me closely now. Not smiling. Not yet.

"You're very controlled," she says. "Especially for someone who's just been through what you have."

I lean forward slightly, elbows on my knees. My voice stays even. "You don't get to talk about control. Not after what you people do." Her eyebrow twitches. Interesting. I found something. She pauses, then shifts tactics like flipping a switch.

"Alright," she says gently. "Let's try something else. How do you feel about being here, Nick?"

I stared at her. Is she joking? I let out a short breath through my nose and looked away, shrugging once. Then I glance back, just long enough for her to see the answer she won't get.

She smiles. Slow and creepy. Like she's pleased I didn't answer.

"You know," she says conversationally, "students who struggle with authority often have complicated family dynamics. Fathers with high expectations. Uncles who exert... influence."

My chest tightens. *Uncle.* The word lands wrong. Heavy. Like it's pressing on something sore and half-healed inside me.

She notices immediately.

"Oh," she says softly. "Did I touch on something sensitive?"

I don't respond. I can't. My pulse is too loud in my ears.

Images flicker just out of reach, voices raised, a room that feels too big, someone saying my name like a warning. My uncle's face should be there, but it's blurred. My father's too. All feeling, no clarity. Dr. Matilda's eyes gleam faintly.

"We'll stop here for today," she says. "You're dismissed."

I'm already standing before she finishes the sentence. I don't look back. The door clicks shut behind me, sealing the room away. The hallway feels colder than it should.

As I walk, one thought claws at the back of my mind, relentless and unanswered.

What don't I remember about my uncle and my father? What happened in that room between the three of us? And why does it feel like, no matter where I go, I'm always standing in the middle of the fallout?

Chapter 47

Push and pull.

Dahlia.

The halls feel different after the ball. Quieter, somehow. Like the walls are holding their breath, waiting for something else to break. My shoes echo too loudly against the floor as I walk, arms wrapped around myself even though it isn't cold, desperate to find a way to cover myself from bleeding eyes.

I'm tired and hurt and sick of all the questions that torment my mind. *I just wish that for even a second, someone would give me some peace and tell the truth.*

"Stop."

The word cuts clean through my thoughts. The pledge. I halt automatically, spine straightening as my eyes flick to the front of the hall where the words loom large and unavoidable. I started reciting without thinking, voice flat, rehearsed. I've said it so many times it doesn't even feel like a language anymore, just sound. Halfway through, I see him. Nick stands a few feet away, leaning against the wall like he doesn't care that the pledge exists, that rules exist, that anything exists.

His face is angled slightly down, but I can feel his attention on me. Heavy and focused.

My chest tightens.

I finish the last line, forcing the words out through my teeth. The second I'm done, I turn, rolling my eyes like I don't care, like he's nothing and walk back the way I came.

I don't get far. I can hear him chasing me. His hand closes around my arm. The contact is sudden. Firm. I flinch hard, yanking my arm back on instinct, heart slamming into my ribs. Fear flashes hot and sharp before anger rushes in to cover it.

"What do you want, let go of me!" I snapped.

"Dahlia," he says quickly, reaching out to me again.

"Don't... don't touch me." I gently warn.

"Wait. Let me explain."

I let out a bitter laugh without stopping. "Explain what?"

"Please," he says, stepping in front of me now. His voice drops. "Just hear me out. The other night–"

I shoved him. Not hard enough to hurt, not like it would. To be honest it hurt me more than it probably did him. But hard enough to make a point. My hands tremble as soon as I do it.

"Yeah, let's talk about the other night, you couldn't even stay twenty minutes with me!" The words spill out, messy and loud before I can stop them. "I woke up twenty minutes later and you were gone. Gone. Do you hate me that much? Or do you just, what, enjoy toying with me?"

He doesn't answer. Something about the way he's standing, too still, shoulders tight, makes me finally really look at him.

My breath catches. There are bruises along his jaw. Fading purples and yellows near his cheekbone. A split at the corner of his lip. My anger stumbles.

"Oh..." I step closer without thinking, hands lifting, my feet reaching to my tip toes, the only way I can come even halfway to his height towering over me. "Oh my gosh. Nick, what happened? Did Wesley-"

I gently turn his chin so I can see his face properly. He flinches. Not subtly. He jerks back like my touch burns. My hands fall uselessly to my sides. His eyes go cold, walls slamming up so fast it's almost audible. He takes a step back, then another, creating distance like it's oxygen.

"You know what," he says, backing away but keeping his eyes locked on mine, "I don't need this."

My throat tightens.

"I don't need your concern," he continues, voice sharp, defensive, cracked around the edges. "Or all your weird emotions. Just-" He shakes his head once. "Just stay away from me."

The words hit harder than I expected. He turns and walks away, not looking back. I stand there, stunned, heart pounding painfully against my ribs.

"Fine!" I shout after him, the word breaking as it leaves my mouth.

Chapter 48

B.F. (Bitch Fight)

Angeline.

I don't remember deciding to fight.

I remember Alyssa's voice first, sharp, bored, aimed to wound.

"Careful," she says loudly. "If Angie gets stressed, she might disappear to the bathroom again."

I keep walking. I truly do try to.

"Don't pretend you're cured," she adds, smirking. "One cookie and you're back on your knees."

I stopped. She steps closer, eyes flicking past me, counting witnesses. Then she smiles. Cruel. Pleased.

"Freddie didn't seem to mind though," she says lightly. "We hooked up last week. Guess he wanted a girl who eats."

Something inside me snaps. Final. I turn.

"Don't." I say, but my voice isn't mine anymore. She tilts her head.

"Glare all you want, Angie... Freddie wouldn't even last with someone like you. You're too scrawny, he'd break you in

217

bed. He needs someone stronger, someone like me who can consume food."

"Stop acting like such a slut Alyssa." I spit out.

I don't know where that even came from. "We all know Freddie wouldn't hook up with the scraps of the school." I smirk.

She steps close, all in my face. I look into her sharp cat eyes. I don't know were all this confidence is coming from. Maybe it's the adrenaline, or I have finally just given up trying to make my peace in this shit hole.

I sigh, then turn and walk away. This is not worth being late to a class and being forced into that white room again for punishment.

"Hey. I'm talking to you." She calls out.

I just keep walking.

"What? did I hit a Nerve?"

"Leave it Alyssa, I don't have time. Neither do you. Maybe we can pick this up at lunch time again hm?"

"Aw don't be like that Angie."

Just ignore her.

"Don't be a bitch, Angie."

A second later, something slams into my back shoving me forward.

I stop. Peek at the clock. 5 minutes until class.

"There she is... aww worried about getting another detention?"

I turn, my pulse spiking.

"Go on then... run off to class."

"No no... you're obviously here to say something to me Alyssa. So say it. Stop stalling."

She snickers. "You know what your problem is? You walk around acting like you're the victim, but nobody's doing this to you. People just genuinely don't like you. Especially Freddie."

"Fuck off Alyssa."

For the first time all morning, that cocky look gets wiped off her smug face. Her friends laugh behind her.

Then–

Crack.

Her palm collides with my cheek. The force turns my head sideways, my jaw instantly aching.

She just stares at me. Waiting for me to cry. To walk away and prove her right.

Silly bitch.

I lose control. My fists fly, grabbing the first thing in reach. Gasps erupt as I slam her into the lockers. Metal shrieks. Her head snaps back hard enough to echo. She screams, hands flying but I've already got a fistful of her hair.

I yank. Hard. She shrieks again, higher this time, stumbling as I drive her back into the lockers, once, twice. The metal dents. Her feet scrambled uselessly against the floor.

"Take it back," I say. My voice is low now. Dead calm. She sobs, trying to pry my fingers loose. I tighten my grip and rip again. Something tears free in my hand. A chunk of hair.

Her scream turns animal.

"Take it back," I repeat, shaking her once, slamming her again. "Say it."

"You're crazy!" she cries.

I shove her down.

She hits the floor hard, curling in on herself, arms over her head. I stood over her, breathing steadily, my hands shaking but still clean. Untouched.

My hand moves. The slap cracks down the hallway like a gunshot. Her head snaps sideways. Before she could scramble away, my fists pound down on her arms. My breath ragged. I don't know how many times I hit her. I just know people are screaming now.

"ANGIE!" Freddie's voice cut through it, sharp, panicked. He's there instantly, stepping between us, arms out, protective.

"That's enough," he says, fierce. Not to me. To everyone else. He turns just enough to look at me. His voice drops. "Princess. Look at me. I've got you."

I step back. Alyssa is still on the floor, sobbing. Her hair is ruined and uneven, jagged, bald patches visible where it's been torn out. Mascara streaks down her face. Her lip is split from the impact. She looks... wrecked. Her boyfriend of the week pushes through the crowd.

"What the hell happened?" He demands.

"She attacked me!" Alyssa wails, pointing weakly. "And he's lying to you Angie! Freddie and I—"

Freddie's eyes widened, catching onto what she was going to say.

"That's a lie," he says calmly. Ice-cold. "I've never touched her. How can I in this fucked up school? Let alone HER."

The boy looks at Alyssa. Really looks. At the missing chunks of hair. The way she can't meet his eyes.

"You lied?" he asked.

"I was protecting us!" she sobs.

What the fuck does that even mean?

He shakes his head once, walking off. "We're done."

Alyssa collapses completely, howling as her friends rush in, hands hovering uselessly, trying to cover the damage that can't be undone. Freddie turns to me and scoops me up without asking, one arm under my knees, the other solid around my back.

"Freddie." I start.

"Shh," he says, already moving.

Chapter 49

Boys will be boys.

Angeline.

Lunch feels... weirdly good. Dahlia and I sit cross-legged on the grass, unwrapping sandwiches like nothing in the world is wrong, laughing way too loudly about Alyssa's face when security finally showed up.

"I can't believe you did that to her hair!" Dahlia giggles. "Like, missing. Entirely."

I grin. "I think I'm legally a legend now."
She snorts. Then Nick and Freddie drop down across from us. Nick sits directly opposite Dahlia. His knee scrapes hers barely, accidentally but it might as well have been a gunshot. She freezes. Then stands up so fast she almost knocks over her drink.

"Lia, wait-" I call, but she's already walking away, shoulders tense, not looking back.

Freddie and I both turn slowly to Nick. We're about to ask what the hell was that when Nick pushes to his feet too and walks off in the opposite direction without a word. Silence.

Just Freddie. Chewing. Loudly. Crunch. Crunch. Crunch. I stared at him. He stares back. Still chewing. Unblinking.

Then, completely serious, he says, "Wanna make out?"

I blink. "What–"

Wes appears out of nowhere and smacks the back of Freddie's head.

"OW– what the hell?" Freddie grunts.

I shoved Freddie's shoulder, laughing. "You're actually disgusting."

He grins, rubbing his head. "You didn't say no."

I groan, dropping back onto the grass. "I hate all of you."

Chapter 50

Sensitivity.

Wes.

The hallway smells like floor cleaner and burnt coffee, the kind that settles in right before afternoon classes. It clings to the back of my throat as we walk.

Angie moves between Dahlia and me, talking with her whole body, hands slicing through the air as she jumps from one story to the next. Her energy fills the space, bright and loud and alive.

Dahlia nods along beside her, a small smile tugging at her lips. But it doesn't quite reach her eyes. There's a distance to her, like part of her is somewhere else entirely, trailing a few steps behind.

Then Freddie and Nick fall into step with us.

Freddie starts talking immediately, his voice echoing around the halls like normal. Nick bumps his shoulder into him, smirking.

I feel it before anything even happens. That shift. That *this is going to go wrong* feeling settling low in my stomach.

Freddie shoves Nick, playful but careless. Nick stumbles sideways.

Right into Dahlia.

It's nothing, really. Barely a touch. Just a brush of shoulders.

"Sorry, Dolly!" Freddie calls instantly, already laughing it off like it's part of the joke.

But Dahlia... She goes rigid.

The smile drops. Her shoulders pull in tight, like she's bracing for something that isn't there anymore. She doesn't say a word. Doesn't even look at any of us.

She just sharply turns and disappears down the next hallway, head lowered, arms close to her sides like she's trying to make herself smaller.

The space she leaves behind feels too big.

Angie scoffs under her breath. "Jesus," she mutters, and swats Nick's arm. "Seriously?"

Nick barely reacts. Just shrugs, that lazy half-smile still sitting on his face.

"What?" he says. "You're telling me she can't even handle that?"

I wince.

So does Angie– but hers turns into something sharper. She stops walking. Turns fully toward him.

"Nick. Don't." Her voice is tight, controlled, but there's weight behind it. "You don't get to decide what's 'nothing' for her."

Nick opens his mouth, ready to fire something back, but she cuts in before he can.

"She's not fragile," Angie says. "She's just... careful. When you start to say stuff like that? It sticks."

Nick huffs, rolling his shoulders like he can shake it off. "Relax. I was joking."

But his eyes flick down the hallway where Dahlia disappeared.

Just for a second. Something in his *big dick energy* slips.

The smirk falters, like it was never fully real to begin with. His jaw tightens. And for a moment, he just looks... tired.

Not angry, not amused.

Just worn down.

He drags a hand over the back of his neck. "I'll catch you guys later," he mutters.

Then he turns and walks off, hands shoved deep into his pockets, shoulders hunched like he's bracing against something no one else can see.

Angie exhales slowly through her nose. "He's such an ass."

Freddie snorts. "Yeah," he says. "A deeply broken ass."

I glance back, just once, watching Nick disappear into the crowd.

"Like a big ass crack" Freddie chuckles to himself resulting in Angie and I just glaring at him.

Chapter 51

Don't dream it's over.

Wes.

The dream feels thick, like I'm stuck in fog. I'm moving, but I'm not thinking about it. My legs just go, steady and automatic, like they already know where I'm meant to be.

My arms swing in the same slow rhythm, over and over. I don't even know if my eyes are open or closed anymore.

I can't tell.

"Wes... wake up."

It's quiet at first, distant enough that it barely reaches me. Then it comes again, sharper this time.

"Wes." Hands grab my shoulders, shaking harder now, but I'm already moving. I'm out of the dorm room, into the hallway, my pajamas dragging behind me like they're caught in something I can't feel. The air is colder out here, that sterile, chemical smell clinging to everything.

My fingers trace the wall as I walk.

"Wes, stop-" Angie's voice is right behind me now, tight and panicked. She grabs onto me, trying to pull me back, turn me, slow me down.

"You're sleepwalking, come on- please!"

My body sways under her grip like I might fall, but I don't stop. I can't. It's like I'm not the one in control anymore, just something being pushed forward, step after step, with no way to fight it.

Then a solid clanking sound echoes around the walls, around the bends of the long hall. Footsteps. Heavy. Measured. Metal against the floor.

Guards.

It cuts straight through everything. Angie feels it too; her hands tighten instantly, her whole body going tense.

"Shit..." She breathes, and suddenly she's pulling at me harder, trying to drag me off course. But my body resists without meaning to, still pushing forward, still locked on whatever path it's decided on.

"Wes- stop, please-" she whispers, desperate now, her voice dropping low as the footsteps get louder, closer, too close.

They're coming this way.

Angie digs her heels into the ground, arms wrapped around me as she tries to haul me back. I feel heavy, like dead weight, making it harder for her, and still I keep moving, still trying to walk straight into them. Her breathing turns shaky, uneven, and I can feel the panic in the way she grips me tighter. At the last second, she jerks me sideways, pulling me hard enough that we both stumble into a stack of crates.

She shoves me down into the shadows behind them just as the guards pass.

Her hand clamps over my mouth, the other gripping my shirt so tight it hurts. I can hear my breathing, loud and uneven, and it feels like it's echoing off the walls. The guards are right there, close enough that I can hear the slow, steady rhythm of their boots, the faint jingle of keys, one of them clearing his throat. If I moved, if I made even the smallest sound, they'd see us.

Angie doesn't move at all. She's completely still against me, like if she just stays quiet enough, we'll disappear.

The footsteps keep going. Past us. Further down the hall.

Only when the sound finally fades does she let go, her body sagging slightly as she leans into me for a second.

"Jesus... you're heavy," she whispers, her breath still unsteady. I mentally groan.

"Wes- no-" she breathes, but I've already slipped out of her grip.

I keep walking.

Down another hallway, through a side door, my feet not even hesitating. It feels like I've done this before, even though I know I haven't. Stairs, then another turn, and then I stop in front of a keypad. My hand lifts without thinking. The numbers come easily, like something I've known for years but don't remember learning.

Each sound feels too loud in the silence. Angie keeps glancing over her shoulder, like she's expecting the guards to come running any second.

"Hurry..." she whispers.

The lock clicks.

The door opens.

Cold air rushes in, sharp and biting, hitting my skin like a shock. It feels real in a way nothing else has. I step outside, and something shifts.

Then I run.

Fast, hard, barefoot against the ground, rocks biting into my feet as grass slips under me. My lungs start burning almost immediately, dragging in cold air too fast, but I don't slow down. I can't. The buildings shrink behind me, the lights blurring until everything turns into dark and distance.

I just keep going. One mile, two- I don't even feel my legs anymore, just the motion, the need to get as far away as possible.

Eventually, my body gives out. I stumble and hit the ground hard, chest heaving as I try to pull air back into my lungs. My heart is pounding so hard it hurts, everything spinning around me as I lie there, completely spent.

"Wes—" Angie drops beside me, grabbing my shoulders again, shaking me—but gentler this time.

"Wes, wake up. Wes—please—" My eyes flutter open slowly, awareness creeping back in piece by piece.

"Angie…?" My voice comes out rough, confused. "What—
I… I couldn't stop running…"

She lets out a breath that turns into a half-laugh, half-sob, shaking her head like she can't believe it.

"We did it. We actually did it." Her grip tightens slightly. "You led us out."

That's when I really look.

There are no fences. No walls. Just trees stretching out into the dark, open land with nothing blocking it off.

Something cracks open in my chest. Relief hits first, sharp and overwhelming, followed by disbelief, then something bigger than both of them. I push myself up, legs shaking, barely holding me, but it doesn't matter. The air feels different out here, colder, cleaner. Free.

Angie stands and grabs my hand, pulling me up the rest of the way.

"Come on," she says, breathless, eyes bright. "Let's go."

And this time, when we run, it's not because we have to.

Chapter 52

No one in sight.

Nick.

Freddie walks, owning the chicks of this school with his so-called *'charm'*. I mean I know he cares for Angie, but they're not really a thing. *Dude can have some fun every once in a while.*

He's talking and pointing with his hands, animated as hell, rambling about something that happened in the gym showers that I'm only half listening to.

It's cute how he picked that up from Angie.

Hold on, what the hell am I saying? Cute? God.

"...and I swear, if the water gets any colder, I'm suing the school for emotional damages," he says. "I don't care if that's not a thing. I'm obviously rich enough to do it!"

I huff despite myself. "You'd lose."

"Yeah, but I'd lose passionately."

We rounded the corner toward our first class, and I instinctively scanned the crowd. It's automatic now. Habit.

No Dahlia.

My jaw tightens before I can stop it. Usually she's with Angie, laughing too loud, or pretending not to notice me while absolutely noticing me. Today, nothing. Just students funneling down the hall like usual. Freddie notices my silence.

"You good?" he asks, glancing over. "You went all broody just now. Getting your daily dose of deep tormented rough guy I see."

"I'm fine," I say too quickly.

We passed the cafeteria entrance. Empty tables being wiped down. No Angie. No Wes. No Dahlia hovering awkwardly near the doors.

"That's weird," Freddie mutters. "We didn't see anyone at breakfast either."

"Maybe they slept in," I say, shrugging.

Freddie gives me a look. "In this place?"

Fair point.

We keep walking. The space beside me feels louder than it should. I tell myself it's nothing- coincidence, bad timing, people having their own lives. But something itches at the back of my mind.

"You ever notice," Freddie says more quietly now, "that every time things feel calm here, it's usually right before something goes sideways?"

I snort. "That's called paranoia."

"Or pattern recognition," he counters. "Very different."

I shake my head. "Don't start. Worrying doesn't help."

He studies me for a second. "You sure you're not just telling *yourself* that?"

I don't answer right away.

Freddie slows his pace to match mine, bumping my shoulder lightly. "Hey. Whatever happens here, you know I've got your back, right?" The sincerity in his voice catches me off guard.

"Yeah," I say finally. "I know."

And I mean it.

That's the thing about Freddie. He doesn't pry. He doesn't push. He just... stays. Even when things get ugly. Especially then. We reach our classroom doors. Still no sign of the others. I glanced down the hall one last time, a familiar twist settling in my chest.

"It's probably nothing," I mutter, more to myself than him.

Freddie grins. "See? You do worry. Just a little."

I shoved past him into class. "Shut up."

Chapter 53

Cheers!

Wes.

We'd been tramping along these stupid train tracks for hours, my legs burning and my stomach threatening mutiny, when, finally, a tiny station appeared in the distance. A proper town, with lights and, more importantly, a sign that said *"Liquor."*

"Hey look–" I started until Angie cut me off after her eyes tracked were I was pointing.

"Run!" Angie yelled before I could even suggest taking a civilized stroll.

I cursed under my breath but ran anyway. Not just because of the alcohol, although, yeah, that was a bonus but because her reckless grin made my blood pressure spike. If anything happened to her, I knew Freddie would kill me.

We ducked into the little lit up shop; Angie immediately flipped into distraction mode. She leaned on the counter, elbows together, tilted her head with a smile that made the cashier, an older guy with way too much cologne, look like he'd just hit the jackpot.

"Oh, hey," she said, batting her eyelashes, "Do you... uh... recommend anything special tonight? Something... strong?"

Something special tonight? Strong? What – has she never been in a liquor store before?

I felt my jaw tighten. Strong enough to knock him out if he gets any closer, I thought, scanning the store for escape routes. Her voice was smooth, flirty, but it was also dangerous. Not for her, but for me. My brain screamed, *'Do NOT let him leer at her'.*

The cashier leaned in, eyes lingering a little too long on her, as they draped down her body. His mouth twisted into an ugly smirk, and he leaned close to her on the counter. I felt my stomach twist.

"Uh... yeah, we've got some nice–"

I stepped forward, casually nudging Angie behind me like she was a priceless artifact.

"She's asking. For me." I grinned at1 him, wrapping my arm around her. I felt her eyes roll.

Angie snorted, suppressing a laugh. "Oh.. uh, James, You're so protective. It's adorable. Don't you want me to make friends?"

James?

"I do want you to make friends, Alyssa" I muttered, and her head whipped around so fast at the fake name I had to squeeze my mouth shut from a chuckle.

"Just... not with him." My eyes narrowed down back onto the old sleez of an old man.

I could already see Freddie's expression if he were here, pure horror and betrayal that someone had dared flirt with her.

Meanwhile, Angie kept chatting with the guy, leaning just enough to keep his attention. "Hmm...maybe I should try Something... exciting, something new." She winked at him.

Exciting was the code word for, *'grab as much shit as you can'*.

I knew what she was doing. While she talked, I slipped a couple of bottles into my backpack. My heart was racing. My mind was half in protective mode, half in sheer panic that she was enjoying the chaos.

Seconds later, we were bolting. Angie laughed, throwing a victory grin over her shoulder, and I sprinted behind her, backpack bouncing, my muscles screaming. Mission accomplished.

We're sprawled on the gravel with bottles in our hands, trying to make a fire.

Trying being the important word here.

About six empty bottles of... I don't even know what lay next to us as well.

I'm hunched over a pathetic pile of sticks, aggressively rubbing two of them together like I've suddenly become some kind of survival expert. Nothing's happening. Not even smoke. Just me, committing fully to looking like an idiot.

"Wow," Angie says, sitting cross-legged and swaying slightly like the ground is optional, "you're officially the worst fire-starter I've ever met."

"Hey," I shoot back, not even stopping, because commitment is key, "I'm good at lots of things. This just isn't one of them."

"You mean any hands-on thing," she says, smirking. "This is actually painful to watch. Like a toddler with matches. A confident toddler."

"I am confident," I mumble, still rubbing. "Confidence is like... eighty percent of fire."

"It's really not."

I stop. Stare at the sticks. Then just flop back onto the gravel with a dramatic sigh.

"Okay. You do it then, Miss Outdoor Survival Queen. I accept defeat."

"Finally," she mutters, crawling closer and immediately nearly tipping sideways before catching herself on my knee.

"God, you're useless."

"Wow. That's so rude," I say, not moving to help her at all.

She starts messing with the sticks, way too focused for someone who can barely sit upright.

"Some brotherly competence would've been nice, but whatever. I'll save us."

"Saved by the flirt queen," I slur, immediately hiccupping after like it's punctuation.

She snorts. "Oh, shut up. You love it."

"I do not love it," I say, pointing at her and missing slightly. "I... hate- it. I hate it. So much." I pause. Blink. "...maybe a little love. But that's the alcohol talking. Not me. Don't listen to him."

"I'm listening to him," she says, grinning. "He's honest."

"He's a liar."

"You're cute when you're drunk," she adds, like she's just dropped a fact.

I sit up way too fast. The world tilts a bit. "I am not cute. I'm..." I try to gather dignity and completely fail, "-I'm a man."

That just makes her lose it. Full laughing now, head dropping forward, shoulders shaking like it's the funniest thing she's ever heard.

We go back to the fire.

Or, like... the idea of a fire.

It turns into a pattern, me trying again like I've learned something, her muttering insults under her breath, me getting offended for about three seconds, then forgetting why I was offended.

At one point, a tiny flame actually sparks.

We both freeze.

"Oh my God," I whisper, leaning in way too close. "Don't breathe. No one breathe."

"I'm not breathing," she whispers back, also immediately leaning in.

The flame flickers. Grows. For one perfect second, we've done it.

Then Angie laughs.

Just one small laugh. The wind catches it instantly. The flame jumps sideways into the dry grass.

"Oh- oh no-"

"OH NO-"

We both scramble at the same time, smacking at it with sticks like that's a solution either of us planned. I nearly fall over, she almost hits me in the face, we're both half-laughing, half-panicking.

"Stop hitting me!"

"I'm not hitting you, I'm saving your life!"

"You're making it worse!"

"Shut up and blow on it!"

"I am blowing on it!"

"You're blowing it towards me!"

Somehow, by pure luck and zero skill, it goes out. We just... stop. Look at each other. Then completely lose it.

Like, can't breathe, stomach-hurting, tears-in-your-eyes laughing. The kind that makes everything feel lighter for a second.

We end up collapsed back on the gravel again, still laughing, when sirens cut through the air.

Loud.

VERY close.

"Oh, seriously?" I groan, dragging myself up and squinting into the distance like that'll help.

Angie doesn't even look worried. She just grabs my hand and pulls me up, spinning it like we're about to start dancing instead of running from something. "Relax, Wes. Worst case, we run."

"I hate running," I mutter automatically.

"You love running," she says, already tugging me a step forward.

"I literally just said-"

But I don't pull my hand away.

Not that she'd let me.

Her laugh echoes out across the tracks, loud and reckless, and for a second, I forget about the sirens, the rules, all of it. She's a complete disaster—dangerous, ridiculous, impossible—and somehow, I'm the one standing here with her.

And yeah... Freddie would absolutely kill me if he knew.

Chapter 54

Dang it.

Angeline.

We were running. No, not running, flying. My lungs burned, my legs screamed, and every breath felt like fire in my chest. Wes was beside me, pulling me along like he was afraid I'd somehow trip and get left behind.

The sirens were right behind us now. My heart was a jackhammer in my ribcage. "Wes!" I gasped. "Where are we going?!"

"Anywhere but here!" he shouted, but we both knew it was pointless. The town lights blurred past, and our shoes slipped on the cracked pavement as we stumbled over debris. I almost went down once, Wes caught me by the waist, dragging me up before I could hit the ground.

"Thanks!" I panted, my chest heaving. "Seriously, Freddie is gonna kill you if he ever finds out-"

"No time!" he snapped, eyes darting left and right. "Just keep moving!"

We zigzagged through streets, darting down alleys, but somehow, we ended up exactly where we didn't want to be, the school. The gates loomed like a trap, and before we could even breathe, lights flashed and uniforms surrounded us.

Shouts cut through the chaos: "Stop! Don't move!"

My stomach dropped. My pulse raced. I looked at Wes, ready to argue, to run, to do anything, but it was too late.

One of the guards raised a syringe. The liquid gleamed in the dim light, and before I could think, it was pressed against my neck.

"Angie- NO! LET HER GO!" Wes yelled, his voice rough. I've never heard him so angry. "Angie! Run! Please- ANGIE!"

"No! Wait-" I tried to scream, but my words were swallowed by panic. My vision blurred, edges of the world melting.

Wes grabbed my arm, struggling, his own body trembling. "Angie, don't- don't let go!"

I couldn't move. My legs buckled like jelly. My arms felt heavy, my fingers numb. The world tilted and my heart was still pounding, screaming that I needed to fight, but my body refused.

"Wes..." I gasped, panic rising in my chest. "I- I can't..."

The last thing I remember before the darkness took me was Wes's face, twisted in frustration and fear, screaming my name over the chaos. And then... nothing.

Everything was gone.

Chapter 55

The damsel *in* distress.

Freddie.

"Honor, loyalty, obedience..." I muttered along with the class, but my words were hollow, echoing against my skull. My eyes weren't on the teacher. They were on the empty chair. Angie's chair. Every time I blinked, it felt like it had been emptied forever, like the world had decided to swallow her whole.

I tried to focus. I really did. Notes blurred into a meaningless mess, the teacher's voice fading into the background.

Where is she?

Finally, the class ended, and I bolted out of the room before anyone could stop me. My legs carried me down the halls, heart hammering like a war drum. I asked every passing student, every guard. No one had seen her. Panic clawed at me with every step. I had been looking for hours, so long that it was now twilight.

And then I saw her.

Through the window of the outer gate, she was being carried inside. Her body was limp, the way someone carries a bag of laundry. My chest constricted.

How did she escape?

I tore through the corridors to the dorm, adrenaline fueling every step.

"Nick!" I practically shoved the door open. "She's back... they're bringing her in! Come on!"

He jumped up, eyes wide and alert. We didn't wait for a plan. We didn't wait for permission. We ran.

The night air hit us as we slipped past shadows, the smell of damp earth and smoke from the distant fire lingering. A guard patrolled the gate, lights sweeping over the grounds. As we crept up, he turned the wrong way, and Nick didn't even hesitate. One punch, one unconscious guard, sprawled on the ground.

I gritted my teeth and lifted Angie in my arms, careful not to jostle her too much, rushing with Nick before the other guards came over. Her weight was lighter than I remembered. "Jesus princess..."

She's here. She's alive.

We made it back to my dorm safely. I laid her down gently on the bed, checking her over. Breathing steady, chest rising and falling. Safe. For now.

"Angie…" I whispered.

She stirred, eyelids fluttering open. Her voice was hoarse, confused.

"Freddie… Nick…" she croaked. "I…Wes…we…we got caught…" she slurred.

"Is she *drunk?*" Nick interrupted.

We finally managed to sober her up and she told us everything. Every detail she could remember, the sprint, the panic, the injection. And then she stopped. Her eyes widened, fear creeping in.

"Where is Wes?" she asked, her voice boomed with confusion.

"I don't know." I said honestly. "But we'll figure it out. Right now, we just need you safe."

Angie shivered, pulling the blankets tighter around her, and I realized how fragile she seemed. I sat beside her, hands hovering, not wanting to smother but not wanting her to feel alone either. The thought of anyone taking her, putting their hands on her…

No, never going to happen again.

Chapter 56

Wake ups and make ups.

Angeline.

We were packed into the assembly hall like sardines, the high ceilings echoing every shuffled foot and cough.

Wait, why haven't I noticed this before?

As I looked around at my fellow peers, I noticed that some of them look kind of, lifeless... I mean they really look like zombies with nothing going on up there. They sat with perfect posture, skin almost drained of color and I can't remember the last time I heard some of them talk.

However, to counter that, suddenly the speakers boom as the students who have basically become mute all start chanting the school's slogan in perfect unison, almost like they were hypnotized.

Holy shit, I really am crazy.

Just as my thoughts started to get louder, the headmistress's shadow stretched across the floor, tall and rigid, her heels clicking like a metronome of dread.

"Attention," she began, her voice cold, smooth, and deliberately slow, like she wanted every syllable to sink into our bones. "It has come to my attention that some students believe the boundaries between the sectors are negotiable."

A shiver ran down my spine. The way she said negotiable made it sound like we were dealing in forbidden sins.

"I will make this perfectly clear," she continued, eyes sweeping over us, stopping just long enough on Wes and Nick to make my skin crawl. "Boys are not to enter girls' dormitories. Girls are not to enter boys' dormitories. Any violation, any will be met with... isolated detention."

She paused, letting the words hang in the air like smoke. "Do I make myself understood?"

A chorus of obedient murmurs filled the room. Everyone nodded, afraid to meet her gaze for too long. I swallowed hard. There was something... wrong about the way she smiled when she said detention. It wasn't a friendly warning. It was a promise.

The assembly ended, and we shuffled out like sheep, the weight of her gaze lingering on our shoulders.

Lunch was quiet at first. Too quiet, considering how chaotic yesterday had been. I noticed Nick leaning forward, eyes locked on Wes like a hawk.

Finally, he snapped. "Wes, how did you and Angie get out?"

Wes blinked at him, expression blank, almost fragile. "Oh, so we're talking now? Look, I don't remember. I swear, Nick. Nothing. It's all... gone."

Nick's hands curled into fists, his chest rising and falling. He looked like he wanted to punch a wall... or Wes. I couldn't help myself.

"Nick," I said quickly, stepping between them. "I know you're desperate to find a way out of here, okay we all are, but I believe him. He didn't plan this. We don't know how we got out. Just... let it go."

There was a pause. Nick's shoulders slumped slightly, and Wes gave a shaky nod. Around us, the group's tension broke, Freddie and the others exchanging glances before murmuring apologies.

"Sorry, Wes," Freddie muttered. "We shouldn't have doubted you."

Wes's lips quivered into a small, tired smile. "It's fine. I know you guys worry."

Nick leaned back, running a hand through his hair. The anger in his eyes softened, the last remnants of the ball's tension resurfacing. "Look," he said, glancing at Wes, "about... everything at the ball. I was a dick. I- yeah. Sorry, man."

Wes shrugged, relief flickering across his face. "Yeah, me too. Things got... out of hand."

Finally, after what felt like a nightmare of a day, I had a little weight lifted off my shoulders.

Chapter 57

Banshee.

Dahlia.

I shouldn't be here.

I know that before my hand even lifts to knock. The boys' dorm feels wrong in a quiet, prickling way, too still, too clean, like the air has been wiped down. But I need to talk to Freddie. About Angie. About the photos. About whether he really *dealt with* it or just hid it somewhere I can't see.

I knock. Once. Then again. Nothing. I glanced down the hall, heart thudding. No guards. No nurses. Just me and the door.

"Of course," I mutter. "Of course it's unlocked."

I push it open carefully and step inside.

The room smells like cologne mixed with the smell of boys. *Ew.* Beds unmade. Freddie's things are scattered completely everywhere. I take one step in, then another, scanning quickly around their desks, trash can, under their beds. When suddenly I feel a haunted presence.

"You really ought to listen to assembly announcements, silly girl."

The voice is right behind me. I don't even have time to turn.

Pain explodes at the side of my neck, sharp, invasive, immediate. My hand flies up too late. The nurse's grip is iron-strong, fingers digging in as something cold floods my veins.

"No!" I gasp, but the word dissolves.

The room folds inward.

I woke up sitting upright.

That's the first thing I notice. My hands can move freely, but as I go to get up, I look down to see my legs and feet strapped with restraints to the chair I'm sitting on. My head lolls forward slightly before I force it up, blinking against the bright, even lighting.

This isn't the basement.

The walls are white, but not empty. There are panels. Monitors. A chair bolted to the floor. A glass window I can't see through from this side. It's clean. Clinical. Used.

A pair of headphones rests in my lap.

My fingers are shaking.

A light turns on.

This whole thing felt oddly familiar... but I couldn't exactly remember why.

PHASE TWO: ESCALATION - flashes briefly on a screen in front of me, then disappears.

A nurse comes in, snatching the headphones out of my hands, sliding them over my ears and tightening just a bit too much.

Sound begins softly.

Two voices. Teachers, maybe. Talking over each other. I can't make out the words just the tone. Authority. Irritation. Then another sound threads in. Someone crying, distant, muffled, like it's happening behind a wall.

I swallow.

My breathing echoes loudly in my own head.

Another sound joins. A boy shouting. Anger. Fear. A scuffle– something slams into something else. Then an alarm starts. Stops. Starts again. Stops. My shoulders tense. I try to keep my breathing steady, but it stutters anyway. A light on the wall flickers.

I freeze.

The sounds overlap more now. Nothing clear. Nothing I can focus on. Just noise piling on noise until my thoughts start slipping, sliding off each other. I focus on the floor. Count tiles. One, two, three. The volume increases. Not sharply. Carefully. Like they're testing how far they can go without me noticing. My ears begin to ache. I force myself not to flinch. If I flinch, it resets. If I dissociate, they mark it.

There is no correct response. The sound jumps suddenly, violently louder. I gasp despite myself.

Pain lances through my head. Something warm trickles down the side of my face. I don't wipe it away. I don't move. My hands curl into fists in my lap so tightly I can feel my nails stabbing me.

"Stop! Please... stop! I–I can't!" I scream.

A voice cuts through the chaos, calm and precise.

"Name five things you hear."

My mouth opens. Nothing comes out.

"Say them clearly!"

"I–" My voice shakes. "I hear... voices. An alarm. Crying. Shouting. Breathing."

"Now say the first five names that come into your head. Out loud."

"Nick. Angie. Freddie. Wes... *Alana*."

I repeat them. Louder. Slower. Again, and again. Every time my voice trembles, they make me start over. Every time my breathing changes, the light flickers. Every time my focus slips, the sound surges.

Eventually, without warning, the headphones are gone. Silence slams into me harder than the noise ever did. I sway slightly, dizzy. Blood drips from my ears down to my cheeks, dark against my skin, spotting the front of my shirt.

The door opens. The nurse steps in, smiling softly, like we've just shared something pleasant.

"You did better than most." she says.

She placed a small cup of water in my hands. A biscuit on the table in front of me. My fingers shake so badly the water ripples. She doesn't seem concerned.

"Take your time." she adds gently.

I stare at the floor, ears ringing, heart still racing, knowing one thing with terrifying clarity. They're learning how I bend.

Chapter 58

FREEDOM... Well, sort of.

Wes.

The town smelled like warm bread and faint metal, like the academy itself had left a tiny fingerprint here. The sun hung low, golden but not harsh, making the cobblestones glow beneath our feet. For once, I didn't feel the academy breathing down my neck. Not completely.

Freddie trudged beside me, hands stuffed into his jacket pockets, eyes darting nervously every few seconds. Classic. But when I nudged him with my elbow, he cracked a slight grin. I'll take it.

"Hey," I whispered, leaning closer so no one else would hear, "Do you think it's weird nothing's happened to me and Angie, since we left?"

He sighed, shoulders shaking. "Well, if you keep bringing it up, then something will definitely happen!"

"I just can't help it. I feel like something really bad is coming."

Freddie rolled his eyes. "We've been here for so long now, how could something bad possibly be worse than isolated detention."

"Yeah, well if you hadn't noticed, not all of us have had the privilege of only getting a haircut as their punishment." I scowl.

"Shit. Sorry man, I forgot. Look just think about something else. Nothing's going to happen to you guys." Freddie reassured.

We ducked into a small market alley, surrounded with other students and guards circling, keeping us all controlled and monitored. The smell of roasted nuts made my stomach growl. Freddie's eyes went wide at the stall selling tiny pastries.

"I... don't- look at me, I'm not buying anything!" he said, but I could see him already reaching for one.

"Yeah, 'buying anything' with what money?" I said, sneaking one too.

"Seriously, they let us come to 'town' and don't even give us money to buy anything!"

"Well, look where we are, it's a town, not detention. Eat something illegal."

He bit into his pastry carefully, like it might explode. "This is... amazing. Why is this illegal?"

I shrugged. "Because the academy says it is. That's reason enough."

We sat on a low wall, legs dangling, stealing bites and talking. Small talk turned into more. I asked him about home, a real home, not the academy. He told me about a messy room, a dog he used to walk at sunrise, a favorite comic he never finished. I told him about rooftops, a skateboard I shouldn't have had, a crush I embarrassed myself over in middle school.

"You're... way weirder than I thought," he said, smiling sideways.

"Trust me," I whispered, nudging him, "I haven't even told you the worst stuff yet."

"It's been getting better. My memory." He continued.

"Oh yeah?"

"Yeah, although I keep having those fuzzy feelings. Like all the blood heads to my brain. That causes me to forget. But I... can't say the same for the rest of the student body. No one talks about anything but the academy anymore."

"Maybe we're the only sane one's left." I mutter.

We laughed. Hard. The kind of laughter that makes your chest hurt, like a secret rebellion in a world designed to crush it out of you. And for a few minutes, we weren't students under evaluation. We were just... two kids in town, stealing a tiny sliver of freedom.

We walked toward the town gate after that, enjoying the warm glow of the late afternoon sun on our backs. At the gate, we both knew the routine: scan the barcode, head inside for evaluation, and obey the rules. But even then, it didn't feel suffocating. Not with him beside me.

I scanned my neck first, then Freddie did his. The numbers flashed 0. Perfect.

I glanced at him and whispered, "See? Easy."

For a moment, I thought maybe we could survive this place. Together.

And that's when everything went wrong.

We were just stepping through the final gate, laughing quietly about some joke I'd made about the cafeteria's "mystery stew," when the scanner flashed red.

I froze. Freddie's eyes widened beside me.

"What?" he whispered, panicked.

I glanced down at the guards device. My number zero before had changed. *One.*

The scanner wouldn't read me. My stomach dropped.

I tried again. Beep. Nothing.

Before I could say anything, Freddie grabbed my sleeve. "Wes, what is it?

Pain ripped through my skull like someone had shoved fire down my spine. My knees nearly buckled.

"GOD-" I screamed, grabbing at my neck.

"Wes!" Freddie yelled, but before he could do anything, a guard shoved him backward. Hard.

I barely had time to register his terrified glare before another set of hands gripped my shoulders and forced me upright. One hand went to my head, tilting it back. The agony intensified, blinding. I could barely think.

The guard inspected my neck, fingers tracing the barcode as if it were a live wire. My screams tore from me involuntarily.

"It's changed! Code 5!" he barked into his walkie. "Immediate evaluation. Nurses. Code 5!"

Freddie's voice was sharp and frantic in my ears. "Wes! What's happening? Please, someone tell me!"

I tried, but the words wouldn't come. My vision flickered, pain clouding everything.

"Just hang on man, help is coming!" Freddie assured.

The guard tilted my head further, and the scanner beeped in protest, red and insistent. I felt the heat behind my eyes spiking again. Nurses rushed toward us, a blur of white and movement. One reached for my arms, another for the scanner, murmuring instructions in clipped, professional tones. The nurses lifted me gently but quickly, scanning, checking, adjusting. With guards barking orders before my mind went completely blank.

Chapter 59

I remember.

Dahlia.

The room smelled faintly of honey, like it was trying to be calming but failing miserably. Dr. Matilda sat across from me, tablet perched on her knees, smiling in a way that made my skin crawl.

"So," she said, tilting her head, "your little isolation escapade. Was it fun being alone with your thoughts, Dahlia?" The words were sugary, but the edge beneath them made me shrink back instinctively.

I forced myself to sit straighter. "It... wasn't fun," I muttered.

Her smile didn't falter. "Oh, but don't be so dramatic." She scribbled in her tablet, eyes flicking up to glance at me, flicking at me a small glimpse of her real eyes.

Then she leaned forward, voice silky but sharp. "Tell me, Dahlia... did you want to hurt yourself in the classroom that day you got sent to the nurses office? Accidental or otherwise? Or are you just incompetent at staying safe?"

I flinched, gripping the armrest of the chair. Her tone... she was mocking me. She wasn't concerned; she was testing me. My stomach twisted. "It was accidental." I said softly, keeping my voice low.

"Accidental," she repeated, head tilting, smile still plastered on. "Hmm. You don't exactly look convincing. You like to play games, don't you? Or maybe you just enjoy... pain." Her eyes glinted, and I shivered.

"Can you tell me about the things that trigger you?"

I swallowed hard, my mouth suddenly dry. I wanted to lie. I wanted to shrink and vanish. But the memories came anyway.

My father yelling, the smell of blood, my mother's silent despair. "Yelling... violence... fear." I whispered.

"Mm," she said, nodding like I'd confirmed some theory she'd already decided on. "And you enjoyed it, yes? Watching, obeying, learning to survive? Isn't that fun to be molded into... someone special?"

I clenched my hands in my lap. "It wasn't entirely my favorite childhood memory." I said, but my voice cracked. "I... wasn't always here," I murmured. "I was... someone else. A different life. My father, he..." My voice faltered.

The images of his hands, his commands, the way he forced me to watch, to learn, to become something I didn't want to be. "He's... he's brutal. But... he's also... loves me? Or something like it. I don't know. I don't understand him."

Dr. Matilda nodded. The words tumbled out.

My past life running like a movie through my mind. My childhood in the mafia, trained to assassinate, to obey, to survive. The life of fear and privilege twisted into duty. My mother's silent suffering, my father's impossibly high expectations. My attempts to run, to escape, were crushed by his devoted followers.

I closed my eyes, water overflowing. *I... remember everything. The killings. The lessons. The warnings. I'm... supposed to be hardened. Strong. But I... sometimes just want to... to be normal.*

"Have you had thoughts of harming yourself, Dahlia? Suicidal thoughts?"

"Again, really? Didn't we just do this?" I ask. She just blinks at me.

I sigh. "Look- like I said before, that was accidental. I'm not suicidal, and I don't dream about cutting myself up. Accidental thoughts? Maybe. But that was not on purpose."

She grinned bigger and thought for a moment. "Tell me, what were you thinking when you cut your hand? Were you thinking of your father?"

I froze. The room felt smaller. Her words weren't just questions, they were weapons. My stomach was lurched at the thought of him. And yet... some part of me still craved his approval, hated myself for it, didn't know how to reconcile either.

"I... don't know," I whispered. My voice felt fragile even to me.

She smiled that same maddening smile.

"Good answer. Indecision suits you. It keeps you... useful. Keep that indecision. It keeps you pliable, doesn't it?"

I shifted uncomfortably in the chair, aware that my body wanted to recoil, wanted to run, but I stayed. I had to. Every word from her was a scalpel, cutting through my carefully built armor. I hated her, but I couldn't leave, not yet.

"And yet," she said, voice soft, too soft, "You're still gentle. What happens when the world tests you? When someone shouts, or fights, or... betrays you?"

I swallowed hard. The memory of isolation, my father's fury, everything... flooded back. My chest tightened. "I... survive," I whispered. "I... do what I have to."

Her smile widened, a little too satisfied. "Yes, yes, that's right. Survive. But remember... survival isn't enough. You're special, Dahlia. Dangerous. And everyone around you... oh, they'll see it soon enough. Won't they?"

The words lingered, cold and sticky in the air. I shifted in my seat again, heart hammering, realizing just how much of me she'd seen, how much she seemed to enjoy seeing.

Chapter 60

The tables have turned.

Freddie.

The bell's already gone when I get back on campus, but I don't slow down. My legs feel like they're still running even after I stop.

Wes's screams are still stuck in my head.

My first thought isn't Nick.

It isn't a teacher.

It's *Princess*.

Angie's the only one who will be able to give me some peace of mind.

I head straight for the library, bag bouncing against my hip, heart punching my ribs so hard it almost hurts. The library is quiet in that thick, unreal way, lamps casting soft circles of light over rows of desks. I spotted them immediately. Angie leaned back in her chair like rules don't apply to her, Dahlia beside her, legs tucked under the table, studying.

Relief hits me so hard my chest tightens.

I don't even sit properly. I drop into the chair opposite them and lean forward, hands shaking.

"Okay," I say, way too fast. "Something happened."

Angie's expression switches instantly, no jokes, no attitude. Just sharp focus. "That's never a good way to start, Freddie."

Dahlia looks up, brows knitting together. "Where's Wes?"

"That's... why I came to find you."

They're both watching me now. Waiting.

"We went into town," I start, rubbing my neck. "Nothing stupid. Just food. Everything was fine until we went to leave."

Angie's jaw tightens.

"They scan the barcodes every time you exit town," I say. "You know that. Neck scan. Quick. Normal." My voice wobbles despite my effort to keep it steady. "Wes leaned forward like usual, and the scanner just... did nothing."

Dahlia's pen freezes mid-air. "Nothing how?"

"It beeped wrong, like it didn't recognize him."

Angie swears under her breath.

"The guard frowned and scanned it again," I continued. "And again. Then he told Wes to tilt his head lower. That's when Wes started yelling."

My hands curl into fists under the table.

"Like... real yelling," I say quietly. "Not joking. Not dramatic. Pain. He grabbed his neck and dropped to his knees, like something was tearing through him from the inside."

Dahlia's face drains of color.

"I panicked," I admit. "I didn't know what to do. I just stood there watching him scream while people stared like he was broken machinery."

Angie leans forward now, elbows on the table. "What did the guards do?"

"They were rough," I said immediately. "One of them grabbed his head and yanked it down to force the scanner closer. Wes was begging them to stop. He couldn't even hold himself up. They said his number had changed," I whisper. "Like that was possible. Like it was his fault."

Silence presses in around us.

"They pulled him up by the arms and dragged him away. Told me to return to school immediately. Ordered me. I tried to follow but they blocked me."

Dahlia's hands are shaking now.

"I shouldn't have left him," I say, guilt flooding my chest. "I should've fought them. I should've–"

Angie stands so suddenly her chair screeches across the floor. "No."

I look up at her.

"That is not on you," she says, voice hard and unwavering. "They took control. You did what you could."

"I watched him scream," I say, quieter now. "And I walked away."

Angie steps closer, lowering her voice. "You walked away because they made you. There was nothing else you could have done."

"That's not true, Angie, I could have done anything! To tackle the guards, to help him get away!"

Dahlia swallows. "Nick is going to lose his mind."

As if the universe is listening, a shadow falls across the table.

Nick.

He doesn't look at me. His eyes lock straight onto Dahlia. "I need to talk to you." he states. "In private."

Dahlia doesn't move. "We have nothing to talk about."

Angie turns slowly, eyes narrowing, then smiles. "Yes, you do," she says sweetly. "You're going to go talk to him. No questions asked."

Dahlia exhales, defeated. She pushes her chair back and stands. "Fine."

Nick turns moving out of the way, allowing Dolly to walk in front of him first, they stalk off between the shelves. The moment they're gone, my shoulders sag.

Angie sits back down across from me, softer now but still solid. "Okay," she says. "Every detail. Times. Words. Everything you remember."

I swallow. "You really think you can help?"

She meets my eyes without hesitation. "I know I can."

Chapter 61

Vandalism is a crime!

Angeline.

The dorm is oddly quiet. That's the first thing I notice after Freddie leaves to shower. The study door clicks shut behind him and the silence rushes in, heavy and uncomfortable, like it's been waiting for him to go.

I sit on my bed and pull my diary out from under the mattress. I tell myself I'm just checking something. I opened it. The light from the desk lamp hits the page at an angle, and that's when I see it. Smudges. Not ink. Not mine. Fingerprints.

I tilt the page slowly, watching the faint oily marks catch the light. Someone touched this. Recently. Carefully enough to think they wouldn't be seen.

My fingers start flipping faster.

The edges of some pages are torn, tiny, deliberate rips near the spine. Pencil marks are lighter in places, erased and rewritten. Words I *know* I wrote differently. My grip tightens over the pages.

"No," I whisper, flipping again. "No, no, no!"

The more I look, the worse it gets. Whole pages are gone.

Not cleanly removed either- ragged edges left behind, like teeth marks. I count pages, panic building, breath coming too fast. They didn't just read it. They *edited* it. I start flipping harder now, the sound sharp in the quiet room, my hands shaking as anger floods in hot and fast. The study door reopens.

Freddie steps out, towel around his waist, hair damp. "Uh- Angie?"

I don't look up. "They took them."

He blinks. "Took what?"

"The pages," I snapped, finally looking at him, eyes burning. "They took pages out of my journal."

He crosses the room quickly. "Okay, hey- calm down, Princess. Talk to me. What pages?"

I shoved the diary at him, finger stabbing the spine. "This one. And this one. And-" My voice cracks. "The one about the therapist."

Freddie's expression shifts. "The therapist?"

"The one who got my name wrong," I say, words tumbling over each other. "I wrote it down. I had her name in there. It was proof that she was trying to mess with me."

He flips through slowly, brow furrowed. "Okay... but- couldn't you just rewrite it?"

"No!" I shout. "I can't. I dated it. I don't remember when it happened. I don't remember her name. That page *mattered*."

My hands clenched into fists. "They erased it, Freddie. Like it never happened. Oh fuck!"

He exhales, then closes it gently and sets it down.

"Angie," he says softly, kneeling in front of me so we're eye level. "Princess. This whole school is your evidence that they're manipulating us."

I shake my head, tears burning. "That's not the same."

"I know," he says quickly. "I know it feels like it was the one thing you had control over. But listen to me, don't let them make you spiral over a page."

I look at the journal again, at the missing pieces, the fingerprints I can't unsee.

"They were inside my head." I whisper.

Freddie looks at me softly.

"They don't get to stay there," he says firmly. "Okay? We'll be smarter. We'll adapt. But you- you don't let them win this."

I nodded, even though my chest still feels hollow. Because if they can rewrite my words...

What else do they think they're allowed to erase?

Chapter 62

I'll be here the whole night.

Nick.

The rooftop is quiet, stable and totally transparent. That must be why I like it so much. It's cold and hard with concrete, it's just us and somehow, we found ourselves up here.

More than likely an off-limits area.

Rain drifts down softly, barely more than a mist, catching on the stars instead of hiding them. The sky is too clear for a night like this, dark velvet split with silver. It should feel peaceful.

It doesn't.

Dahlia sits beside me, knees drawn to her chest, arms wrapped loosely around herself. She looks smaller up here. Not fragile... but guarded. Like she's constantly waiting for the world to tilt the wrong way.

I clear my throat. "Yesterday," I say, keeping my eyes on the edge of the roof. "I saw you in the halls."

She stiffens. I feel it more than see it.

"You walked straight past me," I continued. "Didn't even look up." I swallow. "And there was blood. On your sleeve."

She finally turned to me, disbelief flickering across her face. "Really?" she says flatly. "That's what you want to talk to me about?"

I frown. "What?"

"Not what happened after the dance?" she asks, her voice sharp now. "Not the way you disappeared like I didn't exist?"

My jaw tightens. I turned to her fully. "Tell me."

She hesitates. The light rain beads in her hair, darkening it, sliding down her cheek like something she refuses to wipe away.

"It's nothing," she mutters.

"Dahlia."

She exhales, defeated. "I... cut myself on the infirmary door. It wasn't," She shakes her head. "It doesn't matter."

Something hot and ugly rises in my chest. "That's bullshit," I snapped before I could stop myself. "You don't just bleed in hallways for nothing. Tell me the truth. What really happened!"

Dahlia looks at me confused, her eyes almost screaming with wonder, "Why do you even care?!"

Why did I care? I couldn't give a reason. But whatever it was, it was driving me crazy. *She* was driving me crazy.

"I really need to know!" I roar.

Her shoulders jerk. She flinches.

The sight of it hits me like a slap. "Why do you do that?" I ask, frustration bleeding into my voice. "Why are you always flinching like I'm about to hurt you?"

Her face goes pale.

"You remind me of someone." she says quietly.

The rain feels heavier suddenly. "Who?"

She stands so abruptly her knee bumps the bench. "I shouldn't have said that."

"Dahlia,"

She gets up and turns to leave.

I drop my head back, hands flying up into my hair in pure frustration. "God," I mutter.

She flinches again. Harder this time.

I look at her sharply, ascending to my feet, "Please," I bark, then soften despite myself. "Please. Will you just talk to me?"

She spins around, eyes blazing up to mine. "Talk to you?" she snaps. "You think I should be the one talking to you? That's rich. We've been here for months, Nick, and you couldn't even spare me a glance."

I open my mouth. "Because you..."

"You act like I'm invisible unless I do something wrong!"

"Because you get scared at every little thing!" I cut in, defensive and angry and already regretting it.

Her breath catches.

I can see she's planning to leave. I can't let that happen. I can't let her go, without knowing how I feel. She slowly turned and as she did, it was like all the adrenaline in my body erupted and concussed my heart.

"Fuck it." I whisper to myself.

Before I knew it, I marched over to her, grabbing her arm, pulling her into me. Learning in, to do something I've been craving for so long.

But as I do, I see the fear in her eyes. It was so sudden. What's wrong with me? Ugh, now I've done it.

I stop myself from getting any closer, throwing my hands up next to my shoulders, slowly backing away.

Dahlia gives me an empathetic look but shaking her head in slight confusion, "Nick, why would you–"

"I'm sorry, I'm– I didn't mean that."

Dahlia chuckles to herself, shaking her head again but at the sky before turning to me.

"I'm scared of everything. How could you say that?" she whispers. "You don't even know me."

I look at her then. Really look at her. The way she's holding herself together by sheer will. The rain soaks into her clothes like she doesn't feel it. The hurt she's trying so desperately not to show.

My shoulders drop. My voice follows.

Looking down at her my eyes toughen, my lips just as much, "Maybe it's better that way," I say quietly as I cowardly look away. "Maybe it's best I don't."

The words taste wrong the moment they leave my mouth.

She turns away. I do too, me toward the edge of the roof, her toward the side stairwell. The space between us stretches, heavy and aching.

We stopped at the same time.

"I'm sorry," I mumble, barely loud enough for the rain not to steal it.

She doesn't turn back. "Yeah…" Her voice is dry. Empty. "You don't know how much I've heard that in my life."

Then she's gone, footsteps sharp against the stairs, leaving the rooftop colder than it was before. And I stand there under the stars, wishing I'd said anything different.

Chapter 63

Listening to the wind.

Wes.

I walk up the last few steps of the metal staircase to the rooftop. The taps echo loudly in the cold air. I'm still limping a little, neck stiff, skin there burning like it remembers even if I try not to.

I reach the top of the stairs and start walking across the roof when an angry Dahlia storms past me.

Her eyes are red. Her jaw is set like she's holding something back that might actually break her if she lets it out.

She doesn't even look at me.

"Lia-" I start, but she's already gone down the stairs, boots thudding on the metal, anger rolling off her in waves.

Great.

When I arrive at the top, Nick is already there. He's sitting on the edge of the roof, his legs dangling and head hanging low. He doesn't turn when he hears me.

"Don't jump. It's not worth it man." I joke.

"I really screwed it up this time." he mutters.

I walk over anyway, leaning against the concrete wall beside him. "She'll come back."

Nick laughs, sharp and humorless. "That's what I thought last time." He drags his hand down his face. "Every time I open my mouth, I make it worse. I scared her. Pushed her away. I don't know how to stop doing that."

For a second, I didn't say anything. The wind cuts across the roof, cold against my throat, and I wince before I can stop myself.

Nick notices.

He turns, eyes narrowing. "Your neck."

"It's fine," I lie automatically.

"Bullshit."

I sigh and straighten, fingers brushing my neck, just where the barcode sits. The skin still feels wrong. Too tight. Too hot.

"It changed. I say quietly.

Nick freezes. "What changed?"

"My number." I swallow. "When we tried to leave town, it wouldn't scan. They made me tilt my head down and then–" My jaw clenches. "It felt like something ripped through me. Like my neck was on fire from the inside."

Nick's jaw tightens.

"They dragged me down," I continued. "Held my head there while the scanner kept beeping. Said my barcode didn't exist anymore. Said it was wrong."

"What do you mean it didn't exist?" Nick snaps.

"I mean they acted like *I* wasn't supposed to." I glanced at him. "Like I was a mistake."

The words hang between us.

"Apparently while I was in town they must have thought I got one of my main memories back but who knows, they might be lying. My number changed which is why it wouldn't scan. They took me into this room, strapped my head and body down. They zapped the old barcode off my neck. It burned through me, blistering my skin, and for what felt like hours, maybe an hour, maybe two, they kept at it before finally putting the new one back on top. Every second of it was- well I'll be honest, pure hell. But I guess I've learnt one thing from that- no more tattoos!" I nudged his shoulder.

Nick turns away, breathing hard. "I should've been there."

"You couldn't have been," I say. "Freddie tried. They ordered him back."

Nick laughs again, bitter. "Everyone keeps ordering us around like we're property."

I nodded. "That's kind of the point."

Silence settles in, heavy but not uncomfortable. The city lights blink in the distance, indifferent.

After a moment, I cleared my throat. "You know what the worst part was?"

Nick doesn't look at me, but he listens.

"For a second," I say, "I thought they were going to erase me. Like... wipe the slate clean. New number. New person. No memories. No, me."

Nick finally turns, eyes sharp. "They can't do that."

"They can do whatever they want," I say simply. "That's what it taught me."

"But even throughout all of that, you know what scared me the most?" I ask, looking at him. "Forgetting... losing you guys."

Nick exhales slowly, then shakes his head. "We're not even acting like a proper group right now. I keep scaring Dahlia off like an idiot."

"You didn't scare her," I say. "You scared yourself, and she caught the fallout."

That gets his attention. He looks at me properly now.

"She cares," I add. "That's why it hurts."

Nick presses his lips together, eyes glassy. "I keep wrecking things."

"So do I. Apparently."

A beat passes.

Then I grin, slow and dangerous. "Hey."

Nick raises an eyebrow. "What."

"I've got an idea."

That makes him wary. "I don't like that tone."

"Cheeky," I say. "Not violent. Promise."

He snorts despite himself. "I don't believe you."

Chapter 64

The perfect crime scene.

Nick.

We were rounding the corner near the east wing, moving like professional thieves– or at least, that's what Wes seemed to think.

"Remember the plan," I whispered, crouching behind a row of lockers. "In and out. Quick, clean, no drama."

Wes leaned over, eyes sparkling. "Drama makes it fun."

Famous last words.

He darted ahead too fast, too eager, and didn't notice the staff member leaning against the wall, scrolling on their staff device.

"Hey!" The staff barked, grabbing him by the arm before he could even blink.

Wes froze mid-step, eyes wide, panic flashing. My stomach made a weird flip. The guy can fight like it's a video game, but get caught sneaking? Instant deer-in-headlights.

I stepped beside him, brushing my hand lightly over his shoulder, steadying him, not obvious. "Follow my lead. Stay calm."

The guard reached for his walkie-talkie, asking us, "It's almost lights out, what are you two doing up so late out of your sector?"

I gave a small shrug, casual. "Uh... we were just... on our way checking the notice board. Very official, top priority."

Wes leaned toward me. "Should I nod?"

"Only if you want to die." I hissed.

The guard scowled but waved us along, turning away. "Move."

Once we were out of sight, Wes slumped against the wall like he'd just survived a zombie apocalypse.

"Thanks, man... I thought I was done for," he said, running a hand through his hair.

I nodded toward the notice board ahead. "Okay, mission time. Quick and clean."

Wes grinned, cracking his knuckles. "Finally. Let's do this."

We crept up to the board. The usual drab school notices stared back at us: rules, schedules, mandatory club sign-ups. Perfect target.

I pulled the roll of tape and the stack of goat posters from my bag. "You know the drill. One quick swap, no slipping, no leaving fingerprints."

Wes snorted. "Yeah, yeah. You know, this isn't my first rodeo."

"Why does that not surprise me."

We got to work. I held the old posters steady while Wes stuck the new one, a goat in a tuxedo, monocle firmly in place, right over the dull schedule for the school assembly. He stepped back, admired his work, then leaned over like he was whispering secrets to the goat.

"Perfect," he whispered. "Shadows of legend."

I smirked. "More like goats of legend."

Wes laughed, high and ridiculous, and I had to shove him lightly before he made enough noise to get caught. "Focus," I hissed.

He gave me a mock salute. "Copy that, Captain Shadow."

We finished, stepped back, and surveyed the board. The goat stared out like it owned the school. And honestly? It probably did.

"Mission accomplished.".

"Best shadows ever." Wes replied, punching me lightly on the shoulder.

I snorted. "Bro, you're more of a boulder then a shadow."

"You know what, I'll take that as a compliment!" He smirked.

Chapter 65

I need to punch something.

Nick.

The sunlight hits my face, taunting any sleep I was trying to get. My head feels heavy, a hangover of thoughts I don't even want to name. I roll over and the bed's empty on the other side, Freddie's gone again. Probably up and running laps or already pretending to study. Typical.

I swing my legs off the bed and reach for my shirt... and that's when a certain someone bursts in.

"What are you doing?" I blurt, springing up. "You can't just- this is my dorm! You can't-"

She waves me off like I'm a stubborn fly.

"Relax. I checked the hallway. It's too early for the nurses' rounds. No one's coming."

"Angie you can't just barge in!" I insist, rubbing my face. "Seriously, this isn't-"

"We need to talk," she interrupts, eyes sharp. "About what happened between you and Dahlia."

I freeze. My stomach twists. "I... I don't-"

"Nick," she presses, leaning against my desk all serious, "you pushed her off the rooftop. Well- not literally but mentally. That fight, you scared her and you scared yourself."

My hands clench into fists at my sides. "I'm not... I'm not going to talk about this." I wave around the air roughly.

"Not About her."

Angie steps closer, voice soft but cutting. "What, are you scared? Scared of your feelings for her?"

I swallow hard, my throat suddenly tight. I want to lie, deflect, run. But the truth catches me in my chest and refuses to leave. I just purse my lips and stay quiet.

"You're pushing her away," she says softly. "Because you're scared. And that's... that's killing both of you."

I look down at my hands, ashamed. "I need you to go."

She tilts her head, studying me like she's weighing my stubbornness against my honesty. Then she shrugs.

"Fine. But... you need to fix whatever is going on with you. Before you do anything else."

"I don't want to hurt her." I blurt out as the door creaks open.

"Then don't Nick, but don't just let her believe you want to then." And just like that, she's gone, leaving the dorm too quiet and my chest too full.

I sit on the edge of the bed, staring at the floor, thinking about her words, about Dahlia, about the part of me that's too scared to be honest... even with myself.

Chapter 66

I told you green was my favorite color.

Freddie.

Lovely loneliness at last.

I shut my door behind me and dump my bag on the floor. The room smells the same as always, but my eyes catch something on the bed.

Green. Money? No. A lighter innocently positioned next to a bag with my favorite thing in the world. Good old weed. Its just sitting there on my bed like someone had left them out for me.

I stare at them for a beat. I reach for a memory of when I might have dropped them here or even left them accidentally. My head's fuzzy.

Did I leave them here? I can't remember.

It doesn't matter.

Shrugging, I reach out and grab them. Whatever. It's not like I'm gonna lose my mind over this. Just a little fun. A little escape.

I toss the tiny baggy in my pocket, like it's nothing, like it's always been there. My chest feels a little lighter already, and the day just got a bit more interesting.

Yeah, fuck it. Let's see how it goes.

Chapter 67

M.I.A.

Wes.

I scanned the cafeteria again. No Freddie. Not at our usual table. He wasn't at the library corner either. Just nowhere.

"Where is he?" I muttered, more to myself than anyone.

Dahlia frowned beside me. "He should've been in class... right? You had history together?"

I shrugged. "Yeah, with me and Nick. Don't know where Nick got off to either."

"Lucky", she responded, "I had chem, it was awful, nothing makes sense in that class."

We made our way to our table, taking our seats, greeting Angie, when Nick stormed in, eyes scanning, face tight with worry. He sank onto a bench beside us, fists clenched.

"He's not in class," he said, voice low but tense. "We should've seen him. Something's wrong."

"You weren't either Nick- were you looking for him?" I ask him.

"Yeah, because unlike someone," he glared at me harshly, "I waited for him at the dorm. Like normal. We always walk together since we found the stupid guards don't ask us to *'recite the pledge'* more when you're with someone." he mocks.

Dahlia snickers. And just for a moment, I see the anger on his face lighten when he glances at her.

Angie leans forward, resting her chin on her hand, voice calm. "Maybe he's just... late? Maybe he got held up somewhere?"

"No," Nick snapped. "This isn't like him. He doesn't disappear. Something's going on, and we need to find out what."

Dahlia shifted in her seat, eyes darting between Nick and me. "Should we... go look?"

Nick shook his head, jaw tight. "Not yet. I want to talk to someone. Someone who knows what's happening."

I watched him, a little worried. He's usually calm in a fight, but the way he is practically vibrating with anger now... he was storming right towards trouble. I don't know why he's so upset about this. Sometimes men go M.I.A too. Just need some personal space or some shit...

"Why are you so upset about Freddie going M.I.A though-" I start when he stands up suddenly, practically throwing the chair scraping across the floor, and stormed toward the hallway.

"I'm going to find someone!" he barked over his shoulder.

Dahlia jumped up immediately. "Nick! Wait!"

I stayed where I was, frozen, watching her sprint after him as he disappeared down the corridor.

A moment later, even over the chatter of the students filling the hall, I heard raised voice. Angie and I just glance at each other and the empty chairs before jumping up to go to follow the trails of noise. Much to my suspicion, of course it could only lead to one person. Nick. He was confronting a nurse, hands clenched at his sides.

"Where is he? What have you done to him?" Nick demanded, pacing like he could force an answer out of her by sheer will.

The nurse's expression didn't waver.

"Mr. Deveraux," she said, voice cold and steady. "If you continue this line of questioning about Mr. Kensington, I will schedule an isolated detention session. Understand?"

What a *bitter bitch*.

The nurse soon hurried away as Nick angrily stormed off further down the hallways, with Dahlia following. Angie softly tapped my back, nudging her head in the direction back to the cafeteria.

"C'mon, they need their time to talk. Work things out."

I nodded. "Yeah, lets go. See if she can cool him down."

Chapter 68

Shit happens when you party naked.

Freddie.

I push the out of order sign out of my way as I shove into the last bathroom stall. I flick the lighter and within seconds, I feel like I can breathe again. The smoke curls lazily around me, the world blurring into a warm, hazy bubble where nothing matters except the pull and the calm rush.

I lean back against the brick wall, closing my eyes, letting myself drift. A grin creeps across my face. Yeah... this is perfect. Just me, the smoke, and the quiet.

Then the bubble bursts.

A door slams behind me. I open my eyes and my chest drops. I peak into the massive mirror hanging from the roof and see two guards and a nurse storming through the toilet stalls one by one, shoving every door open until they reach mine, moving like predators. The nurse has that cold, unreadable look, and one of the guards is holding that... thing, a needle gun, sleek and lethal looking.

I push my back into the wall harder to shove through it or maybe it will swallow me whole. My heart hammers practically through my chest and I drop everything and raise my hands for impact.

"What... what the hell!"

It's too late.

They're on me before I can react. The nurse grabs my arms and holds me still, pressing me further against the wall, and the guard leans in, pressing the needle gun against my neck.

"No! Wait!" My words die in my throat.

A sharp jab. Pain explodes along my neck, hot and immediate. My knees buckle, hands flailing, but the world tilts, tilts, tilts...

And then nothing.

Chapter 69

Drowning in endurance.

Freddie.

They tell me it's not about punishment. That's how I know it is. The second I opened my eyes and got my senses back, I knew I was fucked. The white walls just stared back at me as cold gust from the air conditioner made my skin prickle. My eyes darted around and my head ached and pounded in my ears. Then footsteps came from behind. I wriggled and tried to wrestle my way out of the restraints, but in response I just heard a small giggle.

Did that bitch just giggle at me?

The giggly nurse smiles as she pulls a table across with a clean tray on it, before plopping down a clear bag of–

"Evidence." She vocally labels.

It's just out of reach, but close enough that I can see everything inside it. Close enough that I know it's deliberate.

"You introduced a foreign substance into your body," she says lightly, like we're chatting. "So today, we will reset you."

Reset. Like I'm equipment.

The chair I'm being held against my will in is medical and upright. Cold metal is biting through the fabric of my uniform. My hands are being held palm up which is unusual. It doesn't hurt yet. Another nurse brings over two small clear cups. Sealed containers. Cotton swabs. Nothing labelled. My pulse quickens.

"You weren't dependent before." The first nurse continues pleasantly.

"That means this will work faster."

My stomach drops. "Work how?"

She doesn't answer. She opens one of the containers.

The smell hits me instantly, sharp, chemical, wrong. Not enough to make me gag, but enough that my body reacts before my brain can catch up. My stomach tightens. My mouth waters.

A flash of memory slams into me.

The crisp weight of stacked notes in my hand. The thrill of buying something forbidden with money I wasn't supposed to touch. The rush that followed, sharp and sweet but behind it, the judgment, the whispers, the cold stare of my family cutting me off from everything I'd ever had. No money. No protection.

My jaw tightens. The nurse notices.

"There it is," she says, pleased. "Association."

She grabs my mouth with her gloved hands and squeezes so hard my jaw practically pops open. She jams a swab in and rakes it around the inside of my mouth. Harder than necessary. Bitter. Acrid. The taste spreads immediately, tongue, throat, everywhere. I jerk back on instinct.

"Still," she says gently, tightening the restraints a notch. "This only hurts if you resist."

The bitterness intensifies. My mouth floods with saliva, my stomach is lurching like it's confused about what it's supposed to do.

Poison.

The word echoes around my head. *Oh god. There trying to kill me.*

She steps back and let's go of me, and I start spitting up whatever I can muster.

The monitor I didn't notice beside me before starts to beep faster.

"Good," the second nurse murmurs. "Response confirmed."

Then the chair tilts backward. Blood rushes to my head. The taste crawls up the back of my throat. I swallow without thinking and instantly regret it, the bitterness blooms sharper, nausea twisting deep and fast.

"What is this?" I snap. "Did you give me poison?"

The nurse pats my arm.

"Nothing harmful-" she starts sweetly.

"don't you dare touch me! Ill kill you!!" I scream weakly at her and she rips her hand back. My throat feels like its shredding itself up, and my breathing become scratchy.

"Relax Frederick. Your body is doing all the work. This is natural." The second nurse replies.

Minutes drag. Or seconds. I can't tell.

Another container pops open. The smell is stronger this time. Closer. Right under my nose. My stomach cramps violently. Sweat breaks out along my spine. I clamp my jaw shut, fighting the urge to gag, to give them exactly what they want.

"Notice how quickly pleasure becomes discomfort," the nurse says over my ragged breathing. "Your brain learned the wrong shortcut."

I snarl something ugly. I don't even know what to say. The chair tilts again. Just a fraction, but it's enough. Nausea surges so hard my vision blurs, that fuzzy feeling again. Tears sting my eyes, not from fear– from fury. From being trapped. From being made weak over something I never needed. A retch tears out of me before I can stop it. They react instantly. Not alarmed or angry. Pleased.

"Perfect," one of them says softly. "Aversion achieved."

They don't let me vomit. They hold me there, head back, mouth burning, stomach rolling, until the sensation peaks and my body starts to shake on its own. Silent. Humiliating. Endless.

I try to focus on anything else. Princess. Her laugh. The way she looks at me like I'm still me. I have to get out. She'll be waiting. I can't disappear in here.

The room starts to tilt again. My chest tightens. My vision tunnels. Something snapped in my body and suddenly I'm not in control anymore. My muscles lock, then jerk. Foam gathers at my lips. I can hear myself making a sound I don't recognize.

The nurses don't rush.

"Stop faking." one says calmly.

"He's escalating."

The chair is still tilted. Blood pounding. My head feels like it's splitting open. I can't breathe right. I can't tell them. Then- darkness. When I come back, the chair is upright. My throat is raw. My head throbs. My hands tremble uselessly in the restraints. The nurse wipes my mouth gently with a cloth.

"This part always feels dramatic," she says kindly. "But it fades."

"Why?" I rasp.

She meets my eyes, smiles steadily.

"Because next time you think about using," she says, "your body will remember this instead."

They release me slowly. Methodically. My legs barely hold me when I stand. My stomach is still churning, my mouth tasting bitter and wrong no matter how much I swallow. As they lead me out, the nurse calls after me brightly, "Drink water! And don't worry, repeated exposure is very effective.

The door closes, and I'm right back where I started. Alone.

Chapter 70

Don't give me those eyes.

Nick.

My fists are clenched so hard my knuckles ache. I pace fast, too fast, like if I slow down, I'll explode. The nurse's voice keeps replaying in my head- calm, controlled, threatening. Isolated detention. Like Freddie's already been erased and I'm next in line. I can't hold it anymore. I slam my fist into the wall, not hard enough to hurt myself, but enough that it slightly satisfied me.

"Nick!"

Her voice cuts through it.

I don't turn. "Go away, Dahlia."

Footsteps hurry. Then- impact. She shoves me back, hard, my shoulders turning, hitting the wall with a dull thud. It knocks the air out of me more than the anger.

"What the hell is wrong with you?" she snaps. "You can't just confront them like that!"

Something in me breaks loose.

"He's missing!" I yell, the words ripping out raw. "Freddie doesn't just skip class. He doesn't disappear. And you saw her- how she talked about him like he was already gone!" My voice cracks and I hate it. "I'm not just angry, I'm..." I swallow. "I'm scared."

She doesn't flinch. Not when I raise my voice. Not when it spills ugly. I noticed that. It makes me stop. I drag my hand down my face, breathing hard.

"You don't understand what I'm feeling, Dahlia. And you never will. Why don't you just leave me alone?"

She shakes her head, her eyes steadily on mine. "I do understand, Nick. You just always assume I can't, and I won't, but I do." Her voice softens. "I forgive you."

That's what does it. Not the words. The way she looks at me, with those eyes- like she sees the mess under my skin. My guard drops before I can stop it.

"Then we need to do something," I say, urgent again. "Because I just know something is happening. We need to help him."

She grabs my arm before I can pace away, yanking me back. "And how exactly do you plan on doing that? Even if he is in trouble, the nurses will just take you too. What's your big plan- run in and beat everyone to a pulp and carry him out like a damsel in distress?"

I sigh, the tension slipping just enough to breathe. "Well... I'd only planned on beating everyone to pulp."

She snorts despite herself. A small, surprised giggle escapes her. I laugh too, quiet, stupid, relieved. For half a second, the world shrinks to just us. Her hand still on my arm. My eyes flick to her lips, then back to her eyes. The space between us feels charged, fragile.

Then,

"BREACH. ALL STUDENTS REPORT BACK TO SECTORS IMMEDIATELY."

The speakers scream it. Dahlia stiffens and I realize she's still holding me.

Just as I'm trying to lead her away, a scrawny malnourished student stumbles around the corner. Blood is everywhere matted in his hair, smeared across his face, pouring down his leg at the wrong angle. He's limping, dragging himself forward. As I scan the kid, I notice something familiar...

That color, that grey, I remember seeing Dahlia for the first time wearing that grey. Why would this guy be wearing the disheveled same clothes we woke up in? It's not uniform...

Snapping out of it, I look down to see him gripping a knife, slick with fresh red. It drips onto the floor with every step.

The lockdown alarm blares again.

Dahlia is still frozen, completely still. Her pupils are blown wide, the light gone from her eyes like someone switched her off. Like she's waiting for instructions. For permission, for something that isn't coming.

What the fuck could she be waiting for?

"Dahlia." I say sharply. She doesn't move.

I grabbed her shoulders. "Come on, we need to go. Now!" Nothing.

Panic claws up my throat. I shake her harder than I mean to. "COME ON, LET'S GO!"

The knife's reflection glints. The blood keeps dripping. And she's still frozen in my arms.

Chapter 71

The switch has flipped.

Dahlia.

The alarm is too loud. It drills straight through my head until there's nothing else... no walls, no people, just noise and the need to wait.

BREACH. REPORT. IMMEDIATELY.

I stay still. Still is *safe*. Still is *correct*. My lips move on their own. Names. The ones they made me say. Over and over. Proof I was listening. Proof I was good. I don't realize I'm whispering until a voice cuts through the ringing.

"Dahlia."

Hands on my shoulders. My vision stutters. I blink hard, the hallway snapping back into focus in jagged pieces. Nick. The lights. Blood on the floor. Panic hits all at once hot and choking. I grab his arms like they're the only solid thing left, my fingers digging in.

He cups my face, forcing me to look at him.

"What did they do to you?" he whispers.

The question lands too deep. *What have they done to me?* Someone screams, a small broken voice just echoing, inching closer. I turn to find the voice and see another student point at Nick and I, covered in blood, holding an old friend.

"You! You know what they've done! The needles, the white room, you're helping them! Let me go! Let me out! I just want to see my family!" The young student screeches.
Foam falls from his mouth, his eyes filled with terror as he hyperventilates racing toward us, tripping over the IV cables still attached to his body. His leg is definitely not meant to be bending that way. The bone sticking out of his calf doesn't even bother him. He just stumbles instead, and his budging red eyes glare at us as he yells. The knife glints in his own hand, shaking and dripping the familiar liquid.

Nick turns at the now running student. Everything happens at once.

"Nick! –" I cry out as the student just runs harder, and nick only takes a glance at me. I reach to grab his arm, but he shoves me hard instead, sending me stumbling into the wall. My back slams into it as he steps in front of me, hands up. The knife flashes. Everything fractures into pieces. The sound of shoes scraping. That horrible, wet choking noise from the boy. He dodges, blocks, moves fast, knocking the guy off balance and down to the floor.

I try to scream but nothing comes out. My mouth just opens and shuts, useless, silent. My chest tightens, my breathing going uneven, sharp and quick. I grab at my head, fingers tangling in my hair like I can hold myself together, like I can stop this.

I can't breathe. I can't—

Then, a sharp, slicing sound rips through the air.

I flinch hard, my hands coming up automatically, wiping at my face—but it just spreads. It's thick. Sticky.

My stomach drops. Slowly, too slowly, I look down.

It's all over my arm, dotted and smeared across my skin, dripping between my fingers. Too much. There's too much of it.

My breath locks in my chest.

"No..." I whisper, shaking, my voice barely there. "Nick...?"

I try to wipe it off, rubbing at my arm harder and harder like it'll come off, like it's not real—but it just smears more, darker, everywhere.

My hands start shaking. Not small shakes—violent, uncontrollable. My chest heaves, breaths coming too fast, like I'm choking on them. Tears stream uncontrollably down my cheeks, mixing with the smeared blood and dropping onto the white tiles red.

I can't think. I can't move. My eyes snap up, blurry, searching—

"Nick?!"

But I see him on the ground, just lying there. Blood is splashed along the wall and is dripping onto the floor. I look at the student, who is standing above him breathing heavy, raising the knife for another hit–

The panic vanishes like a switch has been flipped. The fear drains out of me, leaving my head clear and empty. Something else rushes in instead. Rage, cold, focused, absolute. I don't feel my hands clenched. I don't feel my heart race. Whoever this kid is?

He's going to pay.

Chapter 72
Nobody look!

Nick.

Pain explodes across my hand.

Burning hot. Sharp enough to steal the air from my lungs.

My teeth grit on instinct and I jerk back with a hiss, staring down at the slice across my palm where the blade caught me. Blood wells immediately, warm and slick, dripping between my fingers. I barely register it. The student uses my distraction as an opportunity and shoves me hard onto the ground. But when I turn and look up, I freeze.

Because Dahlia is standing.

She's upright, shoulders squared, fists balled so tightly her knuckles have gone pale. Her breathing is shallow, eyes dark and locked onto the figure in front of us like something inside her has snapped clean through fear and landed straight into survival.

"Dahlia." I start.

She moves before I can finish.

She intercepts him with a force that knocks the breath from my chest just watching it. She tackles him hard, sending both crashing to the floor. The sound is sickening, a sharp grunt of pain.

And then... she's on him. Her fists come down repeatedly, relentlessly, raw. No hesitation. No sound except the dull impact and her ragged breathing. She's not screaming or crying.

For a second, I just stood there, stunned, heart pounding so hard it hurts. This isn't the girl who froze in my arms moments ago. This is someone colder. Someone trained by anger.

"Dahlia." I gasp, forcing my legs to move. My injured hand screams in protest as I reach for her. Blood smears across the floor as I grab her shoulders. "Dahlia, stop. That's enough. He's down!"

She doesn't hear me. I hook my arm around her waist and haul her back with everything I've got, dragging her off his now limp body. She fights me at first, with wild and desperate strength, but then she breaks. Her body goes slack against mine. I pull her into my chest without thinking, turning so my back faces the hallway, shielding her completely. My injured hand throbs violently, the blood dripping onto my sleeve, but I keep it wrapped around her anyway. I don't care. I'll bleed out before I let go.

Footsteps, fast and panicked.

Suddenly, Angie and Wes come sprinting down the corridor, clearly running for our sector, until they skid to a stop. Angie gasps as Wes mutters, "Holy shit..."

I follow their line of sight and realize what they're seeing. My hands.

Bloodied. Knuckles split. Red smeared across my skin and dripping onto the floor. They don't see her shaking against me. They don't see the way I'm holding her, that if I loosen my grip even slightly, she'll fall apart.

Good.

I shift my stance, angling my body more deliberately in front of her, blocking their view.

"Well?" I snap, sharper than I mean to be. "Stop staring. We need to get into the dorm. Now."

My voice comes out steady, commanding, even though my heart is still racing and my hand feels like it's on fire.

They don't argue.

I guided them forward, ushering them down the hall with my body still half turned in, one arm tight around Dahlia, the other clenched despite the pain. Every step sends another jolt through my hand, but I suck it up and keep moving.

I feel her forehead press lightly into my chest. She's here. She's breathing. That's all that matters. I'll deal with the blood later.

Chapter 73

No...no...no!

Angeline.

The dorm is chaotic. Nick is hunched over on his bed, breathing through his teeth, and Dahlia's moving so fast I can barely keep up with her. She shoves him onto the bed and darts out, the door slamming behind her as she goes for the first aid kit outside the sector.

I pace, my hands clenching and unclenching, the room causing a sensory overload, alarm blaring, disinfectant cutting through the air, the distant shuffle of footsteps in the halls. Band-Aids tear and zippers rip as Dahlia returns, tossing the kit onto the floor. She kneels beside Nick, fumbling with gauze and antiseptic, trying to fix him up while he hisses at every touch. But there's only one thing I can think about. One person.

A missing piece of my heart in the shape of him.

"Where is Freddie?!" I shout, voice cracking over the noise. My panic builds with each second. The thought of him out there, alone, makes my chest seize.

308

"Angie, calm down!" Wes said, stepping close, trying to hold me back. "I'm sure he's fine... just breathe!"

I can't breathe. Not really. Not while the alarm screams and my own thoughts scream louder.

Dahlia mutters curses under her breath, shaking her head at the chaos, and I glance at Nick- he's pale, sweat beading along his temples, grimacing through the pain. Every noise hits him harder than anyone else.

And then, he walks in. *Freddie.* Pale. Disheveled. Bruises forming across his arms and neck, eyes wide and tired. My heart stops mid-beat. The room freezes. The alarm, the zippers, the torn bandages, the disinfectant- it all fades into silence the moment he steps inside. I don't move. Wes doesn't move. Dahlia halts mid-kneel, gauze in her hand. Even Nick freezes, jaw tight, staring.

He's here. He's *alive.*

Chapter 74

Everything is wrong.

Wes.

Angie's voice cuts through the dorm like a siren. "Freddie! Where were you? What happened!"

He doesn't answer. His lips barely move, and his eyes are wide, scanning her face as if trying to prove she's really there. His hands move slowly over her arms, up and down, almost reverent, like he can't believe she's in front of him. He's trembling, weak, and the metallic tang of blood in the air makes my stomach twist.

He opens his mouth, but whatever he's trying to say dies in a gagging sound. He bolts to the bathroom, sounds of violent vomiting follow behind him. Angie followed straight after him, banging on the door practically begging him to come out.

It's really doing my head in considering everything else that's going on in this room.

The smell of all the shitty chemicals hits my nose- sharp, and it makes me flinch back instinctively.

Chaos erupts. Everyone freezes for a heartbeat, then shouts and movements flood the room.

Dahlia's voice cuts through the confusion. "Nick? Nickolas, are you with us? Hey! It's okay!"

All eyes swing toward Nick. He's sitting on the floor, silent tears streaking his face, staring blankly at his bloodied hand. The scent of disinfectant mixes with iron and fear. His breathing is shallow, labored, and the fluorescent lights make the crimson on his hand glint unnaturally.

"It was me." he murmurs, voice low and broken.

Dahlia rushes to him, eyes wide, moving cautiously. "What was you? Nick? What are you talking about?"

He repeats it, voice stronger this time. "It was me. I killed him. I remember now."

I notice how Dahlia's hand softens on his wrist, tentative, hesitant. She slowly pulls back, careful, like she's afraid of breaking him but can't leave him alone either.

Then Freddie dashes back into the room. Pale and Shaky. Even the alarms, the zippers, and the chaos around us seem to fade for a moment.

Angie spins toward him, voice sharp and demanding, "You guys owe us a serious explanation!"

Chapter 75

Promises are made to be kept.

Nick.

Wes's hand presses lightly on my shoulder, steadying me, but I can't stop the shaking. "Nick... look at me," he says, voice low, almost gentle, though tight with urgency.

"I–" I start, voice rough, "I don't–"

"You were shielding her," Wes interrupts, firm. "I saw it. I saw the blood on her hands, and I know... it wasn't you. Dahlia did it, not you."

My chest tightens. Relief and anger twist together. I look to Dahlia, who is trying to calm Angie and Freddie down in the corner of the room, my gaze shifting back to Wes.

"Wes, you better not– don't even think about telling the others," I mutter, voice harsh.

He shakes his head, cutting me off before I can finish.

"Nick... I would never do that to Lia. This stays between us. I won't act like I know anything, and neither will anyone else. I promise."

Something in me unclenches. I nod slightly, appreciating the weight behind his words, the promise that I'm not completely alone in this. That he gets it. That he's not judging. The tremor in my hands eases just enough. I don't fully relax, not yet, but the edge softens. I glance at Wes, eyes meeting his, a silent thank you passing between us.

Before I can say anything more, Dahlia comes over, calm but efficiently, kneeling beside me to check my injury. She doesn't speak much, just works with steady hands, tearing the tape, adjusting the gauze, cleaning the blood. I let her, letting the sting and pressure ground me, letting someone else take control for a moment.

Thank Fuck.

Chapter 76

Glass haunts me.

Angeline.

The school has resumed back to its calculated calmness. After finally settling, we regroup like it's a tribunal. Nick gently rested against a wall, Wes sitting on the floor, Freddie on a far chair and Dahlia and I sitting on Wes's bed.

It's weirdly quiet. I mean look at just what happened, why are we all sitting around not communicating?

Oh, who am I kidding, we suck at communicating.

I've had enough, "Okay is someone going to start talking, or should I just ask all the questions?" I huff. "Because I-, we need to know what the hell is goi-"

"I remember." Nick interrupts.

'What?" I replied with confusion. "Remember what?"

Suddenly the atmosphere shifts, turning colder and fragile. Like when you carry a glass plate, trying not to drop it.

"My life. Before Montclair Academy. I- I remember what I did." Nick mutters.

"What do you remember? What did you do?" Wes nudges.

Nick looks at the ceiling, eyes watering, attempting to not let a single droplet fall. He sighs then looks at Lia, almost for confirmation that he can continue. I knew this was serious.

"My dad is a businessman. He's a CEO for some company, it- it doesn't even matter. My whole life, he has given me everything I have ever wanted. But not what I need- needed." Nick's voice becomes shaky, breakable, never like I've ever heard him before. My fingers start to combust, a cold chill icing my spine as he continues.

"I appreciated what I got, but I never actually cared about that sort of stuff. The cars, the clubs, the status. I just wanted a dad. It was just my dad and I; I'm the only child."

"Was?" Dahlia softly asked, gently rubbing Nick's arm.

Nick's eyes squinted as he huffed with pain, struggling to find the words to explain. Freddie rolled his chair over.

"Hey- hey, you can tell us. We're all here listening. Nothing that is said here will ever leave this room. Cross my heart."

This manages to earn a small giggle from Nick, lightening the mood. Seeing Nick break down his walls like this, it meant more than anything that could possibly go wrong. Nothing could ruin this. Us. Our friendship.

I turn to Freddie, smiling at his dumb shaved head and easy light eyes, "Cross my heart."

"Cross my heart." Wes joined. Followed by a sweet Dahlia, locking her eyes entirely on Nick and Nick alone.

"Cross my heart."

Nick looked comfortable around the circle, taking a deep breath before revealing his truth. His full truth.

"My father was getting more aggressive, angrier as the deals he was investing in didn't go well. He would take it out on me. Blaming me for things he was too incompetent to do. And we would go at it. A lot. He said I had a foul mouth and the soap thing that they did to me. Not new, he used to do it to me. Wash out the vulgarity." Nick mocked. "I started acting out, got involved with the wrong people and I landed myself in debt with some really fucked up guys."

Wes looked concerned, the only one of us having the nerve to ask, "How much money?"

Nick shot him a glance with only three words attached to it. I knew instantly.

A. Shit. Ton.

"Any way's I tried to tell my dad, ask him for help." Nick chuckled to himself. "Crazy right?" Nick's hands clench. "That's when it happened. When everything changed. When I-I... We fought. I grabbed something, I don't even remember what and I hit him. There was blood. A lot of it."

Dahlia inhales sharply beside me.

"I panicked," Nick continues. "Took cash and I ran." His voice drops. "Spent the night in some cheap motel and just crashed. When I woke up the next day, I went to some weird local bar and saw on the news that he was found. *Dead*."

There it is. The glass plate has dropped. And shards have cut us all.

Deeply, I try to swallow, to try and follow what Nick has told us, but the thought of a father doing such a thing. It- It makes me sick to my stomach. Nick doesn't deserve this. No wonder he is so guarded.

"I killed him." Nick stood silent for a while. Suddenly picking up, "When I went back, my uncle was there. He said he'd take care of everything. That's all I remember clearly." Freddie gives Nick a sympathetic glance, breaking eye contact within three seconds, Wes's head practically shaking in disbelief.

"No. You're not a killer. There had to have been something else." Dahlia states.

"She's right. You wouldn't just do that." Freddie agreed.

Nick shakes his head, looking at the floor, attempting his best to listen and understand.

No one speaks. I don't think anyone knows how. Then Lia stands. My heart sinks to the floor. No. Not Lia.

"I remember everything too," she says. Her voice is calm. She doesn't look at any of us at first. Her hands are folded neatly in front of her like she's preparing to deliver bad news.

"My father is- he's a bad man." she begins. "Dangerous. He has done- he does terrible things."

I feel my chest start to ache.

"Like what? Dolly what has he done that's so terrible?" Freddie pushes bitterly.

I look at Freddie, annoyed. What was his problem? He never pry's like this? Why would he ask her like that, can't he see that she's struggling? He's been acting differently ever since he walked through the door.

"What is the matter with you!" I demand. "Why are you being like this? What happened to you?" Freddie looks at me dark, almost like he's about to bite back at me for the first time ever. When–

"Guys quit it! Can we please focus on Lia! She's trying to talk!" Wes commands.

"He's right, knock it off." Nick orders sternly.

Shit. Dahlia. I forgot she's right there. She's scared. I feel like an absolute narcissistic bitch.

"Sorry Lia, please continue." I apologized.

"I was trained," she continues. "From a young age. How to fight. How to hurt people. How to survive violence without reacting to it."

Nick's head snaps up.

"Why would he train you for violence?" he kindly asks. Dahlia turns her face to look up at Nick, scared, almost embarrassed that she has to admit this.

"Because he's dirty. Dirty with his money. With his people. With his whole life!" she cries.

"Dirty?" I ask.

Freddie finishes for Dahlia, knowing he's worked it out.

"Wait, like dirty, dirty? Like the mafia dirty?" Thankfully this time I can tell Freddie has changed his tune, more sympathetic this time.

Dahlia just nods, looking anywhere but any of our eyes. I hate that she's embarrassed. I mean if she knew what my mother was like, I'd gladly state how my parent is a selfish materialistic whore.

"My mother wasn't his partner," Dahlia says softly. "She was forced. She was kind. Gentle. She tried to shield me." Her voice wavers.

"I watched him kill her."

The words land like a gunshot. No one breathes.

"He told me it was necessary. That I'd understand when I was stronger." Dahlia swallows. "He said love makes you weak. Pain makes you useful."

My hands start shaking.

"I grew up being hurt and then praised for surviving it. I don't know where fear ends and loyalty begins." Her eyes finally lifted to meet ours. "I tried to run. That's why I'm here. I just know it."

I think I can tell that we all practically want to vomit.

She sits back down. The room feels smaller. The awkwardness, the silence creeps back in. I mean, we don't know how to handle this, Christ, *we're all only seventeen.* We sit in silence briefly, then I stand because if I don't, I'll cry.

"I remember most of mine," I say. "Public life. Smiling. Rules. Image." I laugh bitterly. "My mother cared more about perception than me. I couldn't be one size too big. My throat tightens. I was never allowed to mess up."

I see the group flash me an empathetic look, this just fuels me to go on a rampage for my bitch of a mother even more.

"So, you were right before, she's the reason you were throwing up. Why you do that to yourself." Nick calmly whispered.

Before even thinking I just continued.

"I was never allowed to step out of line. She even tried to set me up with some fucking dickhead to strengthen our family reputations and some shit about allies. I mean what the fuck does that even mean!"

Unfortunately, I forgot how much of a reaction this would ignite out of Freddie.

"What?" Freddie roared. "Please explain to me that what I just heard was bullshit. That you weren't being set up with some tool?"

I look at Freddie, my stomach fluttering at the thought that this bothers him but just only manage to answer him blandly.

"It's true." I hesitate. "But I know something's missing. Something big."

Wes rubbed his face hard. "Yeah. I remember why I'm here too."

Jesus, we're practically having a fucked-up truth relay. But one that definitely, is needed. And long overdue.

"I screwed up in public. Big time. Media everywhere." His jaw clenches. "Dad was up for re-election. I became a liability. Guess pops wanted me out of the way so I couldn't screw up his campaign. Here I am."

Dahlia responds fast, almost star struck, 'Your father is the president? You're the first son!"

Wes looks up, disappointed, "Yeah don't throw a party. This is exactly what I didn't want. Now it's weird. You all think of me differently now, don't you."

Nick walks over to Wes, patting him on the back, "Trust me. This doesn't change anything. None of us are weirded out. Sorry we just frankly don't give a fuck that you live in the white house."

I can't contain myself; I just start laughing. Hard. We all do. Our truths have finally come out. No walls. No layers. Just raw, real, us. All of us. Wait a minute. I suddenly remember there's one more. Save the best for last, I guess. What could go wrong?

I turn, flicking my blonde curly locks out of the way as I eye him up, "Okay funny guy, your turn. We've all gone. What's going on with you?"

Freddie sighs. "I had drugs back home. Before this place. I've struggled with substance abuse."

The room stiffens instantly.

"I am close with my family. They're all really great, but... I, the idiot I am, was bored. It wasn't enough that my family was great to me, I had to go and spoil it by wanting to get high and feel like trash. I mean sure, my dad and I would bump heads sometimes, but I had the perfect life. Why would I screw that up?"

Hearing Freddie this way, it dis-heartened me. The air became thicker, making it harder hearing my friends' lives, how much hurt they had been through and Freddie? I knew Freddie would break me.

"Anyway, I- I went out on a limb one night, after fighting with my old man, and snagged his cash in the family safe and splurged on all the drugs I could find. Fucked up my dad's money credibility. Once he found out, I was cut off. No more allowance, no more freedom, nothing."

I feel sweat rising against the back of my neck, hearing about Freddie's struggle. I've heard about how substance abuse can change a person.

I gently whisper "Tell me, tell me everything. I'm listening. I'll always listen."

Freddie takes a deep breath, restricting his hands from shaking, "I guess my fuck up really hurt my mom, so she agreed to banish me here, because the last thing I remember is looking at her picture in my room. Then I woke up here with you guys."

Nick and Wes cradle around Freddie, as the three of them stand up, embracing in a kind moment of a hug. Dahlia is still sitting; her cheeks being kissed by her sparkling tears running down. My lips twitching with tension, not knowing how to honestly react. My shoulders, legs, chest, everything feels like they're on fire.

I, however, see Freddie's hands slowly shake. Remembering how disoriented he was when he came in. My voice trembles out before I realize.

"What happened to you before you came in here Freddie? You're shaking."

Freddie looked back down to me, backing out of his hug, "I had isolated detention."

Nick quickly flinches, "What? What the fuck?"

Wes interjects, "What for?"

Dahlia and I looked just as confused.

"They caught me smoking."

What?

"That's where the memory of my substance struggle came back. But, yeah, uh, they pulled me into the White room and shoved chemicals down my throat, so I wouldn't do it again, I guess they knew about my problem, since the drugs were in my room earlier when I came in alone."

Is he fucking serious? I stand corrected. Something can definitely go wrong, and it's all his fault.

I snap, quicker than I get up to my feet, "You fucking smoked! What were you doing with drugs in your room? What were you thinking!"

The whole room is quiet. I can tell the others are staring but I don't care. I am seeing red. Nothing will stop Freddie from squirming his way out of this one.

"No! I found the drugs. I didn't bring them in! I'm telling you guys!" Freddie barks back at me, his face and mine only inches away from each other now.

Liar.

"You still hid it." I shot back. "From all of us! You could have told one of us and we would've taken them from you before you did something so stupid! You compromised all of us."

"You wouldn't understand!" he mutters.

That does it.

"Don't say that!" I shout. "You don't get to decide what I understand."

"This place messes with people!" Freddie says, gesturing violently. "I was just trying to survive."

"And the rest of us weren't?" I snap.

I turn and leave before I say something unforgivable.

Wes followed immediately. "Angie... wait."

"I can't," I choke. "Not right now."

He slows, walking beside me instead of chasing. "You don't have to be okay. Just don't disappear."

I don't answer. But I don't tell him to go away either. Behind us, the dorm door stays shut, holding secrets that can never be unspoken, and a group that may never be the same again.

Chapter 77

The aftermath.

Dahlia.

No one moves after Angie leaves.

The room feels hollow, like something essential just walked out with her. Wes lingers near the door for a second before following, and then it's just the three of us left- me, Freddie, and Nick.

Nick stands with his back to us; hands locked behind his neck like he's trying to hold himself together by force alone. He doesn't look angry.

He looks... tired.

Freddie sinks onto the edge of his bed, staring at the floor. All the usual noise is gone from him. No jokes. No shrugging it off. I step closer.

"Freddie," I say gently.

He flinches, then looks up. His eyes are glassy, but he's holding it in.

"I didn't mean to mess things up," he says quietly. "I really didn't."

"I know," I tell him.

He blinks at me, surprised. "You do?"

I nodded. "You were trying to survive. That doesn't make you a bad person."

His shoulders sag a little, like the words took weight off him he didn't know he was carrying.

"Angie's right. I could have got you guys all punished." he mutters.

"No." I say firmly, but softly. "You're still here. That matters."

I slid down and sat next to him on the floor, resting my head on his shoulder. His breathing is still quick, and his body is still quivering.

"We're gonna be okay."

Chapter 78

Crossing the line.

Wes.

I don't mean to ambush them. Okay, maybe I do. Just a little.

I spot Angie and Dahlia halfway down the hall, heads bent together like they always are when something's wrong, but they don't want anyone else to know. They walk slower than usual. Careful. That's never a good sign.

I step out from our sector's doorway and point. "You. Both of you. Now."

Angie startles. "Wes– what the hell?"

"It's been weeks! We can't all avoid each other forever! No questions," I say, already grabbing her wrist and Dahlia's sleeve. "Trust me."

They protest for all of three seconds before I haul them inside and shut the door behind us.

The hall is quiet, until I rip open the door to the boys dorm. Choked sobs and hiccups echo around the room.

Freddie's sitting on his bed, shoulders caved in, face buried in his hands. He's crying, the kind that wrecks your breathing and makes ugly, broken sounds you can't take back.

Angie freezes. "Oh my god."

Dahlia moves first. She always does.

She kneels in front of him, gentle as glass. "Freddie?"

He looks up, eyes red and swollen, and something in my chest twists hard.

"I remember," he chokes. "I remember everything else."

Angie sits beside him instantly, no hesitation, no anger left. Just concern.

"My mom," Freddie continues, voice cracking. "She's… she's dead. She died years ago from cancer."

The word hangs there, heavy.

"She wanted to be a hairdresser," he says, laughing weakly through tears. "She loved it. Practiced on me all the time. Said my hair was her 'masterpiece.'"

His hand lifts, trembling, hovering over his shaved head like he still expects to feel it there.

"My dad hated it," Freddie whispers. "Said it didn't fit the family image. Crushed it. Crushed her."

Angie's eyes fill instantly.

"When they shaved my head," Freddie sobs, "it wasn't just hair. It was-" He gasps. "It was the last thing she ever did with me. It was the last part of me still connected to her. And t-they took it…"

Dahlia presses her forehead to his knee, eyes shut tight. Angie reaches for him and this time, Freddie doesn't hesitate. He leans into her, clinging like if he lets go, he'll fall apart completely.

"I'm sorry," he whispers to her. "About before. About everything."

Angie shakes her head fiercely. "No. I'm sorry. I should've listened."

They hold each other, crying quietly now. I turn away for a second because my throat burns and I don't trust myself to speak. When I look back, something's changed.

Dahlia straightens slowly. Her face is calm but there's steel under it.

"They took too much from us," she says. "All of us."

Angie nods. "We can't stay."

Freddie wipes his face with his sleeve. "So... what. We just accept this until they let us leave after the reform trial?"

"No."

Slowly we all turned around, seeing Nick by the door, pressed rough, veins pulsating slightly.

"We don't." He exhales. "We're going to plan. Together. And then we get out."

Silence. Then Freddie nods, just a small one.

"Tomorrow," Angie says. "We start tomorrow."

Finally, the fear doesn't feel paralyzed. It feels motivating. And that's when I know- we're not just surviving this anymore. We're leaving. Escaping this hell hole.

Chapter 79

Late night raids.

Nick.

"You really think this is a good idea?" Freddie whispers, peering down the hallway like we're about to steal state secrets instead of, you know... pens and granola bars.

"Absolutely," I say, grinning. "I live for adrenaline. And snacks. Mostly snacks."

He raises an eyebrow but doesn't protest, just yet.

"Sounds like I've rubbed off on you Nickolas."

Shit, I think he has.

We creep down the hall toward the storage room, our shoes squeaking just enough to make me wince. Freddie flinches at every tiny sound, and I can't help but nudge him gently.

"Relax. If the guard comes, we tell him it's a highly classified pen inspection. You got this."

Freddie snorts, a short little laugh that makes me grin. "Highly classified pens, huh?"

I open the door slowly. It squeaks.

Freddie freezes mid-step, eyes wide. "Shhh!" he hisses, hands pressed to his chest.

"See?" I whisper back. "This is nothing. Totally normal, everyday activity."

We slip inside. Pens, notebooks, tiny snacks- our loot is modest but perfect. Freddie picks up a chocolate bar, inspecting it like it's a rare gem. I grab a pack of pens.

This is pathetic and lame, but there's nothing else to do in this place. Besides, if stealing some pens and snacks would get Freddie's mind of his mother. I'll keep this up all night if I have to.

And then, of course, the alarm flickers. A soft buzz hums from the corner. Freddie yelps and drops the chocolate. I grab it midair.

"Smooth save. Impressive reflexes, really. You're basically a ninja." He teases.

I glare at him, but the tension in his shoulders eases. "I'm not a ninja."

"Not yet," He nudges. "Give it time. You'll earn your black belt in sneaky snack retrievals."

We laugh quietly, crouched behind the shelves. Then another sound. A door creaks in the hallway. Freddie freezes again. I glanced at him.

"Cover me," I whisper, and he hesitates, then nods. I peek around the shelf, see nothing, and give him a thumbs-up.

"See?" I grin. "Teamwork. You and me. Solid."

He finally laughs, breathy and relieved. "Okay... yeah. I can trust you."

"Of course you can," I say, tossing him a pen like a trophy. "I'm basically a trust guru. Snacks and pens included."

By the time we sneak back out, chocolate and pens in hand, Freddie's shoulders are loose, his smile real. I can feel the tension lift from both of us a little, I don't have to worry at least not for this tiny, ridiculous, perfect little adventure.

Chapter 80

Phase 1.

Freddie.

Dahlia and I slink through the halls like we're ghosts on a mission. I'm counting doors, corners, and cameras while she scribbles notes on a scrap of paper Princess ripped from her stupid diary. Every turn, every shadow, feels like it could be hiding a camera– or worse, a guard.

"Three cameras at this junction, one in the stairwell," I whisper. Dahlia nods, jotting it down.

By the time we reach the cafeteria, the group is already assembling. Nick and Wes are bickering quietly in the corner, while Princess looks like she's secretly amused at the chaos we're creating. Her eyes search around the room until they latch onto mine, and her grin grows.

I knew I still had it.

"We should split into teams," Dahlia says firmly. "Everyone gets a role. Wes, you go solo."

Wes groans so loud it echoes off the walls, earning a death glare from Nick and Angie slapping him on the arm shushing him.

"Why me? Why do I have to go by myself in this creep-ass place?!"

Nick's glare is sharp enough to cut glass. Wes freezes mid-protest, and I can't resist, leaning forward with a grin. "Because someone's got to be brave enough to actually do what the rest of us are too scared to do."

His eyes light up and the stupid, childlike whining flips instantly into smug excitement.

"Ohhh, that's exactly what I want. Someone finally notices my bravery."

Nick mutters something under his breath about idiots, and Wes flops dramatically onto the nearest chair, still grinning.

We move on to the next order of business: the diary.

"We'll use Angie's as our base but need codes and ciphers."

I scribble ideas as Dahlia brainstorms symbols and shorthand we can use.

"Number-letter swaps," I suggest. "Dates for locations."

Dahlia nods. "Perfect. And we'll mark doors and cameras with invisible ink- just enough for us to see."

"I'll grab some from the chemistry lab." Angie adds.

"So, Wes, are you sure you don't remember the access code? Angie, you didn't see him punch it in?" I ask.

Wes and Angie, disappointedly shake their heads.

"Don't worry! Wes won't stop trying to remember." Angie reassured.

"Yeah, I'm trying."

Well, there goes that.

Nick is already muttering under his breath about efficiency, Wes is daydreaming about solo glory, and I'm just enjoying how tight the team feels right now, all chaos and plans and ridiculous schemes. By the time lunch rolls around, we've got teams, codes, and a plan. Wes still complains every step of the way, but secretly, I know he's thrilled.

"Hey Dolly, can I see what we have written down so far?" She shrugs and hands me the diary and I just blink.

"I'm going to need to memorize all of this. At least I don't have a due date…"

Chapter 81

Chem's actually useful?

Dahlia.

The guards don't even pretend not to watch us anymore.

Angie and I sit at a long table near the back of the library, books spread out like we're just two girls studying for exams. My spine stays straight. My hands move slowly. Every page I turn is deliberate, too fast looks suspicious and too slow looks fake.

Boots pass behind us. We just nod at our books as if the medical reference book I'm pretending to read is very exciting. Angie is doing the same, pretending to read aloud about molecular bonding. It must satisfy the guards because they turn with a grunt. The hum of the lights feels louder than usual. My ears track footsteps automatically now.

Suddenly a shadow pauses at the end of the aisle. I stop breathing.

Another guard stands there for a second too long, before one of the previous guards waves him away. I can feel his presence like pressure on the back of my skull as he stares for a moment to long. Angie flips a page loudly, groans under her breath like a frustrated student.

The guard moves on. Only then do I let myself exhale.

Angie shifts closer to me, lowering her voice.

"Lia," she whispers. "Look."

She tilts a book that she's noticed toward me, barely, just enough. The page is torn halfway out, the edges rough like someone ripped it in a hurry. The handwriting is uneven, ink smudged, some words carved so hard into the paper it's almost torn through. My pulse spikes. These aren't normal notes. They're not sedatives.

They control drugs.

My eyes race over the words.

VIREXAL.

Emotional regulation. Flatness. Heavy limbs. Memorie should fade after administration.

I swallow. The guards all laugh somewhere across the room. I flinch, then force my eyes back to the page. My fingers curl into the edge of the table. There are arrows. Observations. *Reactions.*

'*Reacts badly to bases. Breaks down faster when body chemistry shifts*'.

Angie's handwriting is shaking now. "That's–" She starts, then stops as footsteps pass again.

We wait. Boots. Fabric rustling. A cough. Then it's silent again.

Angie exhales sharply.

"Lia, this must be a staff book. Looks like a nurse must have dropped this." she whispers again, disbelief creeping into her voice as she continued, "Why do I always feel better after chem lab?" *Speak for yourself...*

But I feel it too. The spark. The awful, impossible realization settled in. We flip the page.

LUCIDRA.

Lights bright. Sounds warped. Paranoia. Emotional volatility.

The vents. The way air rushes differently in some halls. Unstable with oxygen. Breaks apart faster when there's lots of it.

Angie's eyes flick to the ceiling. "Is this why the vents matter?"

I guess I nodded, barely breathing. We keep going. Each page is worse than the last.

CALMORIN. Muscle failure. Shaking. The Brain is still working.

SOMNEX. Sleep control. Disorientation. Light sensitivity.

VERITOL. Truth drug. Confessions. Pain when lying.

Every symptom. Every punishment. Every reaction we've watched people have, it all lines up too cleanly to be coincidence. My hands started to shake.

"They wanted us steady and still." Angie whispers. "Not running. It's almost like they're playing with us, like it's a game."

"Yeah, and we don't know the rules." I respond.

Another guard passes. This time closer. I snap the book shut and drag a random textbook on top of it, heart slamming so hard I'm sure he can hear it. He pauses. I force myself to yawn. He moves on. The moment he's gone, Angie flips the book again, faster now, urgency overtaking fear. She turns to the front page and freezes.

She swallows. Well, more like a *loud* gulp.

"Dahlia... this is what the book actually is." She tilts it so I can see.

CONFIDENTIAL INFIRMARY REFERENCE

Institutional Behavioral Compliance Compounds

Property of Medical Wing – Unauthorized Access Prohibited.

My chest goes cold.

"There's a note in the margin," Angie whispers, eyes wide. She reads silently, then looks at me.

"They're not healing anyone. They're enforcing obedience."

My head spins. She flips to the last page. Read aloud, barely a breath.

~~"None of these compounds are approved. Their continued use violates every ethical code."~~

The typed sentence is crossed out violently. Beneath it, handwritten: *Which is exactly why they use them.*

Were we not the first ones to try this? Has someone else almost escaped but failed? Could this be hope?

For a long second, neither of us spoke. Then Angie lets out a shaky laugh. "We did it," she whispers. "We actually found something."

Something *real*. I'm never dozing off in chemistry again.

Chapter 82

Mapping the maze.

Nick.

"Wes, lap of the school," I said, hands tucked into my pockets. "Check every door, every keypad. Note any buttons that are worn out, anything that screams 'frequent use.' You're our eyes on the perimeter."

Wes groaned like I'd just sentenced him to exile.

"I still don't think, me, going alone is about bravery! I could get, ugh- ambushed by janitors or something."

I gave him the familiar glare.

"Because you're fast, loud, and they'll underestimate you. Go. And stop whining. Freddie and I will take the rest of the halls."

He stomped off, muttering under his breath, but I caught the flash of excitement in his eyes, he's exactly the one who'd love this. Freddie and I continued down the hallway, pacing slowly, eyes scanning every corner. Cameras. Motion sensors. I scribbled notes, trying not to make it obvious. Freddie mirrored me, jotting down everything he could see.

"Camera at the junction," I whispered, pointing to a black dome in the ceiling. "And another one there, facing the stairwell. Looks like it tilts."

Freddie nodded, peering at it. "That one's angled wrong. Maybe it only covers half the landing."

We ducked around a corner, careful to avoid a patrolling guard. Every footstep echoed in my skull like a drumbeat. Sweat prickled along my neck. The tension was constant, but somehow... This was fun. Tactical, secretive, like we were in one of those old spy movies, Freddie's always pretending to reenact.

We worked our way up and down the halls, marking each camera, each keypad, each suspiciously shiny button. Every corner we checked, every blind spot we noted, it felt like we were building a map of their entire system in our heads.

By the time we regrouped with Wes, I had a stack of notes that could rival a small blueprint. Wes leaned against a wall, looking smug.

"Everything's in my head, Captain Shadow. You don't need paper."

I rolled my eyes, "Sure, Wes. That's why we have backups."

Chapter 83

1...2...3...

Wes.

The girls were sprawled across the study room in the dorm, giggling over who-knows-what, when Nick and I slipped in behind Freddie, careful not to make too much noise.

"Look at you guys," Angie teased, smirking at our serious faces. "Planning another heist?"

"Something like that," I muttered, but my smirk matched hers. Freddie rolled his eyes, but his smirk didn't drop.

We all crowded around a table, throwing ideas back and forth, laughing at bad jokes, stealing pens from each other, and pretending we weren't spying on security cameras like tiny maniacs.

And then... **BLARING.**

The lockdown alarms drilled into us like a punch to the chest. Instantly, the room went from playful to chaos. I can hear Lia gasp and Angie wraps her arms around her.

I get up and sprint towards the door with Nick and Freddie right behind me.

Outside, the scene was... ridiculous. A student, eyes glazed, shuffling down the hallway in full sleepwalking mode. Guards were rushing around, panicking, trying to corral him, while the alarm shrieked in my ears.

"Code 3!" A guard called out to his co-worker. "Disable security alert, while we contain."

I looked to see that the guard was pointing towards the security room, it wasn't too far from sight from our sector door.

Nick froze beside me.

"Look at the cameras." he muttered. Sure enough, the domes had stopped rotating. Almost like someone had flipped a switch.

"Timer," I said, playing with buttons on my watch. "I'll start it. Let's see how long this lasts."

We crouched in the shadows, scribbling notes as the guards struggled to reset the alarm and redirect the student. Eleven minutes later, everything returned to normal. The cameras rotated again, guards stood around looking frustrated, and the sleepwalking kid was escorted back to his room, blissfully unaware.

Eventually when we returned to the table, the girls immediately started asking questions.

"What was it?" Angie asks.

"Well, it was a sleepwalking student, but the guards did something to the camera– they disabled them. They stopped for…" Nick peeks at my watch. "Eleven minutes."

"I still think the front door is the way out," I said, leaning back in my chair. "I think I saw a teacher punch in a code last night to close it for the day. But I couldn't fully make out the combo If we can figure out a way to create the correct order…"

Freddie raised an eyebrow, already doodling a plan in his notebook. Nick was nodding slowly, calculating. And the girls… Well, they were grinning, eyes bright with hope.

Chapter 84
We're screwed.

Angeline.

The speakers blared, jerking me awake.

"All students report to the assembly hall immediately for a quick announcement. You have three minutes. Report to the assembly hall."

My heart leapt. The pounding of boots on doors came seconds later, guards rattling our dorm. Dahlia and I scrambled out of bed, hastily pulling on clothes as we were herded down the hall. My stomach flipped with every step, still half-asleep.

What could be so important that we must rush down to assembly so quickly?

By the time we reached the hall, students were already filing into seats, whispering nervously.

The headmistress stepped onto the stage, the sudden quiet snapping the tension into place. Her voice was smooth, measured. Her eyes scanned the crowd.

"Now, as some of you may have discovered, we have implemented cameras into your dormitories. We haven't had them in the past, but due to higher results of students getting isolation detentions, we felt it was best to do so... for your... safety."

I froze mid-breath. All of us exchanged glances, Nick's jaw tightened, Wes fidgeted, and Freddie looked like he wanted to disappear.

"For those who are now finding out, they do not look like the cameras around the school grounds. We have had some concerns over the fact that we are watching you get dressed in the morning. I promise you; it is not in our interest to watch you change. And maybe consider getting changed in your provided areas, not in the middle of your studies. For those who asked in the anonymous questions box, yes, our cameras can hear you." she says out loud.

Then her eyes locked directly onto mine. I fidget under her stares. She stares at me for a solid minute, gaining attention and extra glances from students.

The color drained from all our faces. My stomach twisted. We had assumed surveillance, but hearing it laid out like this made it... real. Personal. Violating.

"Now, I will only say this once. Please stop talking about your love lives, and your sexual fantasies at the study table. That table is used for... you guessed it, studying! Do not feel alarmed; becoming reformed means embracing change and complying with acceptance, with or without consent."

I bit the inside of my cheek to keep myself from yelling. Her voice echoed the room, calculating, piercing.

"Now, breakfast is being prepared, so please everybody gets dressed and for the few people in the crowd that have caught my attention in their bright-colored pajamas, please go back and get changed, or we will have to give you a warning. Good morning, everybody, and study hard."

We shuffled out like obedient children. I glanced at the group. Everyone's expressions were grim. There was no joking, no whispers, just silent tension.

As we left, we were herded in single file, one by one, to recite the school pledge. My voice cracked the first time I tried. The others stumbled through it too, the weight of the headmistress's words heavy on all our shoulders.

I didn't speak again, just kept my head down and counted every step until we reached breakfast.

Chapter 85

When one door closes, another opens.

Dahlia.

Lunch felt like a blur, my stomach twisting as we made our way from the cafeteria. We slid onto the short grass, voices low.

"We need a new place," Angie whispered, her eyes scanning the school grounds. "Somewhere we can actually talk without being... watched."

We all silently agreed. "Let's split up again, cover more ground quicker." Wes suggested.

We went different ways after that, the boys heading off to their own corners while Angie and I slipped back toward the library. Two guards appeared just as we reached the hallway, their boots clicking behind us like a countdown.

We quickened our pace while keeping our heads down. Inside the library, we claimed a corner and grabbed random books, pretending to study while our hearts raced.

And then, like magic, the guards were called off. They turned and walked away, leaving us alone. Relief flooded through me, and I exhaled sharply.

"Finally," I muttered.

I started walking along next to the shelf, and then- bam. My foot caught on something hidden beneath the carpet.

"What was that?" Angie murmured, crouching to inspect it.

Tracks. Faint, subtle, pressed into the fibers of the carpet, deliberately concealed. My pulse quickened. We traced them carefully, following the path until it ended at a bookshelf. I pressed my hand against the edge, nudging it. Slowly, it slid across, revealing a dark, narrow space behind it, welcoming us with an opening.

Angie's eyes widened. "This... this is perfect."

Chapter 86

Phase 2?

Wes.

The girls barreled into our dorm, practically dragging us behind them.

"You have to come! Now!" Lia was already halfway to the door, Angie bouncing like she'd had too much caffeine.

"What's going on?" Freddie stammered, tripping over his own feet as he tried to keep up.

"You'll see," Angie said, practically squealing, "But it's amazing. You're gonna love it!"

We followed them down the hall, hearts hammering. By the time we reached the library, Dahlia was pressing against a bookshelf. With a shove, it slid aside, revealing a narrow passage.

"Ta-da!" Angie said, arms out like she'd just unveiled a theme park ride. "Welcome to your secret planning room. We've checked everything! There's nothing in this room. Cameras don't see this. Guards don't see this. Basically... it's perfect."

"Why would the school allow this?" Nick questioned.

"They say they're funded by our filthy rich families, right? I guess in the works of constructing this place when they didn't have much bread, they forgot they built this. Left it alone when the money started coming in to design it." Dahlia expressed.

I stepped in, and my chest tightened. Hidden and quiet. Ours. It felt unreal.

Freddie immediately crouched into a corner, pulling out Angie's journal. His pencil hovered like a nervous bird.

"Uh... okay... so front door... sleepwalking... cams?" His words tumbled out in a jumble.

Nick leaned over, raising an eyebrow. "Slow down, man. One thing at a time."

"Yeah, but if I don't write it all down-" Freddie began, eyes wide, scribbling notes like a madman. Lines, arrows, question marks everywhere.

"Okay," I said, stepping up. "Front door is my domain. I've studied it. Everything that happens there goes through me. If we're leaving through the front, I'm the guide. Got it?"

"Got it," Nick said, nodding.

"Got it," Dahlia said, calm but focused.

"Got it!" Angie added, bouncing on the balls of her feet. "Also, if we get stuck, I have ideas. And jokes. Lots of jokes. Humor as a backup plan! You know- the guards get confused by humor."

Nick groaned. "Only you would think of comedy in a hostage escape scenario."

"Exactly," Angie said proudly. "You never know when a punchline could save your life."

Freddie raised a hand. "Um... do we all... walk together? Or... split up? And what if the cams rotate back while Wes-" He cut himself off, eyes darting to me.

"I said everything for the front door goes through me," I snapped, holding up a hand. "We stick together, follow signals, and no one improvises outside their role."

"Signals?" Angie asked. "What is this, the military?"

"Kinda." Freddie mocked.

We argued, suggested, crossed things out in notebooks, whispered, laughed, and occasionally groaned in frustration. Plans clashed. Ideas overlapped. Someone suggested distracting the guards with a fire alarm, someone else wanted to make a rope ladder out of bed sheets.

I rubbed my temples, trying to sort it all out.

"Okay, listen, sleepwalking is a Freddie thing. I handle cams. Exit the front door. Period. Everything else is... negotiable. We'll refine it as we go."

Freddie scribbled furiously, occasionally muttering, "Oh god, okay... okay..."

Angie leaned forward in her chair. "So, we're thinking: cams down... Freddie sleepwalks... Wes guides... doors unlocked? And then we're free!"

"Maybe not entirely free," I said, sighing, but I couldn't hide the grin tugging at my lips. "Mostly free. But guys, we only have eleven minutes, just like that boy that we saw. So, once the cameras are down because of Freddie, we use those eleven minutes to dodge the guards, take them all out and get to floor one, escape through the front door and then we're out."

I could tell the atmosphere had shifted, we weren't scared anymore. I knew that no matter what, these guys would have my back, and that meant more to me than any freedom we *did* or *didn't* gain.

Dahlia smiled at me, eyes shining. "Messy is okay. As long as we stick together."

Chapter 87

Doomsday is close at hand.

Nick.

It's been weeks and assemblies always feel like funerals here.

We sit in neat rows, backs straight, eyes forward, pretending this is normal. Pretending the words don't slide under our skin.

The headmistress stands at the podium, hands folded, always wearing the most calculated bland color anyone can think of, smiling like she's proud of us. *Fucking bitch.*

"In the coming days," she says smoothly, "your final evaluations will be completed. You should all feel very proud. You are on the verge of becoming fully reformed."

The word lands wrong. Fully. My jaw tightens.

"This institution exists to prepare you for a successful reintegration," she continues. "Tomorrow marks the beginning of that transition. In two days, your final reform test will be complete."

Two days in counting.

I glance sideways without moving my head. Freddie is two rows over, rocking slightly on his heels. Angie's posture is falsely perfect. Dahlia doesn't blink once.

We don't look at each other. We don't need to.

We already know.

Back in the dorm, I get this weird somber feeling. I've lived here for almost a whole year; I've made friends I never thought I could have. Met the girl that makes me feel like the man I've always wanted to be. It all happened in this sector. This place.

Oh, what the fuck am I saying? I can't wait to get the fuck out of here and back to sanity.

We're ready. As ready as we'll ever be. That's when Angie goes pale.

"My diary," she says quietly.

Freddie freezes. "What about it, Princess?"

"It's gone."

The word drops like a stone.

"Gone how?" Wes asks immediately.

"I checked everywhere," Angie says, voice tight. "Under my bed. Inside the mattress. It's not there."

Fuck.

That diary isn't just writing– it's codes, patterns, notes we pieced together over the past two months. Times. Rotations. Blind spots. It's our map.

I run a hand down my face. "Did anyone else know where it was?"

Angie shakes her head. "Only us."

Silence presses in.

Dahlia inhales slowly. "We don't have time to panic. Final reform is only a day away. We're escaping tomorrow."

She's right. I hate that she's right.

"If they have it," Wes says grimly, "they've probably had it for a while."

"And they haven't stopped us," Freddie adds. "Yet."

No one argues.

Because what's the alternative? Stay and let them finish whatever they started? We don't say it out loud, but I see it in all of them, the same thought burning behind their eyes. We leave tomorrow. Or we never leave at all.

Later, we're standing in front of the performance board. It hums faintly, lights shifting like it's alive.

Freddie squints up at it.

"Looks like the Mood Ring of Doom just upgraded me to yellow again. Fantastic."

Dahlia snorts quietly. "Don't tempt the Shiny Eye. I saw it blink at you."

Freddie points at it. "I blink back. Establish dominance."

Knucklehead.

Chapter 88

My best friend.

Dahlia.

We're supposed to be sleeping. No talking. No lights. Not anything.

Angie flips onto her side anyway and whispers, "If we die tomorrow, I just want you to know-"

I roll over instantly. "You are not starting like that."

"I wasn't done."

"Finish it in a way that doesn't curse us."

She pauses. "If we die tomorrow... you still owe me five push-ups from that bet."

I snort into my pillow. "Absolutely not. That bet was unfair."

"You said you could beat me."

"I said I might."

She grinned in the dark. "Coward."

We go quiet, both of us listening. Footsteps? A door? Nothing. Just the hum of the building pretending it's asleep.

Angie sits up suddenly. "Okay. Serious question."

I groaned. "I don't like how you said that."

"If we make it out," she says, "what's the first stupid thing you're doing?"

I don't even think. "Running. Just to prove I can. Probably tripping. You?"

She smiles, even though I can't see it. "Standing still. Just to see if anyone yells at me."

A laugh slips out of me before I can stop it- the kind you have to bite back. She grabs a pillow and launches it straight at my forehead.

"Ow."

"That's for every time you said it'll be fine when it very clearly was not."

I rubbed my forehead. "I stand by that."

We're sitting cross-legged on our beds now, facing each other like we used to, back when everything still felt unreal.

"Okay," I say, holding up my hands. "Final ranking."

"Of what?"

"Us. Survival skills."

She raises an eyebrow. "I'm winning."

"No. I'm smarter."

"You panic."

"I panic efficiently."

She laughs, then sobers. "You're the brave one."

I scoff. "I'm terrified."

"Yeah," she says softly. "But you do things anyway."

I look away, heat creeping up my neck. "Don't get weird."

She smiles. "Too late."

I reached under my pillow and pulled out a marker- half dry, that Nick gave me.

She gasps. "Oh my god. No."

I grab her wrist before she can escape. "I'm not writing anything bad."

"I don't trust you."

"You literally trust me with your life."

"That's different."

I drew a tiny star on the inside of her wrist. Crooked. Uneven.

"There," I whisper. "So, if we get separated, you know you're not alone."

She blinks fast. "You're so annoying."

I grin. "You love me."

She snatches the marker and draws a lopsided heart on my wrist. "Matching. Because I'm sentimental and you hate it."

I look down at it, then laugh quietly. "I hate you."

After a moment, she whispers, "Hey."

"Yeah?"

"No matter what happens tomorrow... I'd do all this again. If it means I still get to be your best friend."

My throat tightens. "Okay. That's it. I'm punching you in the morning for emotional damage. Bold of you to assume you're my best friend," I giggle.

She scoffs. "What- you prefer Alyssa over me?"

"Obviously," I say. "I've always pictured a redhead for my best friend."

We both broke, laughing so hard I have to shove my pillow into my face.

"You're insufferable," she wheezes.

But as I lie back down, staring at the dark ceiling, wrist still warm where she drew that stupid little heart, I think, if this is the last night, at least I'm not alone, at least I'm with my best friend.

Chapter 89

Ready, set, go.

Dahlia

Lunch felt like a bubble of calm chaos. I had a tray stacked with real food, green status perks for hard studying and Angie carefully spooned her soup, measured perfectly by her therapist.

"Where is Wes?" Nick asked, looking around.

"Probably late again. Oh, look here he is!" Freddie pointed out.

Wes slid into the seat across from us, rubbing the back of his neck. "Hey guys– sorry, got held back."

"Again?" I asked. This morning, he said the same thing.

"Yeah... something's off today," he replied, looking around.

"Tell me about it," Angie said, eyes narrowing slightly. "The nurses have been eyeing me all morning. I swear they're waiting for me to slip up."

Freddie leaned back, hands empty. Ever since the diary went missing, we have just had to memorize the times. "Okay... so, um... we just say it out loud? Everything?"

"Exactly," I said, nodding. "We say the plan out loud, clearly, confidently. Everyone needs to be on the same page."

"What about the cameras?" Wes asks, "They can hear us?"

"No matter what, we're escaping tonight. Final reform is in a couple hours after we sleep. There's no stopping that. So, we're going to talk about it. Now. Especially since we don't have it in writing anymore." Angie announced.

"Just keep our voices down." I add.

"Right," Nick said, leaning forward. "The front door is the exit. Wes handles cams and timing. Freddie sleepwalks; I cover windows and take care of any guards in our way. Angie... distractions."

"I bounce, joke, lighten the tension," Angie confirmed, tapping her spoon against her tray. "If anyone trips, makes noise, panics? I cover. Easy."

"Signals," I added. "Coughs, nudges, small sounds. Everyone uses them. No improvising outside your role."

"Dahlia stays behind me to keep lookout." Nick announced.

Freddie took a deep breath. "Okay... cam's down... front door... signals... sleepwalking... distractions..."

"Yes, exactly," Nick said. "And confidence. Stick to your part. No hesitation."

Wes nodded. "The front door is my lead. Follow my timing. Everyone else? Step in at your cues. We cannot mess this up. One chance is all we get."

"Got it." Angie said, bouncing lightly.

"Yep." I said, glancing at Freddie, who finally exhaled and nodded.

"We're ready." Nick said, voice low but steady.

Chapter 90

Now or never.

Freddie.

I don't think I've ever been this awake in my entire life.

I'm lying on my back, staring at the ceiling like I'm waiting for my heart to punch its way out of my ribs. Every nurse check feels louder than the last. Boots. Flashlight. Pause. Sector door checked.

I breathe slowly. Slower than I want to. Slower than feels natural. I let my body go heavy, limp, like I've fallen asleep instead of rehearsing the next ten seconds of my life over and over again.

Across the room, Nick doesn't move.

He's on his back too, one arm dangling off the bed like he doesn't care if it gets chopped off. But I know better. I know that stillness. It's coiled. Controlled. Ready.

Wes lets out a soft, fake snore from the other side of the room. Subtle. Professional.

Then...

It's barely a sound. Just a whisper of vibration. But my blood lights up. 2:10AM.

Showtime.

I slide out of bed, slow and loose, letting my feet drag like I don't know where I am. I let my shoulders slump, head tilted, mouth slightly open. I've practiced this. In the mirror. In my head. Every night since we decided.

Sleepwalking Freddie. How hard could it be?

I shuffle toward the door, bump my shoulder against the wall on purpose. Make it believable. Make it messy.

The second my hand wrapped around the handle, I feel it, a pressure change. Like the building noticed me.

The sector door opens. And then red lights flood the hallway.

Alarms scream to life, sharp and ugly, tearing through the quiet like claws. Cameras swivel. I hear shouting real shouting, boots slamming into the floor from the security room down the hall.

"Hey!" a guard yells. "We've got movement!"

Perfect.

I sway forward, arms limp, eyes unfocused, like I've got no idea the world is ending around me. Two guards burst out, already reaching for their radios.

"Student out of dorm," one snaps. "Possible episode."

Behind me, somewhere I know the others are moving. I don't look back. I don't break character. I stumble another step into the hall, heart pounding so hard it feels like it's shaking my bones. This is it. This is the first crack. And I swear, for just a second, I can almost hear my mom's voice in my head, light, warm, proud.

"*Good hair, Freddie*", she used to say. Good timing too. Then I fall forward, right on cue.

Chapter 91

Just our luck.

Wes.

The alarm is still screaming when the cameras die. Every red light in the hallway cuts out at once, like someone yanked the spine out of the system. The hum disappears. The swivel stops. Silence drops so fast it makes my ears ring.

I freeze mid-step. Nick's head snaps up at the exact same time mine does. Our eyes intertwine.

"...What?" he mouths.

"That wasn't..." I whisper. "That wasn't me."

He swears under his breath. "How? You didn't hack the cams and alarms?"

"No!" My fingers are already twitching toward my watch out of pure reflex. "Who the hell just did that?"

For half a second, panic claws up my throat. This wasn't in the plan. Nothing extra is ever good here. Extra means eyes. Extra means traps. Then Nick makes a decision.

"Doesn't matter," he says, low and sharp. "We go. Now."

He's already moving before the words are done, slipping into the shadows toward the girls' side. I peel off the other way. The security office is just ahead, door cracked; lights dim. I edged closer, heart hammering, every sense stretched thin. Through the gap, I see the main monitor bank. Blank. Except for one small timer bar at the bottom of the screen. I squint. Eleven minutes. Exactly.

"Eleven minutes starts now." I mutter.

The number we planned. The number we timed. The number we rehearsed until it lived in my bones. This isn't a coincidence. I don't like that. But I don't have time to think about it. I hit the timer on my watch. Beep. Zeroed.

"Okay," I whisper to no one. "Plan's live."

I move fast now, low and quiet, ducking behind the service wall where the shadows bend weird and the sound carries wrong.

Behind me the girls quickly take cover in my shadow, just as we see Freddie getting taken away by the only three guards in sight, suddenly him and Nick throw quick jabs, taking them all out.

"Clear." Nick signals, "Come on."

"Told you my sleepwalking would change lives," Freddie whispers.

"Shut up," I hissed, but I'm smiling too. "So, the guards?"

"Their taking a nap." he says.

Chapter 92

The Climax is Coming...

Nick.

I don't knock. I tap once, sharp and deliberate and step back into the shadow of the wall. The door opens immediately. No hesitation. Angie first, Dahlia right behind her. Their eyes flick to me, then down the hall.

"Now," I murmur.

They move without a sound. I fall in behind them and slide a knife from the cafeteria into the back of my jeans, the cool weight of it grounding. I don't look at Dahlia. If I do, I'll slow down. I can feel her there anyway, close, steady, real. We move as one unit, which still surprises me. No arguing. No whispering questions. Just quiet feet and controlled breaths as we take the stairs two at a time.

Down one flight. Then another. Floor 1.

The air changes down here. Colder. Cleaner. Like the building is holding its breath. Freddie is already at the front doors when we reach him, crouched by the keypad, Wes hovering close, eyes darting.

"Okay, go. Guards should be on the other side of the school right now, according to our schedule." Angie whispered.

"Tell me you've got it." Freddie whispers.

Wes swallows. "I... I don't."

I step forward, heart hammering, and see it. The keypad is dead. The screen cracked. Wires exposed like nerves.

"You've got to be kidding me." I mutter.

Angie presses her hands to her hips, jaw tight. "The diary said there was a code."

"Yeah," Wes says, voice strained. "There was."

I grab the handle and pull. Nothing. Locked. Solid. My gaze drops to the keyhole.

"...It's keyed." I say.

Silence hits hard. Dahlia exhales slowly beside me. I can feel it more than I hear it. "So, what now?"

I straighten, fingers brushing the knife at my back.

"Now," I say quietly, "we improvise."

Somewhere above us, something shifts. A distant thud. A sound that doesn't belong. The clock is still ticking. And the door is still closed.

Chapter 93

Tick-Tock.

Wes.

The door doesn't budge.

Nick's already tried to break it three times with his body weight, Freddie's bouncing on his heels like motion alone might solve it, and Dahlia's staring at the lock with that quiet intensity she gets when she's forcing herself not to panic.

My watch vibrates softly. Seven minutes left.

I swallow and force myself to speak. "Wait. The photos."

Everyone looks at me.

"The ones on Dahlia's door," I say quickly. "From the basement. The threatening ones."

Dahlia stiffens beside me.

"In the background," I continued, words tumbling now.

"The-There were keys. Hanging on a hook. Old-school keys. I remember because I thought it was weird they'd leave something like that in frame."

Freddie's eyes widened. "You're saying they wanted us to see them?"

"Or they didn't care if we did." Nick mutters.

Both options sucked. Angie glances down the hall, then back at us.

"If there are keys anywhere, they'd be down there."

No one argues. Desperation beats logic every time. We move. Fast, quiet, cutting left through the nurses' office, which luckily didn't require a code.

Nope, just the front door. How convenient.

The door is still slightly ajar, like Dahlia said it was that day. That alone makes my skin crawl.

We descend the stairs.

The basement smells wrong, cleaner and dust, metal and paper. Almost dull bulbs overhead, flickering just enough to mess with my depth perception.

Dahlia leads without hesitation, like her body remembers the path even if she doesn't want it to. I hate that for her. The file room comes into view.

And there they are.

Our files.

Neatly laid out on the table.

Our names are facing up. Pages aligned. Corners squared. Like someone wanted us to look. Like a display.

Freddie steps closer. "What the hell..."

"Don't touch anything." Nick snaps, low and sharp.

Angie drifts to the side, eyes scanning the room. There are two curtains, thin, industrial, pretending to divide space where none should exist.

"I'm gonna check behind this." she whispers, already reaching.

"Angie," I start.

She pulls the curtain back.

What the fuck?

Bodies. Not slumped. Not hidden. Positioned.

I don't know how many. Two. Three. My brain refuses to count properly. They're dressed in matching grey sets, sitting up in capsules. The exact same as the ones we woke up in, that day. They're pale and still. Faces slack, eyes half-open like they were surprised. That's when I really look at them. They're... They're students! Someone gasps. Might be Dahlia. Maybe it might be me. My stomach drops through the floor.

"Oh my god, Dahlia, it's Grace..." Angie whispers.

We turn to see a small, delicate girl plugged, hanging upright, the life almost drained out of her eyes. Next to her, it read her name and a loading battery bar, like it was indicating how much left there was of something to be completed.

The timer on my watch keeps ticking. Five minutes. Whatever this school or place is, whatever it's been doing to its students. I knew that we were next.

Dahlia looks over.

"Oh gosh, that girl you pointed out on the board! It said she was 'successfully reformed.' I don't understand?"

"But that was near the start of the year.." Angie gasped.

"Well, then I guess it takes a long time to become successfully reformed." Freddie said, whilst looking at all the other students in capsules.

Seriously? This is what it looks like to be 'successfully reformed'?

Chapter 94

Answers that don't answer my questions.

Nick.

I don't want to look. That's the first thought that hits me as we stand there, the basement humming softly like it's alive and pretending it isn't surrounded by the dead or almost dead anyway. The bodies are wrong in a way I can't put language to, arranged and intentional. Like props.

Freddie swallows hard. "Okay," he mutters, trying and failing to sound normal. "I officially hate this field trip."

I force myself closer to our files. The smell of paper and antiseptic mixes with something coppery underneath, and my stomach rolls. Wes flips through his first, jaw tightening more with every page. Angie hesitates, then opens hers.

Her eyes scan fast at first... then stop.

She goes very still.

"What?" Freddie says immediately. "What is it?"

Angie blinks once. Twice. Then lets out a shaky breath that sounds almost like a laugh.

"I knew it. I knew there was something missing."

She turns the page toward us. Royal lineage. Diplomatic immunity clauses. Security protocols. Titles I don't recognize but somehow understand anyway.

"…I'm a princess," she says faintly. "Like. Actually."

There's a beat of silence.

Then Freddie squints at her. "Wait, so this whole time I've been calling you Princess…"

Angie looks at him dull.

"I was accidentally being respectful to the crown?" he finishes.

She snorts despite herself. "You bowed exactly zero times."

"Wow," he says, shaking his head. "I've never been this right and this rude at the same time."

That earns a weak laugh from Wes. Even Dahlia's lips twitch.

I don't open mine. I can't.

The file with my name on it might as well be a loaded weapon. I stare at it like it might go off if I touch it. My chest feels tight, like I already know what it says or worse, like it'll tell me something I don't remember but should.

Dahlia notices. She always does.

"Nick," she says quietly, not pushing, not demanding. "Do you want me to?" rubbing my back softly.

I meet her eyes. There's no pity there. No curiosity. Just… steadiness. I nodded once.

She pulls my file toward her and opens it. I watch her face change as she reads. Just slightly. A crease between her brows. A pause.

"What?" I say, sharper than I mean to.

She hesitates, then reads aloud. "Under 'placement justification'... it says the referral didn't come from your father."

My pulse spikes.

"It says," she continues carefully, "'Guardianship authority exercised by closest surviving relative.'"

I already know. I don't know how, but I do.

Dahlia swallows. "Nick... it was your uncle."

Raged, I cross the room to retrieve my file, my gaze softens however when I realize she's still holding it. Gently taking it from her, I resume my heated mood, my eyes piercing to see exactly what it says.

This is how my uncle 'takes care' of it? How could he ever think that sending me to this torture camp would fix what I did to my father.

Chapter 95

It's the final countdown.

Angeline.

Everything blurs after that. The files, bodies. Secrets that feel too big to carry and too sharp to drop. Every second ticks louder in my head, like the building itself is counting us down.

"We need to go," I say, too many times, to no one in particular. "We need to go!"

Nick's jaw is locked. Dahlia's pale but standing. Freddie keeps glancing between us and the stairs like he's daring them to disappear if he looks hard enough.

Then...

"Guys!" Wes calls.

His voice echoes from the hallway outside the file room, causing us all to jump.

I whip my head up. "Wes?"

"There's," he says, then louder, urgent, "There's another door!"

"What?" Nick snaps. "Wes, now is not,"

"Shh! We don't have time for this!" Freddie adds, panic cracking through his usual tone.

But Wes doesn't answer. He's already farther down the hall, peering into somewhere we shouldn't be.

"Wes!" I shouted, anger flaring hot and fast. "You'll get us caught! Get back here!"

Too late. The sound comes first. Boots. Too many. Too close.

"MOVE!" Nick yells.

Everything explodes into motion.

Alarms scream back to life. Red lights strobe against concrete walls. Guards pour into the hallway like a flood, shouting, weapons raised.

We run.

I grab Dahlia's hand without thinking, dragging her with me, heart hammering so hard it hurts. Freddie's right behind us. Nick is swearing, loud and furious.

And then...

A sharp crack splits the air. Not a warning shot. Not a miss. Wes jerks forward.

For half a second, my brain refuses to understand what I'm seeing. Like if I don't name it, it won't be real. Then Wes hits the ground. Hard. Blood blooms fast against the floor, impossibly red against the grey.

"No," I gasp. "No, no, no!"

"WES!" Freddie screams.

Wes is on the ground, body twitching as his hand reaches up to his stomach. His breathing slows and gargled noises come out.

Nick skids to a stop, eyes wild. Dahlia shivers, her grip crushing my fingers.

The guards keep shouting. The alarms keep blaring.

But all I can hear is the ringing in my ears and the horrible, sickening certainty settling in my chest. This wasn't supposed to happen. We were supposed to get out. And Wes... Wes was just standing there, just trying to help, and–

"GO!" Nick roars, grabbing Freddie and yanking him back as more guards close in. "ANGIE, GO!"

Nicks hands hover over Wes's body, searching for the entry wound.

But theres not just one. Two deep red pools of blood are on his clothes.

One on his thigh, one on his stomach.

I gasp and slam my hand over my mouth. My feet won't move.

I'm staring at Wes's body on the floor, at the way his chest isn't rising the way it should, at the blood pooling like it doesn't care who he is or what he meant to us. His eyes staring empty into Nicks. I scream his name as Freddie drags me and Dahlia away, Nick in the far distance attempting to pick up Wes's limp weight or fight off the guards. I don't even know. I do know that everything has been shattered.

Chapter 96

Mission: Failed.

Freddie.

Everything turns into noise.

Real noise. Not the controlled kind they like. Not alarms and buzzers and polite threats. This is chaos, boots pounding, voices overlapping, shots cracking so loud my ears ring.

I see Nick drop to his knees beside Wes. I see his hands shaking as he tries to lift him.

I shove the girls further up the stairs, and when they're not looking, I turn and run back.

"Come on," Nick snarls, like anger alone might fix this. "Come on, Wes,"

Wes doesn't move. He's too heavy in Nick's arms. Dead weight. Limp in the worst way. Something in my chest snaps.

"Nick!" I grab him under his arms and haul back with everything I've got. "It's no use! We've gotta go!"

He fights me. For a second, I think he's going to punch me. His face is wrecked, grief and fury tangled so tight I barely recognize him.

"They shot him," he says, like he needs me to confirm it. "They shot him."

"I know," I choke out. "I know but if we stay, we're next. They're coming for us and they're only around the corner of the hall!"

Another shot cracks somewhere close.

That's what does it.

Nick stumbles as I drag him, then finally, finally he moves. We cling to each other just long enough to get our feet under us, like if we let go, we'll both collapse.

"Where are the girls?" Nick shouts.

"There upstairs! There already upstairs!" I yell back.

As we sprint up the steps, Angie is frantically looking down the steps while pulling Dahlia up.

"GO!" I yell.

Through an opening, up the stairs. Two at a time. My lungs burn. My legs feel like rubber. I don't remember breathing, I just remember moving. For half a second, hope flares. Then we hit back on the first floor. Guards. Two of them. Weapons raised. Faces blank.

"No," I gasp.

"Down!" someone yells.

Hands slam into my chest. I hit the floor hard, air exploding out of me. Someone's knee pins my back. Cold metal snaps around my wrists. Nick is beside me, fighting, swearing, but there are too many of them. The last thing I see before everything goes dark is Angie screaming my name and Dahlia.

I wake up choking on silence.

Pure, thick silence. The kind that presses in on your skull.

My wrists ache. I looked down, cuffed. Metal biting into my skin.

"Nick?" I choke out.

"I'm here."

He's sitting across from me, also cuffed, jaw clenched so hard it looks like it might crack. Guards lined the walls. Four of them. Maybe more. All watching. The room is white. No corners. No windows. Just mirrors. Double-sided. But in the one section where nick is sitting, the wall is lined with holes from his fist.

"Where the hell are we?" I demand voice shaking despite my best effort. "Where did you take us?"

"Where are they?" Nick snaps. "Where's Dahlia? Angie?"

No one answers. My stomach twists.

Wes. The memory hits me all over again, him going down, the blood, the sound.

"They shot Wes." I whisper, my throat tightening like saying it might make it untrue.

Nick's eyes flick to me, raw and hollow.

I swallow hard, staring at our reflections trapped in the glass. We ran. We didn't save him. The people we care about are somewhere we can't reach. The silence doesn't break. It just waits.

Chapter 97

5 dead, 1 stopped breathing.

Dahlia.

White.

Not light, white. Blinding, endless, pressing in from every direction like it's trying to scrub my brain clean. My eyes burn the second I open them and my body jerks upright on instinct, panic snapping through me before I even remember why.

The room spins. A thin mattress. Metal frame. I'm breathing too fast.

"Angie?" My voice comes out broken, already shaking. My hands clutch the sheet like it can anchor me to something real.

She's there. Beside me. Awake, but not really staring at the wall, face drained of color, like she's been left behind somewhere else. Relief hits me so hard it almost hurts.

Then the memory crashes in.

Running. The shouting. The bang, so loud it split the night apart.

"Where are the boys?" I blurt, sitting up fully now, heart slamming against my ribs. "Nick? Freddie? Wes..."

The word Wes feels wrong in my mouth, like I've already lost the right to say it.

My ears started ringing.

We were being shot at.

The image flashes so vividly it makes my stomach lurch, bright sparks, the crack of gunfire echoing off walls, the way my legs stopped feeling like they belonged to me. I remember ducking, hands over my head, convinced the next sound would be the last thing I ever heard. Convinced I was about to die right there on the floor. I remember Nick's voice crashing through the gunshots, trying to guide us towards safety.

"Angie," I whisper, dread curling tight in my chest. "Wes got shot."

Her head turns slowly, like it takes effort. Her eyes finally meet mine and they're glassy, terrified, wrecked.

"Where did he get shot, Angie?" I ask quickly, desperately. If I know where, maybe I can survive it. "His arm? His leg? Where?"

"I don't know," she says, shaking her head, breath coming in short, uneven pulls. "I can't remember... I just," Her voice breaks apart. "I just saw him go down and..."

The memory grabs me too.

Wes running ahead of us.

Someone shouting.

Another deafening bang.

"Oh my god," Angie chokes. Her hand flies to her mouth like she's about to be sick. "His scream..."

My heart stutters.

"He screamed, Dahlia," she says, voice barely there. "He screamed."

Something inside me drops straight through the floor.

If he screamed, if it hurt enough for that, then...

No.

I can't finish the thought. I should have stopped. My thoughts closed me in. I wanted to stop and drag him along, but Nick yelled at us to keep going, because he went back for him.

"Dahlia! GO! I got him! RUN!" Nick yelled.

I looked at him for what I thought would be the last time, while he turned to run back to Wes's limp body.

My hands go numb. The room feels like it's closing in, white walls pressing tighter until I can barely breathe. The sound of gunfire keeps replaying in my head, again, each crack louder than the last. I remember thinking, this is it. I remember being so sure we weren't getting out.

"Where are they?" I whisper, my voice collapsing in on itself. "Why aren't they here? Why is it just us?"

Angie doesn't answer. She stares straight ahead, like if she looks at me, she'll completely fall apart.

The silence is unbearable.

No Wes. No Nick. No Freddie. Just a locked white room and the echo of gunshots still rattling through my skull. And somewhere, I can't see... Wes is bleeding. Or unconscious. Or worse.

Chapter 98

We lost.

Nick.

My wrists have become weak. Being locked in this tight, confined room, there's no way to tell how long we've been here for in these cuffs.

I already tried threatening. The wall got the most of it when no one even flinched or blinked at me.

My brain is already replaying it.

The gunshots.

Real ones. Sharp, violent cracks that echoed down the corridor. Bullets flying so close I felt the air move past my face. The smell of smoke. My legs were shaking so badly I thought they'd give out.

Wes running ahead of us.

Then...

"He went down," Freddie says quietly, like saying it louder might make it true forever. His voice shakes. "Nick... he just, he dropped."

My throat tightens so hard it hurts.

"I ran straight back to him," I say, the words coming out rough, angry. "I didn't even think. I just..." I shake my head. I can still see it. Bullets sparking off the wall. The way my heart was trying to punch its way out of my chest. "I was right there."

Freddie looks at me. "Nick,"

"He yelled at me," I snapped, fury flaring hot and sudden. "He screamed at me to go. Told me to get the girls out." My jaw clenches so hard it aches. "I should've dragged him. I should've stayed."

Another shot rings in my memory and my stomach twists. I remember freezing. I remember choosing. I see it so clearly it hurts. Wes on the floor. Blood. Panic. His face twisted in pain. I swallow hard.

"I left him."

The door slams open before either of us can speak again. Rough hands haul us up. Freddie struggles, swears, but it's useless. We're dragged through identical white halls, everything blurring together.

Another door, thrown open. The girls. Angie shoots to her feet. Dahlia turns, eyes red and hollow, and when she sees me her face crumples with something like relief and devastation all at once.

I can't stand to see her make that face.

Before I can say a word, a nurse steps in behind us, tablet, calm voice, professional face.

"Please remain seated," she says. "You're safe now."

Angie laughs, a broken, hysterical sound. "Safe?" she snaps. "You shot at us!"

"You let him die," Dahlia says, voice shaking violently. "You killed Wes. He screamed... do you understand that? He screamed for his life!"

The nurse stiffens. "I'm sorry for your distress, but–"

"Distress?" Freddie yells. "You murdered our friend! A student!"

The nurse opens her mouth again, when suddenly a suited figure walks in. Tie strictly done, briefcase in hand.

That face. I know I've seen that face before.

The memory blurs as my eyes regain focus on his features.

"President Whitmore?" I mumble. The room falls dead silent. He looks around at us like we're inconveniences. Like we're stains on the floor.

"Really," he says coolly, straightening his jacket. "All this noise? You'd think something tragic had happened."

My blood boils.

"You? You're behind this!" Angie fires, "You knew that this fucked up place was holding kids? Torturing them, practically indoctrinating us!"

"You had our best friend killed, your own son!" I spit. "How do you expect us to listen to a single word you say after that?"

Freddie nods furiously. "You hunted us like animals."

President Whitmore sighs, long and exaggerated, like a bored parent. "Honestly, the dramatics are exhausting.

Sacrifices are necessary. If you can't understand that, hardly my problem."

Dahlia attempts to step forward, hands shaking. "He was a person. He trusted you."

President Whitmore rubs his temples. "Fine," he says flatly. "If this is truly beyond your emotional capacity to process... I suppose we'll dispense with the illusion."

He steps aside, gesturing for someone. The door opens again. A tall figure stepping beside the president.

No. No it can't be...

Wesley.

He's... he's breathing. Alive. Walking. But... But that means.

For a second, I think I'm hallucinating. My heart stops, then drops straight through my body. Angie gasps. Dahlia staggers back like she's been hit.

Freddie whispers, "No..."

Wes looks the same. Composed. His eyes meet mine and there's nothing familiar in them.

Dahlia calls out, her voice wobbling. "But we saw your blood, Wes! We watched you go down!"

"A simple simulation wound. I needed it to look real," he says evenly.

President Whitmore smiles, patting his son on the back.

The shock curdles instantly into rage, hot and violent and unbearable.

Because Wes wasn't taken from us.

He chose to leave us behind.

Chapter 99

Everything has changed.

Wes.

The silence in the room is thick. Thick enough to choke on. I let it stretch for a moment, letting them feel the weight of the betrayal before I even speak. Their faces... pale, wide-eyed, hearts broken, mouths opening and closing like they're trying to yell some fucked up remark at me but can't.

"I suppose I owe you the truth," I begin, voice steady even as my stomach twists with what's coming next. "Everything that has happened here... every moment... I knew. From the start."

They don't move. They're frozen. I can almost hear the gears grinding in their minds.

"I knew who you were. Who your family were. What you'd done or thought you'd done. That's why you were here. Why you were... sent." I let the word hang in the air. "Your parents? They received cards. Introductions. Explanations of the school. A little welcome package, if you will. I sent them myself. The excitement they had when they read their

395

naughty kids would become the perfect image. little drug addict Freddie. Naughty Nick has alotttt of money to repay a certain someone... Dahlia, daddy wasn't very happy when you tried to run away. Angie? Who wouldn't want to wear a shiny crown on her head. maybe its because you're not thin enough."

"HEY-" Freddie can only start to defend weak little Angie when a guard jams the gun to his head, reminding him of how quickly someone's life can be taken.

Nick's hands clench into fists.

"My mission... it started the first day you saw me. I was late to assembly because; well, because that was when I got my memories back. When the staff explained what I was supposed to do."

I pause. Let the memory cut through.

"My punishment? Fake."

"You mean... your scars?" Nick's voice is sharp, hurtful, full of disbelief.

My father steps into view behind me, smiling that smug smile like he's done all the hard work for me. "Ah," he says casually, "that was my personal touch. From when he was a kid."

I groaned, loud enough to echo. "Yes, Dad, thanks for that."

"So, what? Your neck injury in town was fake too?" Freddie roared.

"Oh, no. That was quite real, poor Wesley here, his brain activity was detecting rises in emotional responses to you whilst being monitored. Emotions compromise plans. I can't have that. So, son had to be reconstructed." My dad explained, sounding as malicious as ever.

"I never got punished. I never got therapy. Well, I did once but that was more of a hangout session for me. The rest? All fake. I simply hid out with the headmistress, reporting about you *idiots*. Only when you got close do you realize some flowers are fake."

I see their faces, the confusion, the shock, the hurt. It fuels me. Not because I enjoy it but because it's time they know.

"You want specifics?" I continued. "I knew the entry code to the front door this whole time, hence why the nurses gave me a drug, to make me extremely tired... so I could pretend to be sleepwalking. Angie had been doing extremely well in her progress, so the staff decided to give her another test. I took the diary. I planted the photos on Dahlia's door. The ones with the key in the background; I took those, and that video of Angie... throwing up? I got it from Alyssa. Handed it straight to the staff. I wouldn't go into your bathroom; no. I respect that. But the rest..." I let it hang.

Angie chokes, her voice trembling. "But you can release the video of me anyway..."

"Well really that was the staff's decision."

"Why would you do all of this to us?" Dahlia whimpered.

"It was all a test. They needed to see how your brain activity and body would respond. To perfectly shape you into the requested form. From your parents of course. But please, let me continue. Drugs in Freddie's bed? My doing. And you, Nick..." My eyes locked on him. "You sabotaged yourself enough for me."

Nick's chest heaves. Freddie's face twists in agony. Like I just ripped out a piece of their soul and held it in my hands.

"Wes... you were like a brother to us!" Freddie screams, raw and trembling. "A BROTHER! How could you?"

Nick's voice cracks. "Everything... everything we trusted you with..." He can barely finish. Slight tears sliding down his face, devastated.

Dahlia and Angie stand frozen, gripping each other tightly, holding onto whatever piece of security they can. They can't speak. Not a word. Only silent sobs, clinging to each other like the world itself is ending.

I watch them. And I feel it. The weight of what I've done, or what I've been forced to do. Confusion. Rage. A hollow sort of emptiness. *But this is what I've worked for, it's what I'm owed.*

He never thought I could do it, but I did. I proved him wrong. My father will finally see what I can bring.

I tell myself that to stay calm.

That it's just another part of the job. Another room. Another explanation. Another controlled outcome.

But then I focus on how they're starting merely at me, I feel something crack.

"You don't get to stand there," Nick says, voice shaking, loud and raw, "like you didn't just destroy us."

I swallow. My mouth is dry. "Nick,"

"No," he snaps, stepping forward until the cuffs on his wrists yank him back. "No, don't say my name like that. Don't say it like you didn't watch me fight for you. Like you didn't let me think you were dead."

Freddie laughs suddenly. It's sharp. Broken. Wrong. "You know what the worst part is?" he yells. "It's not the drugs. It's not the diary. It's not even the gunshots."

I look at him.

"It's that we trusted you," Freddie roars. His eyes are red, tears spilling freely now. "I would've died for you. I would've taken anything for you. And you were laughing with the staff? Spying! You're nothing but a rat!" His voice cracks completely. "We were jokes to you?"

"No," I say quickly. "You weren't jokes."

Nick shakes his head, furious. "Then what were we, Wes? Experiments? Pets? Entertainment?"

I open my mouth and for the first time, the truth comes out clean.

"I had no choice! I wasn't supposed to get attached," I admit. The words hit the room like glass shattering. "That wasn't part of it."

They just look at me blankly.

"But I did," I continued, quieter now, my chest tightening. "I didn't plan to. I swear I didn't. Somewhere between the fights and the nights and the stupid jokes I forgot what I was meant to be."

Nick laughs bitterly. "Oh, poor you."

"I will miss you," I say, my voice breaking despite myself. "All of you. I will miss what we had. I will miss–"

Freddie explodes.

"We will miss Wes too," he screams, tears streaming down his face. "The Wes we knew. The one who protected us. The one who bled with us. Not this one."

He steps forward as far as the guards allow him, voice shaking with rage and grief.

"This one can rot in fucking hell."

The words hit harder than any bullet ever did.

Nick's shoulders started shaking. "You were my brother," he whispers, like saying it louder would kill him. "I loved you. Do you understand that? I loved you."

Something in my chest caves in completely.

"I know," I say, barely audible. "And that's the part that's going to haunt me."

"Liar! You're a liar!" Nick roared back.

Dahlia and Angie are still sobbing silently, unable to even look at me. The girls I lied to. The girls who trusted me with their worst moments.

It seems like a lifetime, this moment between the five of us, when suddenly a nurse moves. Hands grab my arms.

Confusion hits me first.

What's going on? I did my part. My father was finally proud of me... right?

"Wait... what? No, this isn't, Dad?" I twist, panic flooding in fast. "You said this was controlled. You said,"

My father doesn't look at me.

Not once.

"Please," I choke, tears spilling now, real and uncontrollable. "Please, I did everything you asked. I did everything. Look- I'll do another year! Another group! I'll be better next time please!"

A staff member's voice cuts through me like a blade.

"Take him to final correction. Basement."

The words don't register at first. Until I looked at my dad... who wasn't looking at me. That made it real.

I started fighting. Really fighting. Sobbing.

"No, no... please! I can fix it! I can still help them! Dad, dad, please..."

Nothing.

As they drag me toward the door, I twist my head back one last time. Freddie is on his knees now, crying openly. Nick is shaking with rage and grief, mumbling my name like it hurts his mouth to say it. I thought betraying them would be the hardest part. I was wrong. The hardest part is knowing they'll grieve me like I died, maybe I will and knowing I deserve it.

Chapter 100

Please tell me it's a nightmare.

Angeline.

They don't even give us time to breathe. The door opens again and the headmistress walks in like she's entering an assembly, not the aftermath of a massacre of trust. Her shoes click softly against the white floor. Calm. Polished. Smiling.

Like nothing just happened.

I'm still holding onto Dahlia so tightly my fingers hurt. My chest feels hollowed out, scraped raw. Nick is on the floor. Freddie is shaking with rage. Wes is gone. The headmistress clasps her hands together.

"I know this feels... overwhelming," she says gently. "But everything you've experienced here has been for your own good."

I feel something ugly coil in my stomach.

"This school exists to help you," she continued, voice smooth, practiced. "To reform harmful patterns. To redirect futures that were headed somewhere... dangerous." She looks

402

directly at us. At me. "Tomorrow, this will all feel distant. Like a nightmare. Forgotten. Forgiven."

I let out a broken laugh. "You think we can forget this?"

She doesn't even flinch. "The mind is remarkably adaptable, Angeline."

President Whitmore steps forward beside her, straightening his buttoned shirt like this is a business deal.

"Authority for the next generation," he says casually, "Is vital. Without control, the future of our young citizens will end in famine. Pain is temporary. Progress is permanent."

My heart starts pounding harder.

"So that's what this is about?" I chuckle, "Being able to mold us young kids into whatever goodly behaved robots you want!" I yell.

"You don't get it do you? A world without control and order is the beginning of our end! Divinity is essential! Whatever your owners require you to be, that is what you must become!" The headmistress hisses.

"Owners? We're not fucking pets!" Dahlia curses.

"You're going to let them kill your son. He won't be Wesley anymore; he'll be a total stranger." Freddie snarls.

President Whitmore shrugs. "Necessary losses."

That's when the guards move. Hands grab Nick first, hauling him up while he fights, screaming, thrashing like an animal caught in a trap. Freddie is dragged next, shouting until his voice cracks. Dahlia sobs as they pull her from me and I scream her name, clawing at the arms holding her.

"No, don't, please..." My words tangle together, useless.

Nurses flood in behind them. White coats. Blue gloves. Syringes that glint under the lights.

"No," I gasp, stumbling back. "No, no, no!"

One of them grabs my arm. I feel the cold touch of alcohol on my skin.

"Relax," the nurse says softly. "This will help."

"I don't want help!" I scream, twisting, kicking, panic ripping through me so hard I can't think. I see Nick being pinned down. Dahlia crying, reaching for me.

The needle comes closer. My vision blurs. My heart is pounding so loud I swear they can hear it. The last thing I see before they force me down is the headmistress watching calmly, like this is exactly how it was always meant to end. And then the needle presses into my skin and everything goes dark like before.

Chapter 101

Rage.

Nick.

Something in me breaks. Not loudly. Not all at once. Whatever cares about consequences just... disappears.

The second I see the needle sink into Angie's arm, something feral claws its way up my spine.

"No."

The word isn't loud. It's deadly calm. I rip forward against the guards and swing, hard, wild, uncontrolled. My fist slams into a jaw. Someone goes down. Another guard shouts my name like that'll stop me. It doesn't. I feel cuffs cut into my wrists, but I don't care. Pain is nothing. Pain is background noise.

I turn and hit again. Elbow. Fist. Head. I don't even see faces anymore, just targets between me and them. Three guards rush me.

I slam into the first, shoulder-first, sending him back into the wall. Someone grabs me from behind and I twist, throwing my head back into their face. Bone crunches. Blood sprays. I snarl, ripping free, swinging again.

"Nick!"

Dahlia.

Her scream cuts through everything.

I whipped around. She's being dragged toward the door, kicking and thrashing like her life depends on it because it does. Two guards have her arms. She's screaming my name, voice cracking, panicking, terrified.

"I'M HERE," I yell back. "I'M COMING!"

A body slams into me from the side. Another from behind. Hands grab my shoulders, my arms, my throat. I fight them, kicking, swinging, biting if I have to but there are too many.

Across the room, Freddie is fighting his own guards. He's not watching me. He's losing it. He rips free from one guard and slams another into the ground, fists flying, roaring like something unhinged. Someone grabs him from behind and he throws them off, blood dripping from his mouth.

Then he sees Angie. She's weak. Slumping. Barely standing as nurses try to hold her upright.

"ANGIE!" Freddie screams.

He breaks away from his guards and charges. He plows straight into the nurses, knocking one to the floor. Angie stumbles, nearly collapsing, and Freddie catches her with one arm, holding her upright with his body while swinging with the other.

"DON'T TOUCH HER!" he screams, feral and desperate.

The room is chaos. Shouting. Screaming. Bodies crash into walls.

I try to get to Dahlia again. I *need* to get to her. I fight like a man possessed; elbows, knees, headbutts, anything to break through. A guard slams a baton into my ribs, and the air leaves my lungs in a sharp gasp, but I keep going. Another grabs my arm and I rip free hard enough to tear skin.

"Nick!" Dahlia screams again. She's crying now. "Please, please..."

I can hear her voice getting farther away.

No. No!

I lunge forward, fingers stretching for her and I'm hit from behind.

Hard. Another guard. Then another. Then another. Too many. They pile onto me, fists and weight and bodies crushing me down. I fight them all, thrashing, screaming, swearing but I can't fight all of them. My vision blurs at the edges from the sheer force of it.

I can still hear her.

"Nick!" she sobs. "Nick please, don't let them take me!"

"I'M TRYING!" I screamed back, my voice breaking apart. "I'M TRYING..."

A guard pins my shoulders. Another locks my legs. Someone presses a knee into my spine. I rage against them like an animal caught in a trap, every muscle screaming, every instinct burning.

"UGHH FUCK!" I roared in pain.

I don't get injected. I don't go down. I stay awake. Helplessly watching her get away. They force my face toward the door, they're enjoying this. Seeing me see her get taken.

The last thing I hear is Dahlia still screaming my name and the sound of it rips something out of my chest that I'm not sure I'll ever get back. And I swear, with every shattered piece of myself, if I get free... I will burn this place to the ground.

Chapter 102

It all clicks.

Dahlia.

Out in the hall, alone, the door closed. Slow. Heavy. Cruel. I can still hear Nick on the other side, fighting, yelling, saying my name like it's the only thing anchoring him to the world. The gap narrows and something inside my chest splits open.

"No!" I stopped pulling. I stopped crying. I still go.

The guard's grip tightens, already confident, already turning me away. That's when the anger surges hot, clean, terrifyingly clear. Not panic. Not fear. Purpose. My knee comes up. My elbow drives back. He chokes. The second guard reaches for his gun. I took it.

The sound of the shot is thunderous in the small room. One drops. Another tries to move. Another shot. I don't think. I don't hesitate. I tackle the third guard, slam him into the wall, punch until my arms burn and he stops fighting. Someone grabs my ankle, scrambling, I see the dagger in his pocket. I stab until he goes limp. Then... silence.

My breathing is ragged. My hands are shaking. Blood streaks my arms and I don't know whose it is anymore. I stare at what I've done for half a second and then I turn. The door is still open, and I run back through it.

Nick is there. He's standing, chest heaving, knuckles split and red. Two guards are down behind him, unmoving, crumpled where he left them. I look over to see Freddie out of breath, finished with his own guards. Nick's feral, his eyes wild, still looking at me like he expects me to vanish any second.

"Dahlia!"

He runs to me and grabs my shoulders hard, scanning my face, my arms, my clothes.

"What did they do to you?" he demands, panic cracking through his voice. "Are you hurt?

Then he sees past me. The bodies. The dagger in my hand. The blood. He stops mid-sentence.

"Oh," he breathes.

Something shifts in his expression, not fear. Not disgust. Understanding. He gently but firmly takes the dagger from my shaking fingers. "Okay," he says quietly, grounding me. "I've got it. You're safe. I've got it."

The moment it leaves my hands; my legs threaten to give out. He steadies me, forehead pressed briefly to mine like he's making sure I'm real. The four of us were alone in this room, terrified as ever.

Then...

Clap. Slow. Deliberate. Clap. Clap. Clap. The sound echoes from the speakers overhead. Lights flicker on, illuminating a glass wall we hadn't seen before. Behind it standing comfortably, watching above like it's a performance.

Our parents. Nick's uncle. My Father. Angie's mom. Freddie's dad. All of them together. Smiling.

"Dad?" I whisper, my voice barely there.

He doesn't answer.

Nick goes utterly still. Then I feel it, the exact second it clicks for him.

"Oh my god," he says softly, staring at his uncle. "It was you."

The smile on his uncle's face widens.

"You killed my dad," Nick continues, voice low and lethal. "The will. The files. He left everything to me." His grip tightens on the dagger. "You couldn't handle that you got nothing, could you?"

That's what the files meant.

Nick doesn't yell. He grabs my hand.

"We're leaving," he says, voice iron hard. "Now."

Freddie lifts Angie, who's barely conscious, her arms weakly looping around his neck. Alarms begin to scream. Red lights flash, bathing the room in chaos.

We run. Down the stairs. Past bodies. Past doors slamming shut, to see that we're now on floor 4.

Chapter 103

Nobody owns me. Not anymore.

Dahlia.

It hits me all at once.

The adrenaline drains out of my body like someone pulled a plug, and suddenly my legs can't hold me anymore. My hands start shaking.

There are small splashes of blood on my hands. Not imagined. Real. Dark. Sticky.

"I..." My breath hitches. "I killed someone."

The words don't sound like mine. My chest caves in and I sob, hard enough it bends me in half. I can't stop seeing it, the way his body went still, the weight of it, the finality. I did it again. I did it *again*.

We managed to finally catch a breath as we hid in a side corridor. Nick is there instantly. He drops the dagger somewhere without looking and grabs me, both hands cupping my head and face. His thumbs brush my cheeks, grounding, frantic.

"Hey, hey look at me," he says, voice shaking. "Dahlia, are you okay? Did they hurt you? Did one of them,"

I let out a sound that's almost a laugh, but wrong. Sharp. Terrified. It scrapes my throat on the way out.

"If he hurt me?" I whisper, staring straight into Nick's eyes. "Look at what I've just done."

My hands lift between us, shaking so badly they blur. "First the lockdown kid. And now him." My voice cracks completely. "I can't control this. I can't control myself."

Tears spill fast and hot.

"I'm... I'm a monster," I choke. "I'm a monster and I'm just like him. Oh," My breath stutters. "He must be so proud of me."

The words poison my mouth. I look past Nick and see Freddie, Angie limp in his arms, her head resting weakly against his shoulder. She hasn't fully woken up yet. My heart twists.

Nick's grip tightens not painful but reassuring.

"No," he says firmly. "No. Dahlia, I know you. We know you. Don't think that way."

Freddie stops in front of us, eyes wet, jaw tight. "Listen to me, Dolly," he says, voice rough but certain. "You are nothing like your father. Not even close."

Nick doesn't hesitate. The words tumbled out like he'd been holding them in forever.

"You're strong," he says. "And you're caring. You're smart. You have courage. You're selfless." His voice softens. "You are beautiful. And you are good."

Angie stirs weakly in Freddie's arms. Her eyes fluttered open just enough to find me.

"You're my best friend, Lia," she murmurs, barely louder than a breath. "You're everything he's not."

Something inside me breaks but this time, it breaks open. I cry again, but it's different. Softer. Shaky. Tears of relief sliding down my face as the people I love most build me back up piece by piece. *They see me.*

I wipe my cheeks with the back of my sleeve, breathing through the tremor in my chest. "You're right," I say quietly. Then louder, stronger. "All of you are right."

I straighten.

"I am nothing like him," I say. "And I never will be. And when we get out of here I'm going to run. I'm never looking back at him." My voice wobbles, but it holds. "I love you guys."

Nick doesn't even think.

"We love you too," he says. Then, it is softer, just for me. "I love you."

Everything else falls away, the alarms, the blood, the chaos. Nick cups my face gently, and I feel the warmth of his hands steady me. Slowly, he leans in, and our lips meet. The kiss is soft at first, hesitant, but it quickly deepens, full of everything we've held back: relief, fear, love, and trust. My hands find their way to his chest, gripping him as if to anchor myself to reality, and he presses me closer, threading his fingers through my hair. For a moment, nothing else exists but us, and I feel a spark of hope I haven't felt in weeks. When we pull back, our foreheads touch, breaths mingling, and I realize... we finally did it.

I press my forehead, to his and whisper, "I love you." He softly greeted me with his lips again.

Freddie smiles, blinking hard then clears his throat. "I'm proud of you, Dolly. I always knew you had it in you." He pauses. "But can we please go back to where you said get out of here and maybe do that... like now?"

A quiet, shaky laugh passes between us. We run, run like there is no tomorrow. Because frankly, there might not be.

Chapter 104

Plan B.

Freddie.

We hit floor 3 and all we see are stunned faces. Students screaming, shoving each other, the hallway lights flashing with nurses forcing kids back into their sectors. The alarm has awoken the entire school. Some panicking, some walking around like robots with strict orders.

We brace, hiding amongst the crowd as we make our way toward the staffrooms.

Angie is strong enough now to just support her legs. She leans heavily on Dahlia, who's supporting her like she's made of glass. I glance at them, my chest tightening. Seeing them like this, both battered, exhausted, and still holding onto each other, makes me want to punch a wall and scream at the same time. But there's no time for that. Not now.

Nick and I split off toward the security room. It's just us boys. The girls disappear toward the first-aid closet across the hall to deal with anything the staff slipped into Angie's system.

By now the alarm has stopped and the nurses are gone, I see them still trying to contain the rest of the student body, strapping them to their beds with restraints, making incisions into needles.

The door to the security room creaks as we push it open. And there it is, our small arsenal of hope. Guns, ammo, knives, batons... anything that could help us take back control. I feel a rush of adrenaline, sharp and satisfying. For the first time in hours, I can do something. Not just run. Not just survive.

"So... Do you think we can keep these later?" I whisper.

"If we survive, yes. And get the big one." Nick grins.

I just laughed at him. "What, so I get stuck with the little gun?"

Nick moves quickly, checking each rack, loading magazines with steady hands. "We don't have long," he mutters, eyes scanning the screens. "Staff will realize we're here any second."

I load my gun, fingers trembling a little, partly from adrenaline, partly from rage. From fear. From the memory of Wes... from all of it.

"Hey, just so you know, you're terrifying when you're angry." Nick smacks my arm.

"Thanks. I aim to impress." I flash my smile at him.

Nick turns to me. His eyes are hard but determined. "Ready?"

I nod, gripping my weapon like it's an extension of my anger. "Let's make them regret ever touching us, and the girls."

Outside, I can hear faint footsteps our girls moving, working, holding each other together. And for a moment, that gives me focus. Gives me purpose.

Chapter 105

Hello, old self.

Angeline.

We slipped into the first aid closet across from the security room, Dahlia and I pressed against the walls like we're in a spy movie. I glance at my trembling legs and sigh.

"Calmorin," I mutter. "Muscle failure, shaking... but the brain still works. That's what I got."

Dahlia snorts. "Well, lucky you. I got 'how-to-make-my-arms-feel-like concrete while forgetting my own name', also known as VIREXAL."

I glare. "Gross. But yes, that's exactly what you and the boys have. Emotional flatness, heavy limbs, memories going fuzzy... basically, you're zombies with credit cards."

Dahlia grabs bottles and syringes from the shelves, moving faster than I can blink.

"Perfect analogy," she says, smirking. "We just need to mix these anti-drug doses before someone notices we're in here doing mad science."

I roll my eyes. "Let's just make sure the zombies wake up before we throw them at the basement, okay?"

We hustle, the cramped space forcing us to bump shoulders and knock over a box of cotton swabs.

"Shh!" I hissed. "Do you want to alert the entire floor or just me?"

Dahlia ducks, snatching the spilled items. "Me. Definitely me."

Once the dose is ready, I inject myself first. Almost instantly, the tremors stop. My muscles feel solid again, and my mind clears like someone turned the lights back on.

"Okay, now for the others," I say, rolling up my sleeve. "Freddie, Nick, come here before I stab you with a candy cane or something."

Freddie pokes his head in the doorway. "Candy cane? I like where your priorities are."

"Don't joke, I will improvise," I snap. "VIREXAL antidote flatness, heavy limbs, fuzzy memories... I'm not letting you turn into walking office chairs."

Nick steps up, grabbing the syringe. "Thanks. Feels weird getting a needle from you after everything, though."

"Relax," I say, grinning despite myself. "I'm not injecting my love potion. Just giving back your brain. Mostly."

Dahlia helps Freddie with his dose. Everyone wobbles a little at first, but soon they're steady, blinking as their clarity returns.

"Wow," Freddie mutters, rubbing his shoulders. "I feel… normal again. For the first time in forever. I might cry from happiness or sheer panic, can't tell yet."

I shake my head. "Save it. Basement. Now. And try not to trip over anything.

We move quickly, whispering like cartoon spies, bumping into shelves, knocking over bandage rolls, but laughing under our breaths at how ridiculous we must look. With muscles working, heads clear, and the anti-drugs finally taking effect, we stick close and head for the basement.

Chapter 106

A gut feeling.

Dahlia.

We're barreling down the stairs again, the concrete vibrating under our boots. The floor shakes with guards pounding after us, their shouts echoing off the walls. My lungs burn, my legs are screaming, but I can't stop.

"Guys! Wait!" Angie's voice cuts through the chaos, sharp and urgent. She's tugging at me and pointing down the hall on floor 2. "I... I just have a gut feeling; there's a window there!"

Nick glances back briefly, eyes scanning the stairwell like a predator. "Probably locked! We have no time!" He swings a gun he's picked up, firing two precise shots. A guard stumbles back into the railing; another drops mid-step. His eyes snap straight to me, making sure I'm still standing.

Freddie's beside me, helping Angie keep pace. "Move it, Angie! Floor 2 to 1!" he shouts. I glance at her; her legs wobble, but she's determined.

The next staircase yawning before us. My stomach twists every time I think of that window, but Nick doesn't hesitate.

"It's not safe!" he yells, firing another round as a guard tries to step out and intercept me. His bullet knocks the man's gun away just in time. Another guard dives toward Angie, and Nick spins, his shot sending the man sprawling.

Floor 1 hits with a jolt. Nick pauses at the nurses' office, gun up. Shots crack, precise and controlled. One guard reaches for me, I freeze, but Nick's bullet ends it. Another hides behind the counter another precise shot, and he drops before he can even raise his weapon.

"Guys, I don't know how much ammo I have left!" Nick yells.

Behind me, Freddie yells, dragging Angie clear of the stairwell to the basement, taking down anyone trying to follow. My stomach churns as I see the bodies, but I keep moving, heart hammering.

"Don't even look!" Freddie snaps, pulling me forward.

Nick glances over at me, eyes hard but protective. "Stay behind me, Dahlia. I've got you."

Two guards stand in our path. Nick and Freddie fire in perfect sync, one guard crumples; the other flails, Nick's shot catches him in the shoulder. Freddie yanks Angie aside, keeping her safe. I glance at her briefly, the ghost of that window flickering in my mind, the maybe freedom she saw, the gut instinct she can't shake but the adrenaline keeps us moving.

Nick and Freddie eventually drop their guns. Useless without ammo. Grabbing each other's hands we run and don't look back, headed for our last chance. Because in all honesty, I'd rather risk my life escaping than become *reformed*.

We're almost there.

Chapter 107

Humanity.

Angeline.

We quickly huddle back in the file room, tossing folders into piles, trying to grab anything that could help us make sense of this nightmare. My hands shake as I fumble through the papers, but then I hear it... Wes.

He's stuck in a glass room, wearing the same grey clothes as it all started. His voice, raw, desperate, full of cracks and pleading cuts straight through me.

"I know you can hear me! Angie! Please! I... I want to say I'm sorry. I wasn't meant to get that close. I really am... I'm sorry, you have to believe me. Please! I'll make it up to you! Just... open the door!"

My heart tightens. I stumble forward, down the hallway, until I'm outside, looking at him through the glass. I freeze, chest hammering.

"Please... you and Lia... you're like my sisters... I need you."

A tear slips down my cheek, and I press my hand to the glass. "Wes..."

Dahlia storms up behind me, hair flying, voice sharp as a blade. "What the hell are you doing, Ange? Hug-fest, or... wait you're not seriously thinking of letting him out, are you?"

"I... we have to help him!" I whisper, shaking.

She grabs my arm, eyeing me like I've lost it.

"Remember the tears you cried when that video played for the whole school? Remember the hell we went through just to get out of that room... all because that daddy's boy thought he could mess with us?"

Wes's voice cracks, desperate. "Lia... look at me... please! You know me!"

Dahlia scoffs, flipping her hair back like it's the most natural thing in the world. "Know you? The Wes I knew is gone. You're someone else entirely. And newsflash? I'm not impressed."

Then he loses it, rage roaring.

"LET ME OUT! ANGIE! OPEN THE DOOR!" He slams his hand against the glass where mine is pressed. I rip back, heart hammering.

I wipe my tears, voice low and steady.

"You have no right to call me Angie anymore, Wesley. Fuck you."

He screams one last time, venom dripping.

"YOU'RE JUST LIKE YOUR FATHER, DAHLIA!"

I didn't know if he meant that, I could hear the desperation in his voice.

Dahlia spins on him, icy fire in her eyes.

"Oh, Wes... I'm nothing like him. I don't betray my friends for fame or some twisted vision you and your fucked up dad have! And if you're lucky, you'll remember that before you become fully reformed!"

She winds her middle finger up like a fishing rod, pure disgust. Then boots pound the floor. Fast. Heavy. Guards.

Freddie and Nick burst out of the file room, shoving a pile of folders into my arms.

"Take these! MOVE!" Freddie yells.

Nick's eyes sweep the hallway, deadly precise.

"Freddie! Here!" Nick shouts, throwing a rifle to Freddie, picking up another himself that he found.

"Dahlia! GET MOVING! Go! NOW!" Nick shouts.

Freddie fires over his shoulder, picking off the closest guard. "MOVE IT!"

The hallway explodes into chaos. Bullets scream, ricocheting off walls. Sparks fly, concrete pings, smoke curls from near misses. Nick moves like a shadow in front of us, every shot precisely, shielding Dahlia and I. Freddie covers our backs, yelling for us to keep moving.

And then Wes screams, louder than the gunfire.

"ANGIE! LIA! YOU HAVE TO RUN! YOU WON'T SURVIVE! PLEASE... YOU HAVE TO RUN!"

Nick shouts back over the chaos, determination cutting through the din. "GO, DAHLIA! TAKE ANGIE, RUN! YOU GUYS CAN MAKE IT!"

Dahlia spins, grin blazing, eyes fire.

"NO WAY! Come on! We're not leaving anyone behind!"

We take the chance. Freddie bolts first, sprinting up the stairs with Angie and me close behind. Nick follows, firing behind him as guards chase.

I glance back, heart skipping. Nick is coming up the stairs, still taking precise shots at the chasing guards. "COME ON, NICK! NOW!" I shout.

Near the top step, he stops firing, taking out the final guard on the level. He hesitates just for a second and I follow his gaze. Wes's tear-streaked face is pressed against the glass, desperate. He forces a small, shaky smile at Nick. Nick lets a tear slip, lifts his gun, and shoots the lock.

The door explodes open. Wes doesn't hesitate. He tackles the nearest guards, taking them down in a flurry, holding them off just long enough for us to move.

Adrenaline tears through me as we sprint back up the basement stairs, hearts hammering, the echo of gunfire and the last thing, Wes's screams chasing us. For once, the impossible feels real.

Chapter 108

Goodbye, - Frederick.

Freddie.

"We're outnumbered up here!" I shouted, my voice tearing through the roar of gunfire.

Floor 1 is hell. More guards flooded the hallway from every direction, boots pounding, voices barking orders, guns raised. Bullets rip into the walls, sparks exploding like fireworks, smoke and dust choking the air. It's way too loud. Too fast. There's too many. Nick slams Dahlia behind him, his body instinctively shielding hers. I fire over my shoulder, keeping the closest guards back, but the numbers don't stop. They just keep coming. My chest hammers so hard it hurts. For one horrifying second, a single thought takes over.

This is it. We're dead.

Bullets scream past my head, close enough that I feel the heat of them. A guard drops. Another stumbles. It doesn't matter. There are still too many. Everything in me is screaming drop, hide, give up.

Then Angie's voice slices through the chaos like a lifeline.

"WINDOW! FOLLOW ME!"

My heart jolts. She saw it. She's thinking. She's leading us out. She has *a gut feeling*.

Dahlia grabs her hand and they run, and I move with them without thinking, muscles burning, lungs on fire, firing back as we bolt for the stairwell. My entire world narrows to one purpose: keep them alive.

We hit the stairs two at a time. Gunfire follows us, deafening, relentless. Sparks ricochet off the railings. Concrete chips fly. My chest is screaming, every breath sharp and shallow.

Suddenly...

Pain, blinding. Like my leg has been ripped out from under me.

I crash to my knees with a scream I don't recognize as my own. Blood blooms instantly, dark and unstoppable, spreading across the stairs.

Nick is there before I even register the fall, arms hooked under mine, hauling me up with brutal force. Every nerve in my body lights up, agony screaming through me, but he doesn't slow. He doesn't hesitate. He just keeps shooting, precise and lethal, dragging me upward step by step, taking out the rest of the guards.

And then I hear it. Her.

"FREDDIE, NO!!"

Angie's scream is broken. Raw. It cuts straight through the gunfire and sinks into my chest like a blade.

Nick drops me against the wall for a second, breath sharp. "Freddie. You need a minute. To get your strength."

"Nick, dude, I'm not goi-"

"Freddie, would you shut the hell up!" He spits. "Don't even say it."

Fucking stubborn asshole. Won't even let me talk.

"Dahlia! Help me over here- fuck, I need help! We need to barricade the hall, shut the doors quickly," Nick yells out. "Grab something from the dorms to hold the door, I can't hold it by myself!"

Dahlia nods and runs to the first door on our left. She starts punching in our personal code to the dorm.

Access denied.

Then she starts tapping random numbers.

Access denied.

She lets out a frustrated groan and suddenly slams her fist into the keypad.

Access denied.

She spins around, and eyes the gun next to me.

"D-dolly don't," I try to stop her, reaching forward, but a sharp pain shoots up my leg, and I let out a roar. However, her hand is already reaching for the murder weapon next to me.

I look at her eyes, but they don't seem there. Well, not her eyes there still there but Dolly. Her eyes aren't as glossy anymore and seem almost darker. I try to reach and grab her hand as she reaches for the gun but when my hand skims hers she doesn't even blink.

Within a heartbeat, she brings the gun up to her eye and shoots the keypad with precise aim. Smoke wafts of the once electrical piece of shit thing they call *personal security*.

What the fuck?

Students in the dorm start screaming as she runs in. Three girls ran out. Dahlia runs after them, grabbing one by her PJ's.

"Help me get what I need to make a barricade, and you get to live!" she yells, pointing the gun to her head.

The student stops screaming and nods in terror and goes back into the dorm. Suddenly, the two came out with chairs stacked up, the gun still aimed at her head. Her face streaked with tears.

I look at nick. Nick just watches the scene ahead of him... without anything to say apparently.

They start to drag the chairs out of the dorm and over to Nick, but the other chick isn't taking her 'helping hand' as kind behaviour.

"DO YOU KNOW HOW TRAUMATIZING THIS IS? YOU POINT A GUN AT MY HEAD, FORCE ME TO MOVE STUPID CHAIRS, THEN WANT ME TO RUN INTO THE DEATH HALL AS IF THERE ISN'T LIKE... A BAJILLION GUARDS DOWN THERE WAITING TO SHOOT MY BRAINS OUT–"

"First, your brainwashed friends made it down their fine."

"DON'T TALK ABOUT MY FRIENDS YOU FUCKING PHYSCO BITCH! THE GUARDS ARE GOING TO CATCH YOUR ASS AND YOUR PHYSCO FRIENDS!!" She fires back.

"Don't you DARE talk about my friends-" Dolly starts screaming back at the student and drops the stack of chairs to walk towards her, gun blazing, when Nick's loud voice interrupts them.

"HEY! GET ME THOSE CHAIRS! YOU," He points at the crying bitch.

"MOVE!"

She squeaks, turning and sprinting down the stairs, squeezing through the small gap left in the door before it slams shut.

Nick grabs the stack of chairs with one hand and rearranges them as Dolly rushes to get more.

Suddenly, Angie is there. She drops beside me like she's been thrown into the floor. She's shaking so hard her hands don't even land right at first. They hover over my leg, press down, slip, try again. Blood everywhere. Too much. Nothing steady. Nothing right. Tears won't stop rolling down her soft rosey cheeks. Like she already knows she's to mourn me.

"No no no-" she breathes. "No, no, no..."

"GO!" I choke out. "GO, run!"

She doesn't move. She looks like she can't even process it. Her hands keep pressing my leg like she can hold something in place that's already gone too far.

But it's getting worse. I can feel it now. Not just pain.

Something quieter.

Worse.

My vision keeps fading at the edges like the world is trying to turn itself off without me agreeing to it. My breathing doesn't feel like mine anymore. It stutters. Stops. Starts again.

"Angie..." I try, but it comes out wrong. "Hey," I gasp, forcing my hand up to her face.

It doesn't make it properly. My arm shakes halfway there, drops, then I try again. This time I catch her cheek. Barely. I cup her face like I can still hold something together.

She's crying so hard she can't stay still.

She lets out a sound that's more painful than a sob, burying her face into my shoulder. Her tears soak into my shirt. I hold her like I might never get the chance again. Because I know I won't.

She... is the one person, the only person in this entire fucked up world that I have ever learnt to love as much as my mother. If it meant knowing that she would survive this, I would take the guards guns and wipe myself clean in the mouth.

I try to wipe her tears. I miss. My thumb drags under her eye instead, useless, like even that is too much now.

"Don't..." I breathe. "Don't look at me like that."

Then she pulls her jacket off in a panic. Her hands are shaking too badly to think. She wraps it around my leg, tries to hold it tight. It slips. She tries again. Too loose. Then too tight. Then wrong again.

A tourniquet. Desperate. Not enough.

"Shh," I whisper, softer now, like I'm trying to slow everything down just so she doesn't break faster than she already is. "Angie- hey. Hey, look at me."

She does. But she's still looking at my leg too. Like she can't stop herself. Like she's already memorizing the end.

"No," I choke, and I grab her wrist.

Too weak. It barely holds.

But I pull anyway, dragging her hand away from my leg like I can physically make her unsee it.

"Don't- don't look there," I breathe. "Look at me." My grip shakes. It slips. And my hand moves without thinking. It goes into her hair. Soft. Clean. I brush it back from her face and the second I do it...

My vision blurs, and Angies hair under my fingers become something else.

Not Angie.

Not here.

My mum.

"Hey baby..." the words aren't loud, there barely there.

But my ears drone every yell and cry out from my surroundings.

For a second, I can smell her perfume. Feel the weight of her hand against my head. Feel the mattress dip beside me.

She's sitting on the edge of my bed. Late afternoon sunlight spills through the curtains, turning everything gold. Her fingers slide through my hair the same way mine are tangled in Angie's now.

Her hands are grazing through my hair.

Soft. Careful. Like she was trying to fix something she knew she didn't have time to fix.

She always used to say she should've been a hairdresser.

She used to laugh while she did it too, like it mattered more than anything else in the world. Like I mattered more than anything else in the world. Even when she was already fading. Even when she didn't have time left. I remember her fingers through my hair like it was normal.

Like she wasn't leaving. Like she wasn't running out of days while I still needed her here. And then I remember after.

The school cutting it too short.

And suddenly it feels like she's closer than everything else. I blink hard. And it hurts. Because I can almost feel her again. Not as a memory. As something close enough to touch if I let go properly.

Angie is still in front of me. Still holding me. Still trying.

But something inside aches. Not painful. Realization.

This is actually happening. And she's watching it.

I bring my hand up to her face again, faster this time, like I can fix it by forcing her to look at me instead. I cup her cheek properly this time. It still trembles.

"I'm okay," I lie automatically, but it sounds wrong even to me now. "I've got you. It's okay princess.."

Her forehead presses into mine like she's trying to hold me in place. Like she thinks if she doesn't let go, I won't either.

And I-

I can't say it. That's the worst part. It's right there. Sitting in my chest like something I've been carrying too long.

I love her.

I love her in a way I never said out loud because I always thought there'd be more time. But there isn't.

And now it's just stuck behind my teeth with nowhere to go. My fingers move through her hair again. Shaking. Slower now. Like I'm running out of permission to stay conscious. "Not here," I whisper, voice breaking harder now. "Not now. Listen to me."

My forehead rests against hers. Barely holding.

"I'm okay..." I breathe. "I'm okay. We will be okay. I always have."

She shakes her head like she refuses to accept any version of this that ends without me. And I can't even blame her anymore. My fingers are still in her hair. Slower now. Like I'm running out of time to stay.

"Angie..." I whisper. Her eyes snap up. And I can't say it. I can't say what's sitting in my chest.

So it just comes out broken instead.

"Don't look back at me, okay?"

Her breath breaks instantly.

"Don't-" I try again, and my hand shakes harder as I hold her face like I'm trying to keep her here with me a second longer. "Don't you dare look back at me like I'm gone. You hear me?"

She nods. But it's falling apart.

"I need you to run," I whisper. "If you look back, you'll stop. And I can't have that. I can't-" My voice cracks completely.

"Promise me, princess."

That word destroys her. Her face collapses like she's been hit. And I feel it too. Because I won't get to say it again.

"Promise me," I whisper again. "Just don't look back."

She nods. Barely. Dolly tries to pull her up.

"No- Lia NO!" Angie yells, shoving her off.

"Angie, we must go! Please Ange!" Dolly pleads, trying to grab her arm again.

"DAHLIA NO! If you're really the friend, I thought you were then go on without me! I'm not leaving him! If this was Nick, you would do the same!" she cries out, her voice trembling.

Dolly just looks at her. Her doll eyes, wide and glossy. Then she looks at me. Tears slip down her cheeks. But she sees the look on my face. She sees the pool of blood around my leg. I can only nod at her.

Suddenly she reaches down and hauls Princess up and starts dragging her off me.

"NO! DAHLIA! NO! FREDDIE! Freddie..." Her angry yells get washed out by the chokes of her own sobs while Dolly tries to pull her along. Angie tries to grab and smack to get her to let go, but Dolly doesn't give up. The blood on her hands smudges everywhere amongst the two girls. My blood. She almost crumples onto the floor but Dolly won't give her up, rubbing her back and whispering soft words to her.

Then she's gone.

Dahlia looks back once. Our eyes locked. She takes one final look. She sees the blood. She sees the way Nick is holding me up. I can see her mouthing my name, probably screaming it, but I choose not to hear it. I couldn't take hearing the tone in her voice. I never thought that I would be the reason for that noise coming from her.

Little Dolly, I will miss her. Her gentleness, her grace, the way she always managed to see me. She was the sister I never had. The one I vowed to protect. The sister I know my mother would have cherished. I cherished her.

She turns forward again and keeps running.

Nick steps away from leaning his weight off the barricade to haul me up again, breath breaking under the weight of it.

"Shit," he grunts. "It must've hit an artery. Come on, Freddie. Nearly there. Just a bit more, man."

"It's no use man- it's-"

"Shut up!" His voice cracks. "Shut up. I will not leave you and I will not let you die!"

I look at him.

Nickolas. I always saw through him. He couldn't hide from me. My built-in best friend. Nick... my true brother. I chose him. He.... He was my true family.

And I don't fight it anymore.

The window lingers at the end of the corridor, close enough to see but too far to reach as everything in me starts to go still.

I look at Nick, easily communicating that this is the end. When I say, the look in his eyes, was more pain than this fucking bullet has brought me.

The guards have finally slammed their way through the makeshift barricade, yelling commands at one another as they start sprinting towards us.

And behind us, the gunfire doesn't stop. And neither does the fear that this is the moment that I will be leaving this earth.

But I'm not really holding on to this moment anymore.

I'm holding on to something else.

Chapter 109

Graduation.

Nick.

Bullets scream past our heads, tearing through the stairwell. Sparks fly off the concrete railing, and smoke stings my eyes. Every step feels like a battle, every heartbeat like a hammer in my chest.

"Hold on, man! Almost there!" I yell, as Freddie groans through the pain. His hand shoots up, trembling but determined, gripping the gun.

Freddie, trying to regain himself, "Nick… I got this," he gasps, voice strained. "Cover me!"

I keep firing, hitting guards back, trying to buy him the few seconds he needs. Sweat burns my eyes, my lungs scream, but I keep moving.

Freddie squeezes through every ounce of strength he has. His gun flashes once, twice and the window shatters. Glass explodes outward, catching the last sunlight in deadly shards.

"Go! Go! Jump now!" Angie shouts, pointing at the shattered window at the top of the stairwell.

Dahlia grabs her arm, and they leap together. My heart nearly jumps out of its own chest watching her free fall.

I shove my head out the window to see them roll on the grass.

Relief flares in me for half a second until I glance back and see Freddie, blood streaking down his leg, grimacing.

"Nick... go... go man." He growls, voice strained, pain twisting every word, life escaping his eyes.

"No way, man. I'm not letting you die out here!"

I look at Freddie, he looks back for the last time, and I know he decides he can't give up.

"Then fucking toss me!" he yells, fire in his eyes. "Now!"

I hesitate just for a heartbeat, but he isn't joking. With all his strength, he pushes against me, gritting his teeth. I grab him, shoulder him against mine, and heave him toward the opening.

"Catch you on the other side, idiot," he hisses, grinning through the blood and pain.

He sails out first, and I hear the thud as he lands on the grass. My chest clenches.

Alive. *Alive.*

"Nick! Now!" Freddie yells from below, pain and laughter tangled together.

I don't wait. I fired a quick round back, taking out all remaining figures in sight. I don't care who got shot in the crossfire. I leap after them, rolling mid-air, gun still in hand.

Sparks and bullets whiz past me as I hit the ground, adrenaline smashing every nerve in my body.

Dahlia and Angie reached for me immediately. I groaned, still gripping my gun. Freddie collapsed beside us, clutching his leg, but alive. I glance at him and mutter through gritted teeth.

"Next time... we take the elevator."

He laughs weakly, blood mixing with sweat, and I can't help but let out a breath I didn't know I was holding.

We're free.

Chapter 110

The reform trials.

Wendy.

I shouldn't have done it.

That's what I tell myself now, standing at the back of the room with my hands folded neatly in front of me, face calm, posture perfect. That's what I told myself *then*, too, right before I did it anyway.

The memory comes back in pieces.

The hum of the security room. The soft glow of monitors stacked too high for one person to watch properly. I remember my fingers hovering over the controls, heart beating so loud I was sure it would trip a sensor on its own.

Eleven minutes. That was all I could give them without raising suspicion. Eleven minutes was nothing, but it was also everything.

I remember thinking of their faces.

Freddie's crooked grin when he thanked me for oatmeal like it was a gift and not a rule. Angie's politeness sharpened by fear she pretended not to have. Wes, always watching, always noticing. Nick's silence; heavy, deliberate. And Dahlia... Dahlia with her careful hands and eyes that carried too much history for someone so young.

I pulled the lever. The cameras went dark. I didn't stay to watch what happened next.

Now I'm here.

The present snaps back into place like a rubber band, stinging. The room is crowded with guards lining the walls, nurses standing straight and still. The headmistress is at the front, voice smooth as ever. President Whitmore stands beside her, hands clasped behind his back, eyes cold and calculating.

"Find them," the headmistress says, calm, certain. "They can't have got far."

"We will not lose them," President Whitmore adds. "They could ruin everything, if this gets out. The only way this works is if we obtain the targets and proceed for full reconstructive reform!"

My stomach turns.

"We must act fast to avoid the publics knowledge. Alert Press Secretary. These little shits... they're *wanted*." he continues. "And they will not jeopardize our mission."

A murmur of agreement ripples through the room. I feel it then, something sour and heavy settling in my throat. A knowing. A line crossed that I couldn't undo.

I think of bleeding ears. Of shaved hair. Of children being commanded to break themselves neatly and quietly. I think of the way they looked at me sometimes, like I was safe. Like I was human. My hands curl into fists before I can stop them.

I don't want to be part of this anymore.

I don't want to stand in the shadows while they hunt the only kids who ever looked back and didn't bend. I don't want to hear words like *key* and *mission* used to justify what's being done to them. I helped them once. I don't know if I'll get the chance again. But as the room is filled with plans and orders and certainty, one thing settles deep in my bones.

I am no longer on their side.

Epilogue

We'll make it to tomorrow.

Dahlia.

It's been hours but we don't stop running until our lungs are on fire and the school feels far away.

Nick was under Freddie's right arm practically dragging him along after Freddie insisted he could go further.

Stubborn mule.

After managing to get away from the gates and lose the remaining guards, we collapsed into a massive underground pipe, rusted and damp, hidden beneath tangled weeds and concrete. The air inside is cold and metallic, echoing with the sound of our breathing. My back hits the curved wall and I slide down, knees trembling, hands shaking so badly I have to press them into the dirt to steady myself.

We made it. That thought doesn't feel real yet.

Freddie is sprawled across the ground near the opening, groaning softly, one hand clamped around his leg. Blood still drips steadily onto the concrete, dark and thick, each drop echoing too loudly in the pipe.

I don't know how he made it. I don't know how he is STILL making it.

Angie is kneeling beside him, chest heaving, hair plastered to her face with sweat and tears.

For a moment, no one speaks. We just breathe. Then Freddie turns his head slowly, eyes finding Angie like she's the only thing anchoring him to the world.

"I love you, Princess," he says hoarsely. Like it's the most obvious thing in the universe. "Have this whole time."

The words hang there, fragile, exposed.

Angie blinks, still trying to catch her breath. "Yeah," she says, voice breathless, almost distracted. "Me too."

Freddie freezes. His groaning stops. His hand loosens on his leg. He stares at her like the world just tilted sideways.

"...Wait," he says slowly. "You love me too?"

She finally looks at him properly, brows knitting together like he's just asked the dumbest question imaginable. "Of course I love you, idiot."

She reaches out instinctively and smacks his leg. Right on the wound.

"FUCK!" Freddie yells, jerking violently, pain ripping through him.

"Oh my god, Freddie, I'm so sorry," Angie hisses immediately, hands flying to him, panic flashing across her face.

Then before any of us can say a word she leans down and kisses him. Slow, not rushed. Not panicking. Like they've been waiting their entire lives for that kiss, and this was the perfect moment. Passionate and delicate, long overdue. His hands covered in her golden curls, her cheeks being greeted with pink again, color I thought we lost from the punishments. I watch as they stare into each other's eyes, like they know they're soulmates and how they don't just love each other, but they are each other's best friend too. It's the first thing since we jumped from that window that has made my stomach feel a little lighter.

"Finally." I huffed, smiling at them hopelessly. They greet me with a smirk after giggling with themselves.

Nick lets out a low whistle. "Wow," he mutters. Then, grinning, "Wait, smack his leg again, Angie."

Freddie snaps his head up. "No," he rushes out. "Absolutely do not smack Freddie's leg again."

Angie pulls back, shrugs casually... and smacks his leg again.

"Fuck!" Freddie hisses, teeth clenched, face contorting.

But then Nick's smile fades.

"Did anyone else see that?" he says slowly, crouching down. "The wound... it flickered. Like a projector glitch."

My heart stutters. Nick kneels fully now, waving his hand carefully over Freddie's leg.

And I see it.

The blood-stained skin flickers just for a second almost static. Like light catching on something that isn't really there.

I turn to look at the slight trail of blood in the tunnel, and it flicks too.

Then the wound disappears. Completely. No blood. No tears. No damage. Freddie exhales a long, shaky breath, head falling back against the pipe.

"Oh, thank god," he murmurs. "I was really committing to the dramatic death thing."

Angie's hand flies to her mouth. I feel cold all over.

"It's a hologram?" Angie asks. "Why would they just... turn it off then? Let us go..?"

"That's how," I whisper. The words tumbled out before I could stop them. "That's how Wes wasn't injured... when we saw him get shot."

Everyone looks at me confused.

"Remember what he said. '*A simple simulation wound.*' It's a bullet that simulates the wound of a real gunshot, causes real pain, and blood but only temporarily. It obviously fades over a certain amount of time. Or with enough distance of the gun perhaps... he got shot in the school, so we must have shot the guard back by our REAL guns- so the weapon that shot Freddie is still in the school... like its lost connection or something." I explained.

"Which is like a mile back." Nick agrees.

"That's what they do at that school," Angie continued, "The punishments... They were experimenting on us! The simulations. They weren't trying to 'fix us', they were convincing us we were injured; that there was something wrong that they needed to remove out of us. Brainwashing us. Manipulating pain responses. Making us think we were weak. Emotionally. Mentally. Physically. They thought we were breakable. Our parents... the way they were just watching us like a comedy show while we were being torn apart inside and out."

I shake my head, pieces clicking together in a way that makes my chest ache. "They're testing us. Conditioning us. Training us to believe we need them. To think we'll fail without their control. You heard the headmistress and President Whitmore!"

Nick scoffs softly. "They expect us to break," he says. "To crawl back."

Freddie lifts his chin, eyes burning. "But we won't."

"No," I say, meeting his gaze.

We're dirty. Exhausted, shaking. But alive.

"They expect us to falter," I say. But we won't. We are stronger than they think."

I look at them, a small smile breaking through our faces despite everything.

"Aren't we, Freddie?"

He grins back, crooked and fearless. "Yeah," he says softly. "They picked the wrong kids."

I grin. "Let them come, they'll find we're not the same kids they tried to control."

Acknowledgment

Thank you guys SO much for reading!! We hope you have had as much fun reading Heirs of Montclair as we did writing it! Your support is truly appreciated! This book means so much to us, not just because of the story itself, but the journey we shared while creating it together. Every chapter holds a piece of the time we would stay up way to late throwing around ideas, building characters, and adding layers of depth to a world that become real to us.

To everyone who supported us during this time and encouraged us to keep going, thank you. For believing in our small ideas as they grew overtime.

I hope during this time between this book and the next you will be mentally preparing yourself for what we have planned. It's gonna be a big ride of emotions! We hope you have gotten to experience the emotion, the laughter and the imagination the same way we did throughout this book. We hope this story stays with you long after you finish the last sentence. Massive thank you to our special cover designer, **Maria necula – coverbound.co** !

If you have any comments, questions or anything about the books, feel free to check out our Instagram account and TikTok below. We would love to hear from you!

This is only the beginning.

About the Authors

The Gwennies are from Australia (cousins Brooke Golfin and Ella Partridge) who share a love of storytelling, but each bring their own spark to the page. Ella rides and loves horses, eats far too much sushi, and has been writing stories since grade 5. Brooke loves watching movies and tv shows, specifically dramas and true-crime documentaries, while also having a deep passion for law, pursuing the study of criminology. Together, they craft stories full of adventure, heart, and a little bit of mischief.

♪ @thegwennies

@thegwennies.official